Rachel Ray
Vol. I

by

Anthony Trollope

Double 9
BOOKS

Rachel Ray
Vol. I
by Anthony Trollope

ISBN: 978-93-64288-37-8

Published by

DOUBLE 9 BOOKS

2/13-B, Ansari Road
Daryaganj, New Delhi – 110002
info@double9books.com
www.double9books.com
Tel. 011-40042856

ABOUT THE AUTHOR

Anthony Trollope (1815-1882) was a renowned English novelist of the Victorian era, best known for his insightful and richly detailed portrayals of 19th-century English society. His prolific writing career produced a vast array of novels, many of which have become classics of English literature. First Novels: Trollope's debut novel, "The Macdermots of Ballycloran", was published in 1847. However, it was not until the publication of "The Warden" in 1855 that he gained significant recognition. Trollope's writing is known for its realism, detailed character development, and exploration of social issues. His characters are often complex and multifaceted, reflecting the diverse nature of human experiences. He employed a straightforward narrative style, often interjecting his own commentary and opinions, which adds a distinctive voice to his works. Trollope's works remain significant in the study of Victorian literature. His keen observations of society, human relationships, and institutional behaviors continue to be appreciated for their depth and insight. Many of his novels have been adapted for television, radio, and stage, keeping his stories and characters alive for new generations. Anthony Trollope's contribution to literature is marked by his ability to combine detailed social critique with engaging storytelling, making him one of the enduring figures of English literature.

CONTENTS

CHAPTER I
THE RAY FAMILY

There are women who cannot grow alone as standard trees;—for whom the support and warmth of some wall, some paling, some post, is absolutely necessary;—who, in their growth, will bend and incline themselves towards some such prop for their life, creeping with their tendrils along the ground till they reach it when the circumstances of life have brought no such prop within their natural and immediate reach. Of most women it may be said that it would be well for them that they should marry,—as indeed of most men also, seeing that man and wife will each lend the other strength, and yet in lending lose none; but to the women of whom I now speak some kind of marriage is quite indispensable, and by them some kind of marriage is always made, though the union is often unnatural. A woman in want of a wall against which to nail herself will swear conjugal obedience sometimes to her cook, sometimes to her grandchild, sometimes to her lawyer. Any standing corner, post, or stump, strong enough to bear her weight will suffice; but to some standing corner, post, or stump, she will find her way and attach herself, and there will she be married.

Such a woman was our Mrs. Ray. As her name imports, she had been married in the way most popular among ladies, with bell, book, and parson. She had been like a young peach tree that, in its early days, is carefully taught to grow against a propitious southern wall. Her natural prop had been found for her, and all had been well. But her heaven had been made black with storms; the heavy winds had come, and the warm sheltering covert against which she had felt herself so safe had been torn away from her branches as they were spreading themselves forth to the fulness of life. She had been married at eighteen, and then, after ten years of wedded security, she had become a widow.

Her husband had been some years older than herself,—a steady, sober, hardworking, earnest man, well fitted to act as a protecting screen to such a woman as he had chosen. They had lived in Exeter, both of them having belonged to Devonshire from their birth; and Mr. Ray, though not a clergyman himself, had been employed in matters ecclesiastical. He was a lawyer,—but a lawyer of that sort that is so nearly akin to the sacerdotal profession, as to make him quite clerical and almost a clergyman. He managed the property of the dean and chapter, and knew what were the rights, and also what were the wrongs, of prebendaries and minor canons,— of vicars choral, and even of choristers. But he had been dead many years before our story commences, and so much as this is now said of him simply to explain under what circumstances Mrs. Ray had received the first tinge of that colouring which was given to her life by church matters.

They had been married somewhat over ten years when he died, and she was left with two surviving daughters, the eldest and the youngest of the children she had borne. The eldest, Dorothea, was then more than nine years old, and as she took much after her father, being stern, sober, and steady, Mrs. Ray immediately married herself to her eldest child. Dorothea became the prop against which she would henceforth grow. And against Dorothea she had grown ever since, with the exception of one short year. In that year Dorothea had taken a husband to herself and had lost him;— so that there were two widows in the same house. She, like her mother, had married early, having joined her lot to that of a young clergyman near Baslehurst; but he had lived but a few months, and Mrs. Ray's eldest child had come back to her mother's cottage, black, and stiff, and stern, in widow's weeds,—Mrs. Prime by name. Black, and stiff, and stern, in widow's weeds, she had remained since, for nine years following, and those nine years will bring us to the beginning of our story.

As regards Mrs. Ray herself, I think it was well that poor Mr. Prime had died. It assured to her the support which she needed. It must, however, be acknowledged that Mrs. Prime was a harder taskmaster than Dorothea Ray had been, and that the mother might have undergone a gentler ruling had the daughter never become a wife. I think there was much in the hardness of the weeds she wore. It seemed as though Mrs. Prime in selecting her crape, her bombazine, and the models of her caps, had resolved to repress all ideas of feminine softness;—as though she had sworn to herself, with a great oath, that man should never again look on her with gratified eyes. The materials she wore have made other widows very pleasant to be seen,—with a sad thoughtful pleasantness indeed, but still very pleasant. There was nothing of that with Mrs. Prime. When she came back to her mother's cottage near Baslehurst she was not yet twenty years old, but she was rough with weeds. Her caps were lumpy, heavy, full of woe, and clean only as decency might require,—not nicely clean with feminine care. The very stuff of which they were made was brown, rather than white, and her dress was always the same. It was rough, and black, and clinging,—disagreeable to the eye in its shape, as will always be the dress of any woman which is worn day after day through all hours. By nature and education Mrs. Prime was a prim, tidy woman, but it seemed that her peculiar ideas of duty required her to militate against her nature and education, at any rate in appearance. And this was her lot in life before she had yet reached her twentieth year!

Dorothea Ray had not been wanting in some feminine attraction. She had ever been brown and homely, but her features had been well-formed, and her eyes had been bright. Now, as she approached to thirty years of age, she might have been as well-looking as at any earlier period of her life if it had been her wish to possess good looks. But she had had no such wish. On the contrary, her desire had been to be ugly, forbidding, unattractive, almost repulsive; so that, in very truth, she might be known to be a widow indeed. And here I must not be misunderstood. There was nothing hypocritical about Mrs. Prime, nor did she make any attempt to appear before men to be weighted with a deeper sorrow than that which she truly bore; hypocrisy was by no means her fault. Her fault was this; that she had taught herself to believe that cheerfulness was a sin, and that the more she became morose, the nearer would she be to the fruition of those hopes of future happiness on which her heart was set. In all her words and thoughts she was genuine; but, then, in so very many of them she was mistaken! This was the wall against which Mrs. Ray had allowed herself to be fastened for many years past, and though the support was strong it must be admitted that it could hardly have been at all times pleasant.

Mrs. Ray had become a widow before she was thirty; and she had grieved for her husband with truest sorrow, pouring herself out at first in tears, and afterwards expending herself in long hours of vain regrets. But she had never been rough or hard in her widowhood. It had ever been her nature to be soft. She was a woman all over, and had about her so much of a woman's prettiness, that she had not altogether divested herself of it, even when her weepers had been of the broadest. To obtain favour in men's eyes had never been in her mind since she had first obtained favour in the eyes of him who had been her lord; but yet she had never absolutely divested herself of her woman charms, of that look half retreating, half beseeching, which had won the heart of the ecclesiastical lawyer. Gradually her weeds and her deep heavy crapes had fallen away from her, and then, without much thought on the matter, she dressed herself much as did other women of forty or forty-five,—being driven, however, on certain occasions by her daughter to a degree of dinginess, not by any means rivalling that of the daughter herself, but which she would not have achieved had she been left to her own devices. She was a sweet-tempered, good-humoured, loving, timid woman, ever listening and believing and learning, with a certain aptitude for gentle mirth at her heart which, however, was always being repressed and controlled by the circumstances of her life. She could gossip over a cup of tea, and enjoy buttered toast and hot cake very thoroughly, if only there was no one near her to whisper into her ear that any such enjoyment was wicked. In spite of the sorrows she had suffered she would have taught herself to believe this world to be a pleasant place, were it not so often preached into her ears that it is a vale of tribulation in which no satisfaction can abide. And it may be said of Mrs. Ray that her religion, though it sufficed her, tormented her grievously. It sufficed her; and if on such a subject I may venture to give an opinion, I think it was of a nature to suffice her in that great strait for which it had been prepared. But in this world it tormented her, carrying her hither and thither, and leaving her in grievous doubt, not as to its own truth in any of its details, but as to her own conduct under its injunctions, and also as to her own mode of believing in it. In truth she believed too much. She could never divide the minister from the Bible;—nay, the very clerk in the church was sacred to her while exercising his functions therein. It never occurred to her to question any word that was said to her. If a linen-draper were to tell her that one coloured calico was better for her than another, she would take that point as settled by the man's word, and for the time would be free from all doubt on that heading. So also when the clergyman in his sermon told her that she should live simply and altogether for heaven, that all thoughts as to this world were wicked thoughts, and that nothing belonging to this world could be other than painful, full of sorrow and vexations, she would go home believing him absolutely, and with tear-laden eyes would bethink herself how utterly she was a castaway, because of that tea, and cake, and innocent tittle tattle with which the hours of her Saturday evening had been beguiled. She would weakly resolve that she would laugh no more, and that she would live in truth in a valley of tears. But then as the bright sun came upon her, and the birds sang around her, and some one that she loved would cling to her and kiss her, she would be happy in her own despite, and would laugh with a low musical sweet tone, forgetting that such laughter was a sin.

And then that very clergyman himself would torment her;—he that told her from the pulpit on Sundays how frightfully vain were all attempts at worldly happiness. He would come to her on the Monday with a good-natured, rather rubicund face, and would ask after all her little worldly belongings,—for he knew of her history and her means,—and he would joke with her, and tell her comfortably of his grown sons and daughters, who were prospering in worldly matters, and express the fondest solicitude as to their worldly advancement. Twice or thrice a year Mrs. Ray would go to the parsonage, and such evenings would be by no means hours of wailing.

Tea and buttered toast on such occasions would be very manifestly in the ascendant. Mrs. Ray never questioned the propriety of her clergyman's life, nor taught herself to see a discrepancy between his doctrine and his conduct. But she believed in both, and was unconsciously troubled at having her belief so varied. She never thought about it, or discovered that her friend allowed himself to be carried away in his sermons by his zeal, and that he condemned this world in all things, hoping that he might thereby teach his hearers to condemn it in some things. Mrs. Ray would allow herself the privilege of no such argument as that. It was all gospel to her. The parson in the church, and the parson out of the church, were alike gospels to her sweet, white, credulous mind; but these differing gospels troubled her and tormented her.

Of that particular clergyman, I may as well here say that he was the Rev. Charles Comfort, and that he was rector of Cawston, a parish in Devonshire, about two miles out of Baslehurst. Mr. Prime had for a year or two been his curate, and during that term of curacy he had married Dorothea Ray. Then he had died, and his widow had returned from the house her husband had occupied near the church to her mother's cottage. Mr. Prime had been possessed of some property, and when he died he left his widow in the uncontrolled possession of two hundred a year. As it was well known that Mrs. Ray's income was considerably less than this, the people of Baslehurst and Cawston had declared how comfortable for Mrs. Ray would be this accession of wealth to the family. But Mrs. Ray had not become much the richer. Mrs. Prime did no doubt pay her fair quota towards the maintenance of the humble cottage at Bragg's End, for such was the name of the spot at which Mrs. Ray lived. But she did not do more than this. She established a Dorcas society at Baslehurst, of which she became permanent president, and spent her money in carrying on this institution in the manner most pleasing to herself. I fear that Mrs. Prime liked to be more powerful at these charitable meetings than her sister labourers in the same vineyard, and that she achieved this power by the means of her money. I do not bring this as a heavy accusation against her. In such institutions there is generally need of a strong, stirring, leading mind. If some one would not assume power, the power needed would not be exercised. Such a one as Mrs. Prime is often necessary. But we all have our own pet temptations, and I think that Mrs. Prime's temptation was a love of power.

It will be understood that Baslehurst is a town,—a town with a market, and hotels, and a big brewery, and a square, and street; whereas Cawston is a village, or rather a rural parish, three miles out of Baslehurst, north of it, lying on the river Avon. But Bragg's End, though within the parish of Cawston, lies about a mile and a half from the church and village, on the road to Baslehurst, and partakes therefore almost as much of the township of Baslehurst as it does of the rusticity of Cawston. How Bragg came to such an end, or why this corner of the parish came to be thus united for ever to Bragg's name, no one in the parish knew. The place consisted of a little green, and a little wooden bridge, over a little stream that trickled away into the Avon. Here were clustered half a dozen labourers' cottages, and a beer or cider shop. Standing back from the green was the house and homestead of Farmer Sturt, and close upon the green, with its garden hedge running down to the bridge, was the pretty cottage of Mrs. Ray. Mr. Comfort had known her husband, and he had found for her this quiet home. It was a pretty place, with one small sitting-room opening back upon the little garden, and with another somewhat larger fronting towards the road and the green. In the front room Mrs. Ray lived, looking out upon so much of the world as Bragg's End green afforded to her view. The other seemed to be kept with some faint expectation of company that never came. Many of the widow's neatest belongings were here preserved in most perfect order; but one may say that they were altogether thrown away,—unless indeed they afforded solace to their owner in the very act of dusting them. Here there were four or five books, prettily bound, with gilt leaves, arranged in shapes on the small round table. Here also was deposited a spangled mat of wondrous brightness, made of short white sticks of glass strung together. It must have taken care and time in its manufacture, but was, I should say, but of little efficacy either for domestic use or domestic ornament. There were shells on the chimneypiece, and two or three china figures. There was a birdcage hung in the window but without a bird. It was all very clean, but the room conveyed at the first glance an overpowering idea of its own absolute inutility and vanity. It was capable of answering no purpose for which men and women use rooms; but he who could have said so to Mrs. Ray must have been a cruel and a hardhearted man.

The other room which looked out upon the green was snug enough, and sufficed for all the widow's wants. There was a little book-case laden with books. There was the family table at which they ate their meals; and there was the little table near the window at which Mrs. Ray worked. There was an old sofa, and an old arm-chair; and there was, also, a carpet, alas, so old that the poor woman had become painfully aware that she must soon have either no carpet or a new one. A word or two had already been said between her and Mrs. Prime on that matter, but the word or two had not as yet been comfortable. Then, over the fire, there was an old round mirror; and, having told of that, I believe I need not further describe the furniture of the sitting room at Bragg's End.

But I have not as yet described the whole of Mrs. Ray's family. Had I done so, her life would indeed have been sour, and sorrowful, for she was a woman who especially needed companionship. Though I have hitherto spoken but of one daughter, I have said that two had been left with her when her husband died. She had one whom she feared and obeyed, seeing that a master was necessary to her; but she had another whom she loved and caressed, and I may declare, that some such object for her tenderness was as necessary to her as the master. She could not have lived without something to kiss, something to tend, something to which she might speak in short, loving, pet terms of affection. This youngest girl, Rachel, had been only two years old when her father died, and now, at the time of this story, was not yet quite twenty. Her sister was, in truth, only seven years her senior, but in all the facts and ways of life, she seemed to be the elder by at least half a century. Rachel indeed, at the time, felt herself to be much nearer of an age with her mother. With her mother she could laugh and talk, ay, and form little wicked whispered schemes behind the tyrant's back, during some of those Dorcas hours, in which Mrs. Prime would be employed at Baslehurst; schemes, however, for the final perpetration of which, the courage of the elder widow would too frequently be found insufficient.

Rachel Ray was a fair-haired, well-grown, comely girl, — very like her mother in all but this, that whereas about the mother's eyes there was always a look of weakness, there was a shadowing of coming strength of character round those of the daughter. On her brow there was written a capacity for sustained purpose which was wanting to Mrs. Ray. Not that the reader is to suppose that she was masterful like her sister. She had been brought up under Mrs. Prime's directions, and had not, as yet, learned to rebel. Nor was she in any way prone to domineer. A little wickedness now and then, to the extent, perhaps, of a vain walk into Baslehurst on a summer evening, a little obstinacy in refusing to explain whither she had been and whom she had seen, a yawn in church, or a word of complaint as to the length of the second Sunday sermon, — these were her sins; and when rebuked for them by her sister, she would of late toss her head, and look slily across to her mother, with an eye that was not penitent. Then Mrs. Prime would become black and angry, and would foretell hard things for her sister, denouncing her as fashioning herself wilfully in the world's ways. On such occasions Mrs. Ray would become very unhappy, believing first in the one child and then in the other. She would defend Rachel, till her weak defence would be knocked to shivers, and her poor vacillating words taken from out of her mouth. Then, when forced to acknowledge that Rachel was in danger of backsliding, she would kiss her and cry over her, and beg her to listen to the sermons. Rachel hitherto had never rebelled. She had never declared that a walk into Baslehurst was better than a sermon. She had never said out boldly that she liked the world and its wickednesses. But an observer of physiognomy, had such observer been there, might have seen that the days of such rebellion were coming.

She was a fair-haired girl, with hair, not flaxen, but of light-brown tint,—thick, and full, and glossy, so that its charms could not all be hidden away let Mrs. Prime do what she would to effect such hiding. She was well made, being tall and straight, with great appearance of health and strength. She walked as though the motion were pleasant to her, and easy,—as though the very act of walking were a pleasure. She was bright too, and clever in their little cottage, striving hard with her needle to make things look well, and not sparing her strength in giving household assistance. One little maiden Mrs. Ray employed, and a gardener came to her for half a day once a week;—but I doubt whether the maiden in the house, or the gardener out of the house, did as much hard work as Rachel. How she had toiled over that carpet, patching it and piecing it! Even Dorothea could not accuse her of idleness. Therefore Dorothea accused her of profitless industry, because she would not attend more frequently at those Dorcas meetings.

"But, Dolly, how on earth am I to make my own things, and look after mamma's? Charity begins at home." Then had Dorothea put down her huge Dorcas basket, and explained to her sister, at considerable length, her reading of that text of Scripture. "One's own clothes must be made all the same," Rachel said when the female preacher had finished. "And I don't suppose even you would like mamma to go to church without a decent gown." Then Dorothea had seized up her huge basket angrily, and had trudged off into Baslehurst at a quick pace,—at a pace much too quick when the summer's heat is considered;—and as she went, unhappy thoughts filled her mind. A coloured dress belonging to Rachel herself had met her eye, and she had heard tidings of—a young man!

Such tidings, to her ears, were tidings of iniquity, of vanity, of terrible sin; they were tidings which hardly admitted of being discussed with decency, and which had to be spoken of below the breath. A young man! Could it be that such disgrace had fallen upon her sister! She had not as yet mentioned the subject to Rachel, but she had given a dark hint to their afflicted mother.

"No, I didn't see it myself, but I heard it from Miss Pucker."

"She that was to have been married to William Whitecoat, the baker's son, only he went away to Torquay and picked up with somebody else. People said he did it because she does squint so dreadfully."

"Mother!"—and Dorothea spoke very sternly as she answered—"what does it matter to us about William Whitecoat, or Miss Pucker's squint? She is a woman eager in doing good."

"It's only since he left Baslehurst, my dear."

"Mother!—does that matter to Rachel? Will that save her if she be in danger? I tell you that Miss Pucker saw her walking with that young man from the brewery!"

Though Mrs. Ray had been strongly inclined to throw what odium she could upon Miss Pucker, and though she hated Miss Pucker in her heart,—at this special moment,—for having carried tales against her darling, she could not deny, even to herself, that a terrible state of things had arrived if it were really true that Rachel had been seen walking with a young man. She was not bitter on the subject as was Mrs. Prime and poor Miss Pucker, but she was filled full of indefinite horror with regard to young men in general. They were all regarded by her as wolves,—as wolves, either with or without sheep's clothing. I doubt whether she ever brought it home to herself that those whom she now recognized as the established and well-credited lords of the creation had ever been young men themselves. When she heard of a wedding,—when she learned that some struggling son of Adam had taken to himself a wife, and had settled himself down to the sober work of the world, she rejoiced greatly, thinking that the son of Adam had done well to get himself married. But whenever it was whispered into her ear that any young man was looking after a young woman,—that he was taking the only step by which he could hope to find a wife for himself,—she was instantly shocked at the wickedness of the world, and prayed inwardly that the girl at least might be saved like a brand from the burning. A young man, in her estimation, was a wicked wild beast, seeking after young women to devour them, as a cat seeks after mice. This at least was her established idea,—the idea on which she worked, unless some other idea on any special occasion were put into her head. When young Butler Cornbury, the eldest son of the neighbouring squire, came to Cawston after pretty Patty Comfort,—for Patty Comfort was said to have been the prettiest girl in Devonshire;—and when Patty Comfort had been allowed to go to the assemblies at Torquay almost on purpose to meet him, Mrs. Ray had thought it all right, because it had been presented to her mind as all right by the Rector. Butler Cornbury had married Patty Comfort and it was all right. But had she heard of Patty's dancings without the assistance of a few hints from Mr. Comfort himself, her mind would have worked in a different way.

She certainly desired that her own child Rachel should some day find a husband, and Rachel was already older than she had been when she married, or than Mrs. Prime had been at her wedding; but, nevertheless, there was something terrible in the very thought of—a young man; and she, though she would fain have defended her child, hardly knew how to do so otherwise than by discrediting the words of Miss Pucker. "She always was very ill-natured, you know," Mrs. Ray ventured to hint.

"Mother!" said Mrs. Prime, in that peculiarly stern voice of hers. "There can be no reason for supposing that Miss Pucker wishes to malign the child. It is my belief that Rachel will be in Baslehurst this evening. If so, she probably intends to meet him again."

"I know she is going into Baslehurst after tea," said Mrs. Ray, "because she has promised to walk with the Miss Tappitts. She told me so."

"Exactly;—with the brewery girls! Oh, mother!" Now it is certainly true that the three Miss Tappitts were the daughters of Bungall and Tappitt, the old-established brewers of Baslehurst. They were, at least, the actual children of Mr. Tappitt, who was the sole surviving partner in the brewery. The name of Bungall had for many years been used merely to give solidity and standing to the Tappitt family. The Miss Tappitts certainly came from the brewery, and Miss Pucker had said that the young man came from the same quarter. There was ground in this for much suspicion, and Mrs. Ray became uneasy. This conversation between the two widows had occurred before dinner at the cottage on a Saturday;—and it was after dinner that the elder sister had endeavoured to persuade the younger one to accompany her to the Dorcas workshop;—but had endeavoured in vain.

CHAPTER II
THE YOUNG MAN FROM THE BREWERY

There were during the summer months four Dorcas afternoons held weekly in Baslehurst, at all of which Mrs. Prime presided. It was her custom to start soon after dinner, so as to reach the working room before three o'clock, and there she would remain till nine, or as long as the daylight remained. The meeting was held in a sitting room belonging to Miss Pucker, for the use of which the Institution paid some moderate rent. The other ladies, all belonging to Baslehurst, were accustomed to go home to tea in the middle of their labours; but, as Mrs. Prime could not do this because of the distance, she remained with Miss Pucker, paying for such refreshment as she needed. In this way there came to be a great friendship between Mrs. Prime and Miss Pucker;—or rather, perhaps, Mrs. Prime thus obtained the services of a most obedient minister. Rachel had on various occasions gone with her sister to the Dorcas meetings, and once or twice had remained at Miss Pucker's house, drinking tea there. But this she greatly disliked. She was aware, when she did so, that her sister paid for her, and she thought that Dorothea showed by her behaviour that she was mistress of the entertainment. And then Rachel greatly disliked Miss Pucker. She disliked that lady's squint, she disliked the tone of her voice, she disliked her subservience to Mrs. Prime, and she especially disliked the vehemence of her objection to—young men. When Rachel had last left Miss Pucker's room she had resolved that she would never again drink tea there. She had not said to herself positively that she would attend no more of the Dorcas meetings;—but as regarded their summer arrangement this resolve against the tea-drinking amounted almost to the same thing.

It was on this account, I protest, and by no means on account of that young man from the brewery, that Rachel had with determination opposed her sister's request on this special Saturday. And the refusal had been made in an unaccustomed manner, owing to the request also having been pressed with unusual vigour.

"Rachel, I particularly wish it, and I think that you ought to come," Dorothea had said.

"I had rather not come, Dolly."

"That means," continued Mrs. Prime, "that you prefer your pleasure to your duty;—that you boldly declare yourself determined to neglect that which you know you ought to do."

"I don't know any such thing," said Rachel.

"If you think of it you will know it," said Mrs. Prime.

"At any rate I don't mean to go to Miss Pucker's this afternoon."—Then Rachel left the room.

It was immediately after this conversation that Mrs. Prime uttered to Mrs. Ray that terrible hint about the young man; and at the same time uttered another hint by which she strove to impress upon her mother that Rachel ought to be kept in subordination,—in fact, that the power should not belong to Rachel of choosing whether she would or would not go to Dorcas meetings. In all such matters, according to Dorothea's view of the case, Rachel should do as she was bidden. But then how was Rachel to be made to do as she was bidden? How was her sister to enforce her attendance? Obedience in this world depends as frequently on the weakness of him who is governed as on the strength of him who governs. That man who was going to the left is ordered by you with some voice of command to go to the right. When he hesitates you put more command into your voice, more command into your eyes,—and then he obeys. Mrs. Prime had tried this, but Rachel had not turned to the right. When Mrs. Prime applied for aid to their mother, it was a sign that the power of command was going from herself. After dinner the elder sister made another little futile attempt, and then, when she had again failed, she trudged off with her basket.

Mrs. Ray and Rachel were left sitting at the open window, looking out upon the mignionette. It was now in July, when the summer sun is at the hottest,—and in those southern parts of Devonshire the summer sun in July is very hot. There is no other part of England like it. The lanes are low and narrow, and not a breath of air stirs through them. The ground rises in hills on all sides, so that every spot is a sheltered nook. The rich red earth drinks in the heat and holds it, and no breezes come up from the southern torpid sea. Of all counties in England Devonshire is the fairest to the eye; but, having known it in its summer glory, I must confess that those southern regions are not fitted for much noonday summer walking.

"I'm afraid she'll find it very hot with that big basket," said Mrs. Ray, after a short pause. It must not be supposed that either she or Rachel were idle because they remained at home. They both had their needles in their hands, and Rachel was at work, not on that coloured frock of her own which had roused her sister's suspicion, but on needful aid to her mother's Sunday gown.

"She might have left it in Baslehurst if she liked," said Rachel, "or I would have carried it for her as far as the bridge, only that she was so angry with me when she went."

"I don't think she was exactly angry, Rachel."

"Oh, but she was, mamma;—very angry. I know by her way of flinging out of the house."

"I think she was sorry because you would not go with her."

"But I don't like going there, mamma. I don't like that Miss Pucker. I can't go without staying to tea, and I don't like drinking tea there." Then there was a little pause. "You don't want me to go;—do you, mamma? How would the things get done here? and you can't like having your tea alone."

"No; I don't like that at all," said Mrs. Ray. But she hardly thought of what she was saying. Her mind was away, working on the subject of that young man. She felt that it was her duty to say something to Rachel, and yet she did not know what to say. Was she to quote Miss Pucker? It went, moreover, sorely against the grain with her to disturb the comfort of their present happy moments by any disagreeable allusion. The world gave her nothing better than those hours in which Rachel was alone with her,—in which Rachel tended her and comforted her. No word had been said on a subject so wicked and full of vanity, but Mrs. Ray knew that her evening meal would be brought in at half-past five in the shape of a little feast,—a feast which would not be spread if Mrs. Prime had remained at home. At five o'clock Rachel would slip away and make hot toast, and would run over the Green to Farmer Sturt's wife for a little thick cream, and there would be a batter cake, and so there would be a feast. Rachel was excellent at the preparation of such banquets, knowing how to coax the teapot into a good drawing humour, and being very clever in little comforts; and she would hover about her mother, in a way very delightful to that lady, making the widow feel for the time that there was a gleam of sunshine in the valley of tribulation. All that must be over for this afternoon if she spoke of Miss Pucker and the young man. Yes; and must it not be over for many an afternoon to come? If there were to be distrust between her and Rachel what would her life be worth to her?

But yet there was her duty! As she sat there looking out into the garden indistinct ideas of what were a mother's duties to her child lay heavy on her mind,—ideas which were very indistinct, but which were not on that account the less powerful in their operation. She knew that it behoved her to sacrifice everything to her child's welfare, but she did not know what special sacrifice she was at this moment called upon to make. Would it be well that she should leave this matter altogether in the hands of Mrs. Prime, and thus, as it were, abdicate her own authority? Mrs. Prime would undertake such a task with much more skill and power of language than she could use. But then would this be fair to Rachel, and would Rachel obey her sister? Any explicit direction from herself,—if only she could bring herself to give any,—Rachel would, she thought, obey. In this way she resolved that she would break the ice and do her duty.

"Are you going into Baslehurst this evening, dear?" she said.

"Yes, mamma; I shall walk in after tea;—that is if you don't want me. I told the Miss Tappitts I would meet them."

"No; I shan't want you. But Rachel—"

"Well, mamma?"

Mrs. Ray did not know how to do it. The matter was surrounded with difficulties. How was she to begin, so as to introduce the subject of the young man without shocking her child and showing an amount of distrust which she did not feel? "Do you like those Miss Tappitts?" she said.

"Yes;—in a sort of a way. They are very good-natured, and one likes to know somebody. I think they are nicer than Miss Pucker."

"Oh, yes;—I never did like Miss Pucker myself. But, Rachel—"

"What is it, mamma? I know you've something to say, and that you don't half like to say it. Dolly has been telling tales about me, and you want to lecture me, only you haven't got the heart. Isn't that it, mamma?" Then she put down her work, and coming close up to her mother, knelt before her and looked up into her face. "You want to scold me, and you haven't got the heart to do it."

"My darling, my darling," said the mother, stroking her child's soft smooth hair. "I don't want to scold you;—I never want to scold you. I hate scolding anybody."

"I know you do, mamma."

"But they have told me something which has frightened me."

"They! who are they?"

"Your sister told me, and Miss Pucker told her."

"Oh, Miss Pucker! What business has Miss Pucker with me? If she is to come between us all our happiness will be over." Then Rachel rose from her knees and began to look angry, whereupon her mother was more frightened than ever. "But let me hear it, mamma. I've no doubt it is something very awful."

Mrs. Ray looked at her daughter with beseeching eyes, as though praying to be forgiven for having introduced a subject so disagreeable. "Dorothea says that on Wednesday evening you were walking under the churchyard elms with—that young man from the brewery."

At any rate everything had been said now. The extent of the depravity with which Rachel was to be charged had been made known to her in the very plainest terms. Mrs. Ray as she uttered the terrible words turned first pale and then red,—pale with fear and red with shame. As soon as she had spoken them she wished the words unsaid. Her dislike to Miss Pucker amounted almost to hatred. She felt bitterly even towards her own eldest daughter. She looked timidly into Rachel's face and unconsciously construed into their true meaning those lines which formed themselves on the girl's brow and over her eyes.

"Well, mamma; and what else?" said Rachel.

"Dorothea thinks that perhaps you are going into Baslehurst to meet him again."

"And suppose I am?"

From the tone in which this question was asked it was clear to Mrs. Ray that she was expected to answer it. And yet what answer could she make? It had never occurred to her that her child would take upon herself to defend such conduct as that imputed to her, or that any question would be raised as to the propriety or impropriety of the proceeding. She was by no means prepared to show why it was so very terrible and iniquitous. She regarded it as a sin,—known to be a sin generally,—as is stealing or lying. "Suppose I am going to walk with him again? what then?"

"Oh, Rachel, who is he? I don't even know his name. I didn't believe it, when Dorothea told me; only as she did tell me I thought I ought to mention it. Oh dear, oh dear! I hope there is nothing wrong. You were always so good;—I can't believe anything wrong of you."

"No, mamma;—don't. Don't think evil of me."

"I never did, my darling."

"I am not going into Baslehurst to walk with Mr. Rowan;—for I suppose it is him you mean."

"I don't know, my dear; I never heard the young man's name."

"It is Mr. Rowan. I did walk with him along the churchyard path when that woman with her sharp squinting eyes saw me. He does belong to the brewery. He is related in some way to the Tappitts, and was a nephew of old Mrs. Bungall's. He is there as a clerk, and they say he is to be a partner,—only I don't think he ever will, for he quarrels with Mr. Tappitt."

"Dear, dear!" said Mrs. Ray.

"And now, mamma, you know as much about him as I do; only this, that he went to Exeter this morning, and does not come back till Monday, so that it is impossible that I should meet him in Baslehurst this evening;—and it was very unkind of Dolly to say so; very unkind indeed." Then Rachel gave way and began to cry.

It certainly did seem to Mrs. Ray that Rachel knew a good deal about Mr. Rowan. She knew of his kith and kin, she knew of his prospects and what was like to mar his prospects, and she knew also of his immediate proceedings, whereabouts, and intentions. Mrs. Ray did not logically draw any conclusion from these premises, but she became uncomfortably assured that there did exist a considerable intimacy between Mr. Rowan and her daughter. And how had it come to pass that this had been allowed to form itself without any knowledge on her part? Miss Pucker might be odious and disagreeable;—Mrs. Ray was inclined to think that the lady in question was very odious and disagreeable;—but must it not be admitted that her little story about the young man had proved itself to be true?

"I never will go to those nasty rag meetings any more."

"Oh Rachel, don't speak in that way."

"But I won't. I will never put my foot in that woman's room again. They talk nothing but scandal all the time they are there, and speak any ill they can of the poor young girls whom they talk about. If you don't mind my knowing Mr. Rowan, what is it to them?"

But this was assuming a great deal. Mrs. Ray was by no means prepared to say that she did not object to her daughter's acquaintance with Mr. Rowan. "But I don't know anything about him, my dear. I never heard his name before."

"No, mamma; you never did. And I know very little of him; so little that there has been nothing to tell,—at least next to nothing. I don't want to have any secrets from you, mamma."

"But, Rachel,—he isn't, is he—? I mean there isn't anything particular between him and you? How was it you were walking with him alone?"

"I wasn't walking with him alone;—at least only for a little way. He had been out with his cousins and we had all been together, and when they went in, of course I was obliged to come home. I couldn't help his coming along the churchyard path with me. And what if he did, mamma? He couldn't bite me."

"But my dear—"

"Oh mamma;—don't be afraid of me." Then she came across, and again knelt at her mother's feet. "If you'll trust me I'll tell you everything."

Upon hearing this assurance, Mrs. Ray of course promised Rachel that she would trust her and expected in return to be told everything then, at the moment. But she perceived that her daughter did not mean to tell her anything further at that time. Rachel, when she had received her mother's promise, embraced her warmly, caressing her and petting her as was her custom, and then after a while she resumed her work. Mrs. Ray was delighted to have the evil thing over, but she could not but feel that the conversation had not terminated as it should have done.

Soon after that the hour arrived for their little feast, and Rachel went about her work just as merrily and kindly as though there had been no words about the young man. She went across for the cream, and stayed gossiping for some few minutes with Mrs. Sturt. Then she bustled about the kitchen making the tea and toasting the bread. She had never been more anxious to make everything comfortable for her mother, and never more eager in her coaxing way of doing honour to the good things which she had prepared; but, through it all, her mother was aware that everything was not right; there was something in Rachel's voice which betrayed inward uneasiness;—something in the vivacity of her movements that was not quite true to her usual nature. Mrs. Ray felt that it was so, and could not therefore be altogether at her ease. She pretended to enjoy herself;—but Rachel knew that her joy was not real. Nothing further, however, was said, either regarding that evening's walk into Baslehurst, or touching that other walk as to which Miss Pucker's tale had been told. Mrs. Ray had done as much as her courage enabled her to attempt on that occasion.

When the tea-drinking was over, and the cups and spoons had been tidily put away, Rachel prepared herself for her walk. She had been very careful that nothing should be hurried,—that there should be no apparent anxiety on her part to leave her mother quickly. And even when all was done, she would not go without some assurance of her mother's goodwill. "If you have any wish that I should stay, mamma, I don't care in the least about going."

"No, my dear; I don't want you to stay at all."

"Your dress is finished."

"Thank you, my dear; you have been very good."

"I haven't been good at all; but I will be good if you'll trust me."

"I will trust you."

"At any rate you need not be afraid to-night, for I am only going to take a walk with those three girls across the church meadows. They're always very civil, and I don't like to turn my back upon them."

"I don't wish you to turn your back upon them."

"It's stupid not to know anybody; isn't it?"

"I dare say it is," said Mrs. Ray. Then Rachel had finished tying on her hat, and she walked forth.

For more than two hours after that the widow sat alone, thinking of her children. As regarded Mrs. Prime, there was at any rate no cause for trembling, timid thoughts. She might be regarded as being safe from the world's wicked allurements. She was founded like a strong rock, and was, with her stedfast earnestness, a staff on which her weaker mother might lean with security. But then she was so stern,—and her very strength was so oppressive! Rachel was weaker, more worldly, given terribly to vain desires and thoughts that were almost wicked; but then it was so pleasant to live with her! And Rachel, though weak and worldly and almost wicked, was so very good and kind and sweet! As Mrs. Ray thought of this she began to doubt whether, after all, the world was so very bad a place, and whether the wickedness of tea and toast, and of other creature comforts, could be so very great. "I wonder what sort of a young man he is," she said to herself.

Mrs. Prime's return was always timed with the regularity of clockwork. At this period of the year she invariably came in exactly at half-past nine. Mrs. Ray was very anxious that Rachel should come in first, so that nothing should be said of her walk on this evening. She had been unwilling to imply distrust by making any special request on this occasion, and had therefore said nothing on the subject as Rachel went; but she had carefully watched the clock, and had become uneasy as the time came round for Mrs. Prime's appearance. Exactly at half-past nine she entered the house, bringing with her the heavy basket laden with work, and bringing with her also a face full of the deepest displeasure. She said nothing as she seated herself wearily on a chair against the wall; but her manner was such as to make it impossible that her mother should not notice it. "Is there anything wrong, Dorothea?" she said.

"Rachel has not come home yet, of course?" said Mrs. Prime.

"No; not yet. She is with the Miss Tappitts."

"No, mother, she is not with the Miss Tappitts:" and her voice, as she said these words, was dreadful to the mother's ears.

"Isn't she? I thought she was. Do you know where she is?"

"Who is to say where she is? Half an hour since I saw her alone with—"

"With whom? Not with that young man from the brewery, for he is at Exeter."

"Mother, he is here,—in Baslehurst! Half an hour since he and Rachel were standing alone together beneath the elms in the churchyard. I saw them with my own eyes."

CHAPTER III
THE ARM IN THE CLOUDS

There was plenty of time for full inquiry and full reply between Mrs. Ray and Mrs. Prime before Rachel opened the cottage door, and interrupted them. It was then nearly half-past ten. Rachel had never been so late before. The last streak of the sun's reflection in the east had vanished, the last ruddy line of evening light had gone, and the darkness of the coming night was upon them. The hour was late for any girl such as Rachel Ray to be out alone.

There had been a long discussion between the mother and the elder daughter; and Mrs. Ray, believing implicitly in the last announcements made to her, was full of fears for her child. The utmost rigour of self-denying propriety should have been exercised by Rachel, whereas her conduct had been too dreadful almost to be described. Two or three hours since Mrs. Ray had fondly promised that she would trust her younger daughter, and had let her forth alone, proud in seeing her so comely as she went. An idea had almost entered her mind that if the young man was very steady, such an acquaintance might perhaps be not altogether wicked. But everything was changed now. All the happiness of her trust was gone. All her sweet hopes were crushed. Her heart was filled with fear, and her face was pale with sorrow.

"Why should she know where he was to be?" Dorothea had asked. "But he is not at Exeter;—he is here, and she was with him." Then the two had sat gloomily together till Rachel returned. As she came in there was a little forced laugh upon her face. "I am late; am I not?" she said. "Oh, Rachel, very late!" said her mother. "It is half-past ten," said Mrs. Prime. "Oh, Dolly, don't speak with that terrible voice, as though the world were coming to an end," said Rachel; and she looked up almost savagely, showing that she was resolved to fight.

But it may be as well to say a few words about the firm of Messrs. Bungall and Tappitt, about the Tappitt family generally, and about Mr. Luke Rowan, before any further portion of the history of that evening is written.

Why there should have been any brewery at all at Baslehurst, seeing that everybody in that part of the world drinks cider, or how, under such circumstances, Messrs. Bungall and Tappitt had managed to live upon the proceeds of their trade, I cannot pretend to say. Baslehurst is in the heart of the Devonshire cider country. It is surrounded by orchards, and farmers talk there of their apples as they do of their cheese in Cheshire, or their wheat in Essex, or their sheep in Lincolnshire. Men drink cider by the gallon,—by the gallon daily; cider presses are to be found at every squire's house, at every parsonage, and every farm homestead. The trade of a brewer at Baslehurst would seem to be as profitless as that of a breeches-maker in the Highlands, or a shoemaker in Connaught;—but nevertheless Bungall and Tappitt had been brewers in Baslehurst for the last fifty years, and had managed to live out of their brewery.

It is not to be supposed that they were great men like the mighty men of beer known of old,—such as Barclay and Perkins, or Reid and Co. Nor were they new, and pink, and prosperous, going into Parliament for this borough and that, just as they pleased, like the modern heroes of the bitter cask. When the student at Oxford was asked what man had most benefited humanity, and when he answered "Bass," I think that he should not have been plucked. It was a fair average answer. But no student at any university could have said as much for Bungall and Tappitt without deserving utter disgrace, and whatever penance an outraged examiner could inflict. It was a sour and muddy stream that flowed from their vats; a beverage disagreeable to the palate, and very cold and uncomfortable to the stomach. Who drank it I could never learn. It was to be found at no respectable inn. It was admitted at no private gentleman's table. The farmers knew nothing of it. The labourers drenched themselves habitually with cider. Nevertheless the brewery of Messrs. Bungall and Tappitt was kept going, and the large ugly square brick house in which the Tappitt family lived was warm and comfortable. There is something in the very name of beer that makes money.

Old Bungall, he who first established the house, was still remembered by the seniors of Baslehurst, but he had been dead more than twenty years before the period of my story. He had been a short, fat old man, not much above five feet high, very silent, very hard, and very ignorant. But he had understood business, and had established the firm on a solid foundation. Late in life he had taken into partnership his nephew Tappitt, and during his life had been a severe taskmaster to his partner. Indeed the firm had only assumed its present name on the demise of Bungall. As long as he had lived it had been Bungall's brewery. When the days of mourning were over, then—and not till then—Mr. Tappitt had put up a board with the joint names of the firm as at present called.

It was believed in Baslehurst that Mr. Bungall had not bequeathed his undivided interest in the concern to his nephew. Indeed people went so far as to say that he had left away from Mr. Tappitt all that he could leave. The truth in that respect may as well be told at once. His widow had possessed a third of the profits of the concern, in lieu of her right to a full half share in the concern, which would have carried with it the onus of a full half share of the work. That third and those rights she had left to her nephew,—or rather to her great-nephew, Luke Rowan. It was not, however, in this young man's power to walk into the brewery and claim a seat there as a partner. It was not in his power to do so, even if such should be his wish. When old Mrs. Bungall died at Dawlish at the very advanced age of ninety-seven, there came to be, as was natural, some little dispute between Mr. Tappitt and his distant connection, Luke Rowan. Mr. Tappitt suggested that Luke should take a thousand pounds down, and walk forth free from all contamination of malt and hops. Luke's attorney asked for ten thousand. Luke Rowan at the time was articled to a lawyer in London, and as the dinginess of the chambers which he frequented in Lincoln's Inn Fields appeared to him less attractive than the beautiful rivers of Devonshire, he offered to go into the brewery as a partner. It was at last settled that he should place himself there as a clerk for twelve months, drawing a certain moderate income out of the concern; and that if at the end of the year he should show himself to be able, and feel himself to be willing, to act as a partner, the firm should be changed to Tappitt and Rowan, and he should be established permanently as a Baslehurst brewer. Some information, however, beyond this has already been given to the reader respecting Mr. Rowan's prospects. "I don't think he ever will be a partner," Rachel had said to her mother, "because he quarrels with Mr. Tappitt." She had been very accurate in her statement. Mr. Rowan had now been three months at Baslehurst, and had not altogether found the ways of his relative pleasant. Mr. Tappitt wished to treat him as a clerk, whereas he wished to be treated as a partner. And Mr. Tappitt had by no means found the ways of the young man to be pleasant. Young Rowan was not idle, nor did he lack intelligence; indeed he possessed more energy and cleverness than, in Tappitt's opinion, were necessary to the position of a brewer in Baslehurst; but he was by no means willing to use these good gifts in the manner indicated by the sole existing owner of the concern. Mr. Tappitt wished that Rowan should learn brewing seated on a stool, and that the lessons should be purely arithmetical. Luke was instructed as to the use of certain dull, dingy, disagreeable ledgers, and informed that in them lay the natural work of a brewer. But he desired to learn the chemical action of malt and hops upon each other, and had not been a fortnight in the concern before he suggested to Mr. Tappitt that by a salutary process, which he described, the liquor might be made less muddy. "Let us brew good beer," he had said; and then Tappitt had known that it would not do. "Yes," said Tappitt, "and sell for twopence a pint what will cost you threepence to make!" "That's what we've got to look to," said Rowan. "I believe it can be done for the money,—only one must learn how to do it." "I've been at it all my life," Tappitt said. "Yes, Mr. Tappitt; but it is only now that men are beginning to appreciate all that chemistry can do for them. If you'll allow me I'll make an experiment on a small scale." After that Mr. Tappitt had declared emphatically to his wife that Luke Rowan should never become a partner of his. "He would ruin any business in the world," said Tappitt. "And as to conceit!" It is true that Rowan was conceited, and perhaps true also that he would have ruined the brewery had he been allowed to have his own way.

But Mrs. Tappitt by no means held him in such aversion as did her husband. He was a well-grown, good-looking young man for whom his friends had made comfortable provision, and Mrs. Tappitt had three marriageable daughters. Her ideas on the subject of young men in general were by no means identical with those held by Mrs. Ray. She was aware how frequently it happened that a young partner would marry a daughter of the senior in the house, and it seemed to her that special provision for such an arrangement was made in this case. Young Rowan was living in her house, and was naturally thrown into great intimacy with her girls. It was clear to her quick eye that he was of a susceptible disposition, fond of ladies' society, and altogether prone to those pleasant pre-matrimonial conversations, from the effects of which it is so difficult for an inexperienced young man to make his escape. Mrs. Tappitt was minded to devote to him Augusta, the second of her flock,—but not so minded with any obstinacy of resolution. If Luke should prefer Martha, the elder, or Cherry, the younger girl, Mrs. Tappitt would make no objection; but she expected that he should do his duty by taking one of them. "Laws, T., don't be so foolish," she said to her husband, when he made his complaint to her. She always called her husband T., unless when the solemnity of some special occasion justified her in addressing him as Mr. Tappitt. To have called him Tom or Thomas, would, in her estimation, have been very vulgar. "Don't be so foolish. Did you never have to do with a young man before? Those tantrums will all blow off when he gets himself into harness." The tantrums spoken of were Rowan's insane desire to brew good beer, but they were of so fatal a nature that Tappitt was determined not to submit himself to them. Luke Rowan should never be partner of his,—not though he had twenty daughters waiting to be married!

Rachel had been acquainted with the Tappitts before young Rowan had come to Baslehurst, and had been made known to him by them all collectively. Had they shared their mother's prudence they would probably not have done anything so rash. Rachel was better-looking than either of them,—though that fact perhaps might not have been known to them. But in justice to them all I must say that they lacked their mother's prudence. They were good-humoured, laughing, ordinary girls,—very much alike, with long brown curls, fresh complexions, large mouths, and thick noses. Augusta was rather the taller of the three, and therefore, in her mother's eyes, the beauty. But the girls themselves, when their distant cousin had come amongst them, had not thought of appropriating him. When, after the first day, they became intimate with him, they promised to introduce him to the beauties of the neighbourhood, and Cherry had declared her conviction that he would fall in love with Rachel Ray directly he saw her. "She is tall, you know," said Cherry, "a great deal taller than us." "Then I'm sure I shan't like her," Luke had said. "Oh, but you must like her, because she is a friend of ours," Cherry had answered; "and I shouldn't be a bit surprised if you fell violently in love with her." Mrs. Tappitt did not hear all this, but, nevertheless, she began to entertain a dislike to Rachel. It must not be supposed that she admitted her daughter Augusta to any participation in her plans. Mrs. Tappitt could scheme for her child, but she could not teach her child to scheme. As regarded the girl, it must all fall out after the natural, pleasant, everyday fashion of such things; but Mrs. Tappitt considered that her own natural advantages were so great that she could make the thing fall out as she wished. When she was informed about a fortnight after Rowan's arrival in Baslehurst that Rachel Ray had been walking with the party from the brewery, she could not prevent herself from saying an ill-natured word or two. "Rachel Ray is all very well," she said, "but she is not the person whom you should show off to a stranger as your particular friend."

"Why not, mamma?" said Cherry.

"Why not, my dear! There are reasons why not. Mrs. Ray is very well in her way, but—"

"Her husband was a gentleman," said Martha, "and a great friend of Mr. Comfort's."

"My dear, I have nothing to say against her," said the mother, "only this; that she does not go among the people we know. There is Mrs. Prime, the other daughter; her great friend is Miss Pucker. I don't suppose you want to be very intimate with Miss Pucker." The brewer's wife had a position in Baslehurst and wished that her daughters should maintain it.

It will now be understood in what way Rachel had formed her acquaintance with Luke Rowan, and I think it may certainly be admitted that she had been guilty of no great impropriety;—unless, indeed, she had been wrong in saying nothing of the acquaintance to her mother. Previous to those ill-natured tidings brought home as to the first churchyard meeting, Rachel had seen him but twice. On the first occasion she had thought but little of it,—but little of Luke himself or of her acquaintance with him. In simple truth the matter had passed from her mind, and therefore she had not spoken of it. When they met the second time, Luke had walked much of the way home with her,—with her alone,—having joined himself to her when the Tappitt girls went into their house as Rachel had afterwards described to her mother. In all that she had said she had spoken absolutely the truth; but it cannot be pleaded on her behalf that after this second meeting with Mr. Rowan she had said nothing of him because she had thought nothing. She had indeed thought much, but it had seemed well to her to keep her thoughts to herself.

The Tappitt girls had by no means given up their friend because their mother had objected to Miss Pucker; and when Rachel met them on that Saturday evening,—that fatal Saturday,—they were very gracious to her. The brewery at Baslehurst stood on the outskirts of the town, in a narrow lane which led from the church into the High-street. This lane,—Brewery-lane, as it was called,—was not the main approach to the church; but from the lane there was a stile into the churchyard, and a gate, opened on Sundays, by which people on that side reached the church. From the opposite side of the churchyard a road led away to the foot of the High-street, and out towards the bridge which divided the town from the parish of Cawston. Along one side of this road there was a double row of elms, having a footpath beneath them. This old avenue began within the churchyard, running across the lower end of it, and was continued for some two hundred yards beyond its precincts. This, then, would be the way which Rachel would naturally take in going home, after leaving the Miss Tappitts at their door; but it was by no means the way which was the nearest for Mrs. Prime after leaving Miss Pucker's lodgings in the High-street, seeing that the High-street itself ran direct to Cawston bridge.

And it must also be explained that there was a third path out of the churchyard, not leading into any road, but going right away across the fields. The church stood rather high, so that the land sloped away from it towards the west, and the view there was very pretty. The path led down through a small field, with high hedgerows, and by orchards, to two little hamlets belonging to Baslehurst, and this was a favourite walk with the people of the town. It was here that Rachel had walked with the Miss Tappitts on that evening when Luke Rowan had first accompanied her as far as Cawston bridge, and it was here that they agreed to walk again on the Saturday when Rowan was supposed to be away at Exeter. Rachel was to come along under the elms, and was to meet her friends there, or in the churchyard, or, if not so, then she was to call for them at the brewery.

She found the three girls leaning against the rails near the churchyard stile. "We have been waiting ever so long," said Cherry, who was more specially Rachel's friend.

"Oh, but I said you were not to wait," said Rachel, "for I never am quite sure whether I can come."

"We knew you'd come," said Augusta, "because—"

"Because what?" asked Rachel.

"Because nothing," said Cherry. "She's only joking."

Rachel said nothing more, not having understood the point of the joke. The joke was this,—that Luke Rowan had come back from Exeter, and that Rachel was supposed to have heard of his return, and therefore that her coming for the walk was certain. But Augusta had not intended to be ill-natured, and had not really believed what she had been about to insinuate. "The fact is," said Martha, "that Mr. Rowan has come home; but I don't suppose we shall see anything of him this evening as he is busy with papa."

Rachel for a few minutes became silent and thoughtful. Her mind had not yet freed itself from the effects of her conversation with her mother, and she had been thinking of this young man during the whole of her solitary walk into town. But she had been thinking of him as we think of matters which need not put us to any immediate trouble. He was away at Exeter, and she would have time to decide whether or no she would admit his proffered intimacy before she should see him again. "I do so hope we shall be friends," he had said to her as he gave her his hand when they parted on Cawston bridge. And then he had muttered something, which she had not quite caught, as to Baslehurst being altogether another place to him since he had seen her. She had hurried home on that occasion with a feeling, half pleasant and half painful, that something out of the usual course had occurred to her. But, after all, it amounted to nothing. What was there that she could tell her mother? She had no special tale to tell, and yet she could not speak of young Rowan as she would have spoken of a chance acquaintance. Was she not conscious that he had pressed her hand warmly as he parted from her?

Rachel herself entertained much of that indefinite fear of young men which so strongly pervaded her mother's mind, and which, as regarded her sister, had altogether ceased to be indefinite. Rachel knew that they were the natural enemies of her special class, and that any kind of friendship might be allowed to her, except a friendship with any of them. And as she was a good girl, loving her mother, anxious to do well, guided by pure thoughts, she felt aware that Mr. Rowan should be shunned. Had it not been that he himself had told her that he was to be in Exeter, she would not have come out to walk with the brewery girls on that evening. What she might hereafter decide upon doing, how these affairs might be made to arrange themselves, she by no means could foresee;—but on that evening she had thought she would be safe, and therefore she had come out to walk.

"What do you think?" said Cherry; "we are going to have a party next week."

"It won't be till the week after," said Augusta.

"At any rate, we are going to have a party, and you must come. You'll get a regular invite, you know, when they're sent out. Mr. Rowan's mother and sister are coming down on a visit to us for a few days, and so we're going to be quite smart."

"I don't know about going to a party. I suppose it is for a dance?"

"Of course it is for a dance," said Martha.

"And of course you'll come and dance with Luke Rowan," said Cherry. Nothing could be more imprudent than Cherry Tappitt, and Augusta was beginning to be aware of this, though she had not been allowed to participate in her mother's schemes. After that, there was much talking about the party, but the conversation was chiefly kept up by the Tappitt girls. Rachel was almost sure that her mother would not like her to go to a dance, and was quite sure that her sister would oppose such iniquity with all her power; therefore she made no promise. But she listened as the list was repeated of those who were expected to come, and asked some few questions as to Mrs. Rowan and her daughter. Then, at a sudden turn of a lane, a lane that led back to the town by another route, they met Luke Rowan himself.

He was a cousin of the Tappitts, and therefore, though the relationship was not near, he had already assumed the privilege of calling them by their Christian names; and Martha, who was nearly thirty years old, and four years his senior, had taught herself to call him Luke; with the other two he was as yet Mr. Rowan. The greeting was of course very friendly, and he returned with them on their path. To Rachel he raised his hat, and then offered his hand. She had felt herself to be confused the moment she saw him,—so confused that she was not able to ask him how he was with ordinary composure. She was very angry with herself, and heartily wished that she was seated with the Dorcas women at Miss Pucker's. Any position would have been better for her than this, in which she was disgracing herself and showing that she could not bear herself before this young man as though he were no more than an ordinary acquaintance. Her mind would revert to that hand-squeezing, to those muttered words, and to her mother's caution. When he remarked to her that he had come back earlier than he expected, she could not take his words as though they signified nothing. His sudden return was a momentous fact to her, putting her out of her usual quiet mode of thought. She said little or nothing, and he, at any rate, did not observe that she was confused; but she was herself so conscious of it, that it seemed to her that all of them must have seen it.

Thus they sauntered along, back to the outskirts of the town, and so into the brewery lane, by a route opposite to that of the churchyard. The whole way they talked of nothing but the party. Was Miss Rowan fond of dancing? Then by degrees the girls called her Mary, declaring that as she was a cousin they intended so to do. And Luke said that he ought to be called by his Christian name; and the two younger girls agreed that he was entitled to the privilege, only they would ask mamma first; and in this way they were becoming very intimate. Rachel said but little, and perhaps not much that was said was addressed specially to her, but she seemed to feel that she was included in the friendliness of the gathering. Every now and then Luke Rowan would address her, and his voice was pleasant to her ears. He had made an effort to walk next to her,—an attempt almost too slight to be called an effort, which she had, almost unconsciously, frustrated, by so placing herself that Augusta should be between them. Augusta was not quite in a good humour, and said one or two words which were slightly snubbing in their tendency; but this was more than atoned for by Cherry's high good-humour.

When they reached the brewery they all declared themselves to be very much astonished on learning that it was already past nine. Rachel's surprise, at any rate, was real. "I must go home at once," she said; "I don't know what mamma will think of me." And then, wishing them all good-bye, without further delay she hurried on into the churchyard.

"I'll see you safe through the ghosts at any rate," said Rowan.

"I'm not a bit afraid of churchyard ghosts," said Rachel, moving on. But Rowan followed her.

"I've got to go into town to meet your father," said he to the other girls, "and I'll be back with him."

Augusta saw with some annoyance that he had overtaken Rachel before she had passed over the stile, and stood lingering at the door long enough to be aware that Luke was over first. "That girl is a flirt, after all," she said to her sister Martha.

Luke was over the stile first, and then turned round to assist Miss Ray. She could not refuse him her hand in such a position; or if she could have done so she lacked the presence of mind that was necessary for such refusal. "You must let me walk home with you," he said.

"Indeed I will do no such thing. You told Augusta that you were going to her papa in the town."

"So I am, but I will see you first as far as the bridge; you can't refuse me that."

"Indeed I can, and indeed I will. I beg you won't come. I am sure you would not wish to annoy me."

"Look," said he, pointing to the west; "did you ever see such a setting sun as that? Did you ever see such blood-red colour?" The light was very wonderful, for the sun had just gone down and all the western heavens were crimson with its departing glory. In the few moments that they stood there gazing it might almost have been believed that some portentous miracle had happened, so deep and dark, and yet so bright, were the hues of the horizon. It seemed as though the lands below the hill were bathed in blood. The elm trees interrupted their view, so that they could only look out through the spaces between their trunks. "Come to the stile," said he. "If you were to live a thousand years you might never again see such a sunset as that. You would never forgive yourself if you missed it, just that you might save three minutes."

Rachel stepped with him towards the stile; but it was not solely his entreaty that made her do so. As he spoke of the sun's glory her sharp ear caught the sound of a woman's foot close to the stile over which she had passed, and knowing that she could not escape at once from Luke Rowan, she had left the main path through the churchyard, in order that the new comer might not see her there talking to him. So she accompanied him on till they stood between the trees, and then they remained encompassed as it were in the full light of the sun's rays. But if her ears had been sharp, so were the eyes of this new comer. And while she stood there with Rowan beneath the elms, her sister stood a while also on the churchyard path and recognized the figures of them both.

"Rachel," said he, after they had remained there in silence for a moment, "live as long as you may, never on God's earth will you look on any sight more lovely than that. Ah! do you see the man's arm, as it were; the deep purple cloud, like a huge hand stretched out from some other world to take you? Do you see it?"

The sound of his voice was very pleasant. His words to her young ears seemed full of poetry and sweet mysterious romance. He spoke to her as no one,—no man or woman,—had ever spoken to her before. She had a feeling, as painful as it was delicious, that the man's words were sweet with a sweetness which she had known in her dreams. He had asked her a question, and repeated it, so that she was all but driven to answer him; but still she was full of the one great fact that he had called her Rachel, and that he must be rebuked for so calling her. But how could she rebuke a man who had bid her look at God's beautiful works in such language as he had used?

"Yes, I see it; it is very grand; but—"

"There were the fingers, but you see how they are melting away. The arm is there still, but the hand is gone. You and I can trace it because we saw it when it was clear, but we could not now show it to another. I wonder whether any one else saw that hand and arm, or only you and I. I should like to think that it was shown to us, and us only."

It was impossible for her now to go back upon that word Rachel. She must pass it by as though she had not heard it. "All the world might have seen it had they looked," said she.

"Perhaps not. Do you think that all eyes can see alike?"

"Well, yes; I suppose so."

"All eyes will see a loaf of bread alike, or a churchyard stile, but all eyes will not see the clouds alike. Do you not often find worlds among the clouds? I do."

"Worlds!" she said, amazed at his energy; and then she bethought herself that he was right. She would never have seen that hand and arm had he not been there to show it her. So she gazed down upon the changing colours of the horizon, and almost forgot that she should not have lingered there a moment.

And yet there was a strong feeling upon her that she was sinking,—sinking,—sinking away into iniquity. She ought not to have stood there an instant, she ought not to have been there with him at all;—and yet she lingered. Now that she was there she hardly knew how to move herself away.

"Yes; worlds among the clouds," he continued; but before he did so there had been silence between them for a minute or two. "Do you never feel that you look into other worlds beyond this one in which you eat, and drink, and sleep? Have you no other worlds in your dreams?" Yes; such dreams she had known, and now, she almost thought that she could remember to have seen strange forms in the clouds. She knew that henceforth she would watch the clouds and find them there. She looked down into the flood of light beneath her, with a full consciousness that he was close to her, touching her; with a full consciousness that every moment that she lingered there was a new sin; with a full consciousness, too, that the beauty of those fading colours seen thus in his presence possessed a charm, a sense of soft delight, which she had never known before. At last she uttered a long sigh.

"Why, what ails you?" said he.

"Oh, I must go; I have been so wrong to stand here. Good-bye; pray, pray do not come with me."

"But you will shake hands with me." Then he got her hand, and held it. "Why should it be wrong for you to stand and look at the sunset? Am I an ogre? Have I done anything that should make you afraid of me?"

"Do not hold me. Mr. Rowan I did not think you would behave like that." The gloom of the evening was now coming on, and though but a few minutes had passed since Mrs. Prime had walked through the churchyard, she would not have been able to recognize them had she walked there now. "It is getting dark, and I must go instantly."

"Let me go with you, then, as far as the bridge."

"No, no, no. Pray do not vex me."

"I will not. You shall go alone. But stand while I say one word to you. Why should you be afraid of me?"

"I am not afraid of you,—at least,—you know what I mean."

"I wonder,—I wonder whether—you dislike me."

"I don't dislike anybody. Good-night."

He had however again got her hand. "I'll tell you why I ask;—because I like you so much, so very much! Why should we not be friends? Well; there. I will not trouble you now. I will not stir from here till you are out of sight. But mind,—remember this; I intend that you shall like me."

She was gone from him, fleeing away along the path in a run while the last words were being spoken; and yet, though they were spoken in a low voice, she heard and remembered every syllable. What did the man mean by saying that he intended that she should like him? Like him! How could she fail of liking him? Only was it not incumbent on her to take some steps which might save her from ever seeing him again? Like him, indeed! What was the meaning of the word? Had he intended to ask her to love him? And if so, what answer must she make?

How beautiful had been those clouds! As soon as she was beyond the church wall, so that she could look again to the west, she gazed with all her eyes to see if there were still a remnant left of that arm. No; it had all melted into a monstrous shape, indistinct and gloomy, partaking of the darkness of night. The brightness of the vision was gone. But he bade her look into the clouds for new worlds, and she seemed to feel that there was a hidden meaning in his words. As she looked out into the coming darkness, a mystery crept over her, a sense of something wonderful that was out there, away,—of something so full of mystery that she could not tell whether she was thinking of the hidden distances of the horizon, or of the distances of her own future life, which were still further off and more closely hidden. She found herself trembling, sighing, almost sobbing, and then she ran again. He had wrapped her in his influence, and filled her full of the magnetism of his own being. Her woman's weakness,—the peculiar susceptibility of her nature, had never before been touched. She had now heard the first word of romance that had ever reached her ears, and it had fallen upon her with so great a power that she was overwhelmed.

Words of romance! Words direct from the Evil One, Mrs. Prime would have called them! And in saying so she would have spoken the belief of many a good woman and many a good man. She herself was a good woman,—a sincere, honest, hardworking, self-denying woman; a woman who struggled hard to do her duty as she believed it had been taught to her. She, as she walked through the churchyard,—having come down the brewery lane with some inkling that her sister might be there,—had been struck with horror at seeing Rachel standing with that man. What should she do? She paused a moment to ask herself whether she should return for her; but she said to herself that her sister was obstinate, that a scene would be occasioned, that she would do no good,—and so she passed on. Words of romance, indeed! Must not all such words be words from the Father of Lies, seeing that they are words of falseness? Some such thoughts passed through her mind as she walked home, thinking of her sister's iniquity,—of her sister who must be saved, like a brand from the fire, but whose saving could now be effected only by the sternest of discipline. The hours at the Dorcas meetings must be made longer, and Rachel must always be there.

In the mean time Rachel hurried home with her spirits all a-tremble. Of her immediately-coming encounter with her mother and her sister she hardly thought much before she reached the door. She thought only of him, how beautiful he was, how grand,—and how dangerous; of him and of his words, how beautiful they were, how grand, and how terribly dangerous! She knew that it was very late and she hurried her steps. She knew that her mother must be appeased, and her sister must be opposed,—but neither to her mother or to her sister was given the depth of her thoughts. She was still thinking of him, and of the man's arm in the clouds, when she opened the door of the cottage at Bragg's End.

CHAPTER IV
WHAT SHALL BE DONE ABOUT IT?

Rachel was still thinking of Luke Rowan and of the man's arm when she opened the cottage door, but the sight of her sister's face, and the tone of her sister's voice, soon brought her back to a full consciousness of her immediate present position. "Oh, Dolly, do not speak with that terrible voice, as though the world were coming to an end," she said, in answer to the first note of objurgation that was uttered; but the notes that came afterwards were so much more terrible, so much more severe, that Rachel found herself quite unable to stop them by any would-be joking tone.

Mrs. Prime was desirous that her mother should speak the words of censure that must be spoken. She would have preferred herself to remain silent, knowing that she could be as severe in her silence as in her speech, if only her mother would use the occasion as it should be used. Mrs. Ray had been made to feel how great was the necessity for outspoken severity; but when the moment came, and her dear beautiful child stood there before her, she could not utter the words with which she had been already prompted. "Oh, Rachel," she said, "Dorothea tells me—" and then she stopped.

"What has Dorothea told you?" asked Rachel.

"I have told her," said Mrs. Prime, now speaking out, "that I saw you standing alone an hour since with that young man,—in the churchyard. And yet you had said that he was to have been away in Exeter!"

Rachel's cheeks and forehead were now suffused with red. We used to think, when we pretended to read the faces of our neighbours, that a rising blush betrayed a conscious falsehood. For the most part we know better now, and have learned to decipher more accurately the outward signs which are given by the impulses of the heart. An unmerited accusation of untruth will ever bring the blood to the face of the young and innocent. But Mrs. Ray was among the ignorant in this matter, and she groaned inwardly when she saw her child's confusion.

"Oh, Rachel, is it true?" she said.

"Is what true, mamma? It is true that Mr. Rowan spoke to me in the churchyard, though I did not know that Dorothea was acting as a spy on me."

"Rachel, Rachel!" said the mother.

"It is very necessary that some one should act the spy on you," said the sister. "A spy, indeed! You think to anger me by using such a word, but I will not be angered by any words. I went there to look after you, fearing that there was occasion,—fearing it, but hardly thinking it. Now we know that there was occasion."

"There was no occasion," said Rachel, looking into her sister's face with eyes of which the incipient strength was becoming manifest. "There was no occasion. Oh, mamma, you do not think there was an occasion for watching me?"

"Why did you say that that young man was at Exeter?" asked Mrs. Prime.

"Because he had told me that he would be there;—he had told us all so, as we were walking together. He came to-day instead of coming to-morrow. What would you say if I questioned you in that way about your friends?" Then, when the words had passed from her lips, she remembered that she should not have called Mr. Rowan her friend. She had never called him so, in thinking of him, to herself. She had never admitted that she had any regard for him. She had acknowledged to herself that it would be very dangerous to entertain friendship for such as he.

"Friend, Rachel!" said Mrs. Prime. "If you look for such friendship as that, who can say what will come to you?"

"I haven't looked for it. I haven't looked for anything. People do get to know each other without any looking, and they can't help it."

Then Mrs. Prime took off her bonnet and her shawl, and Rachel laid down her hat and her little light summer cloak; but it must not be supposed that the war was suspended during these operations. Mrs. Prime was aware that a great deal more must be said, but she was very anxious that her mother should say it. Rachel also knew that much more would be said, and she was by no means anxious that the subject should be dropped, if only she could talk her mother over to her side.

"If mother thinks it right," exclaimed Mrs. Prime, "that you should be standing alone with a young man after nightfall in the churchyard, then I have done. In that case I will say no more. But I must tell her, and I must tell you also, that if it is to be so, I cannot remain at the cottage any longer."

"Oh, Dorothea!" said Mrs. Ray.

"Indeed, mother, I cannot. If Rachel is not hindered from such meetings by her own sense of what is right, she must be hindered by the authority of those older than herself."

"Hindered,—hindered from what?" said Rachel, who felt that her tears were coming, but struggled hard to retain them. "Mamma, I have done nothing that was wrong. Mamma, you will believe me, will you not?"

Mrs. Ray did not know what to say. She strove to believe both of them, though the words of one were directly at variance with the words of the other.

"Do you mean to claim it as your right," said Mrs. Prime, "to be standing out there alone at any hour of the night, with any young man that you please? If so, you cannot be my sister."

"I do not want to be your sister if you think such hard things," said Rachel, whose tears now could no longer be restrained. Honi soit qui mal y pense. She did not, at the moment, remember the words to speak them, but they contain exactly the purport of her thought. And now, having become conscious of her own weakness by reason of these tears which would overwhelm her, she determined that she would say nothing further till she pleaded her cause before her mother alone. How could she describe before her sister the way in which that interview at the churchyard stile had been brought about? But she could kneel at her mother's feet and tell her everything;—she thought, at least, that she could tell her mother everything. She occupied generally the same bedroom as her sister; but, on certain occasions,—if her mother was unwell or the like,—she would sleep in her mother's room. "Mamma," she said, "you will let me sleep with you to-night. I will go now, and when you come I will tell you everything. Good night to you, Dolly."

"Good night, Rachel;" and the voice of Mrs. Prime, as she bade her sister adieu for the evening, sounded as the voice of the ravens.

The two widows sat in silence for a while, each waiting for the other to speak. Then Mrs. Prime got up and folded her shawl very carefully, and carefully put her bonnet and gloves down upon it. It was her habit to be very careful with her clothes, but in her anger she had almost thrown them upon the little sofa. "Will you have anything before you go to bed, Dorothea?" said Mrs. Ray. "Nothing, thank you," said Mrs. Prime; and her voice was very like the voice of the ravens. Then Mrs. Ray began to think it possible that she might escape away to Rachel without any further words. "I am very tired," she said, "and I think I will go, Dorothea."

"Mother," said Mrs. Prime, "something must be done about this."

"Yes, my dear; she will talk to me to-night, and tell it me all."

"But will she tell you the truth?"

"She never told me a falsehood yet, Dorothea. I'm sure she didn't know that the young man was to be here. You know if he did come back from Exeter before he said he would she couldn't help it."

"And do you mean that she couldn't help being with him there,—all alone? Mother, what would you think of any other girl of whom you heard such a thing?"

Mrs. Ray shuddered; and then some thought, some shadow perhaps of a remembrance, flitted across her mind, which seemed to have the effect of palliating her child's iniquity. "Suppose—" she said. "Suppose what?" said Mrs. Prime, sternly. But Mrs. Ray did not dare to go on with her supposition. She did not dare to suggest that Mr. Rowan might perhaps be a very proper young man, and that the two young people might be growing fond of each other in a proper sort of way. She hardly believed in any such propriety herself, and she knew that her daughter would scout it to the winds. "Suppose what?" said Mrs. Prime again, more sternly than before. "If the other girls left her and went away to the brewery, perhaps she could not have helped it," said Mrs. Ray.

"But she was not walking with him. Her face was not turned towards home even. They were standing together under the trees, and, judging from the time at which I got home, they must have remained together for nearly half an hour afterwards. And this with a perfect stranger, mother,—a man whose name she had never mentioned to us till she was told how Miss Pucker had seen them together! You cannot suppose that I want to make her out worse than she is. She is your child, and my sister; and we are bound together for weal or for woe."

"You talked about going away and leaving us," said Mrs. Ray, speaking in soreness rather than in anger.

"So I did; and so I must, unless something be done. It could not be right that I should remain here, seeing such things, if my voice is not allowed to be heard. But though I did go, she would still be my sister. I should still share the sorrow,—and the shame."

"Oh, Dorothea, do not say such words."

"But they must be said, mother. Is it not from such meetings that shame comes,—shame, and sorrow, and sin? You love her dearly, and so do I; and are we therefore to allow her to be a castaway? Those whom you love you must chastise. I have no authority over her,—as she has told me, more than once already,—and therefore I say again, that unless all this be stopped, I must leave the cottage. Good night, now, mother. I hope you will speak to her in earnest." Then Mrs. Prime took her candle and went her way.

For ten minutes the mother sat herself down, thinking of the condition of her youngest daughter, and trying to think what words she would use when she found herself in her daughter's presence. Sorrow, and Shame, and Sin! Her child a castaway! What terrible words they were! And yet there had been nothing that she could allege in answer to them. That comfortable idea of a decent husband for her child had been banished from her mind almost before it had been entertained. Then she thought of Rachel's eyes, and knew that she would not be able to assume a perfect mastery over her girl. When the ten minutes were over she had made up her mind to nothing, and then she also took up her candle and went to her room. When she first entered it she did not see Rachel. She had silently closed the door and come some steps within the chamber before her child showed herself from behind the bed. "Mamma," she said, "put down the candle that I may speak to you." Whereupon Mrs. Ray put down the candle, and Rachel took hold of both her arms. "Mamma, you do not believe ill of me; do you? You do not think of me the things that Dorothea says? Say that you do not, or I shall die."

"My darling, I have never thought anything bad of you before."

"And do you think bad of me now? Did you not tell me before I went out that you would trust me, and have you so soon forgotten your trust? Look at me, mamma. What have I ever done that you should think me to be such as she says?"

"I do not think that you have done anything; but you are very young, Rachel."

"Young, mamma! I am older than you were when you married, and older than Dolly was. I am old enough to know what is wrong. Shall I tell you what happened this evening? He came and met us all in the fields. I knew before that he had come back, for the girls had said so, but I thought that he was in Exeter when I left here. Had I not believed that, I should not have gone. I think I should not have gone."

"Then you are afraid of him?"

"No, mamma; I am not afraid of him. But he says such strange things to me; and I would not purposely have gone out to meet him. He came to us in the fields, and then we returned up the lane to the brewery, and there we left the girls. As I went through the churchyard he came there too, and then the sun was setting, and he stopped me to look at it; I did stop with him,—for a few moments, and I felt ashamed of myself; but how was I to help it? Mamma, if I could remember them I would tell you every word he said to me, and every look of his face. He asked me to be his friend. Mamma, if you will believe in me I will tell you everything. I will never deceive you."

She was still holding her mother's arms while she spoke. Now she held her very close and nestled in against her bosom, and gradually got her cheek against her mother's cheek, and her lips against her mother's neck. How could any mother refuse such a caress as that, or remain hard and stern against such signs of love? Mrs. Ray, at any rate, was not possessed of strength to do so. She was vanquished, and put her arm round her girl and embraced her. She spoke soft words, and told Rachel that she was her dear, dear, dearest darling. She was still awed and dismayed by the tidings which she had heard of the young man; she still thought there was some terrible danger against which it behoved them all to be on their guard. But she no longer felt herself divided from her child, and had ceased to believe in the necessity of those terrible words which Mrs. Prime had used.

"You will believe me?" said Rachel. "You will not think that I am making up stories to deceive you?" Then the mother assured the daughter with many kisses that she would believe her.

After that they sat long into the night, discussing all that Luke Rowan had said, and the discussion certainly took place after a fashion that would not have been considered satisfactory by Mrs. Prime had she heard it. Mrs. Ray was soon led into talking about Mr. Rowan as though he were not a wolf,—as though he might possibly be neither a wolf ravenous with his native wolfish fur and open wolfish greed; or, worse than that, a wolf, more ravenous still, in sheep's clothing. There was no word spoken of him as a lover; but Rachel told her mother that the man had called her by her Christian name, and Mrs. Ray had fully understood the sign. "My darling, you mustn't let him do that." "No, mamma; I won't. But he went on talking so fast that I had not time to stop him, and after that it was not worth while." The project of the party was also told to Mrs. Ray, and Rachel, sitting now with her head upon her mother's lap, owned that she would like to go to it. "Parties are not always wicked, mamma," she said. To this assertion Mrs. Ray expressed an undecided assent, but intimated her decided belief that very many parties were wicked. "There will be dancing, and I do not like that," said Mrs. Ray. "Yet I was taught dancing at school," said Rachel. When the matter had gone so far as this it must be acknowledged that Rachel had done much towards securing her share of mastery over her mother. "He will be there, of course," said Mrs. Ray. "Oh, yes; he will be there," said Rachel. "But why should I be afraid of him? Why should I live as though I were afraid to meet him? Dolly thinks that I should be shut up close, to be taken care of; but you do not think of me like that. If I was minded to be bad, shutting me up would not keep me from it." Such arguments as these from Rachel's mouth sounded, at first, very terrible to Mrs. Ray, but yet she yielded to them.

On the next morning Rachel was down first, and was found by her sister fast engaged on the usual work of the house, as though nothing out of the way had occurred on the previous evening. "Good morning, Dolly," she said, and then went on arranging the things on the breakfast-table. "Good morning, Rachel," said Mrs. Prime, still speaking like a raven. There was not a word said between them about the young man or the churchyard, and at nine o'clock Mrs. Ray came down to them, dressed ready for church. They seated themselves and ate their breakfast together, and still not a word was said.

It was Mrs. Prime's custom to go to morning service at one of the churches in Baslehurst; not at the old parish church which stood in the churchyard near the brewery, but at a new church which had been built as auxiliary to the other, and at which the Rev. Samuel Prong was the ministering clergyman. As we shall have occasion to know Mr. Prong it may be as well to explain here that he was not simply a curate to old Dr. Harford, the rector of Baslehurst. He had a separate district of his own, which had been divided from the old parish, not exactly in accordance with the rector's good pleasure. Dr. Harford had held the living for more than forty years; he had held it for nearly forty years before the division had been made, and he had thought that the parish should remain a parish entire, —more especially as the presentation to the new benefice was not conceded to him. Therefore Dr. Harford did not love Mr. Prong.

But Mrs. Prime did love him, —with that sort of love which devout women bestow upon the church minister of their choice. Mr. Prong was an energetic, severe, hardworking, and, I fear, intolerant young man, who bestowed very much laudable care upon his sermons. The care and industry were laudable, but not so the pride with which he thought of them and their results. He spoke much of preaching the Gospel, and was sincere beyond all doubt in his desire to do so; but he allowed himself to be led away into a belief that his brethren in the ministry around him did not preach the Gospel, —that they were careless shepherds, or shepherds' dogs indifferent to the wolf, and in this way he had made himself unpopular among the clergy and gentry of the neighbourhood. It may well be understood that such a man coming down upon a district, cut out almost from the centre of Dr. Harford's parish, would be a thorn in the side of that old man. But Mr. Prong had his circle of friends, of very ardent friends, and among them Mrs. Prime was one of the most ardent. For the last year or two she had always attended morning service at his church, and very frequently had gone there twice in the day, though the walk was long and tedious, taking her the whole length of the town of Baslehurst. And there had been some little uneasiness between Mrs. Ray and Mrs. Prime on the matter of this church attendance. Mrs. Prime had wished her mother and sister to have the benefit of Mr. Prong's eloquence; but Mrs. Ray, though she was weak in morals, was strong in her determination to adhere to Mr. Comfort of Cawston. It had been matter of great sorrow to her that her daughter should leave Mr. Comfort's church, and she had positively declined to be taken out of her own parish. Rachel had, of course, stuck to her mother in this controversy, and had said some sharp things about Mr. Prong. She declared that Mr. Prong had been educated at Islington, and that sometimes he forgot his "h's." When such things were said Mrs. Prime would wax very angry, and would declare that no one could be saved by the perfection of Dr. Harford's pronunciation. But there was no question as to Dr. Harford, and no justification for the introduction of his name into the dispute. Mrs. Prime, however, did not choose to say anything against Mr. Comfort, with whom her husband had been curate, and who, in her younger days, had been a light to her own feet. Mr. Comfort was by no means such a one as Dr. Harford, though the two old men were friends. Mr. Comfort had been regarded as a Calvinist when he was young, as Evangelical in middle life, and was still known as a Low Churchman in his old age. Therefore Mrs. Prime would spare him in her sneers, though she left his ministry. He had become lukewarm, but not absolutely stone cold, like the old rector at Baslehurst. So said Mrs. Prime. Old men would become lukewarm, and therefore she could pardon Mr. Comfort. But Dr. Harford had never been warm at all,—had never been warm with the warmth which she valued. Therefore she scorned him and sneered at him. In return for which Rachel scorned Mr. Prong and sneered at him.

But though it was Mrs. Prime's custom to go to church at Baslehurst, on this special Sunday she declared her intention of accompanying her mother to Cawston. Not a word had been said about the young man, and they all started off on their walk together in silence and gloom. With such thoughts as they had in their mind it was impossible that they should make the journey pleasantly. Rachel had counted on the walk with her mother, and had determined that everything should be pleasant. She would have said a word or two about Luke Rowan, and would have gradually reconciled her mother to his name. But as it was she said nothing; and it may be feared that her mind, during the period of her worship, was not at charity with her sister. Mr. Comfort preached his half-hour as usual, and then they all walked home. Dr. Harford never exceeded twenty minutes, and had often been known to finish his discourse within ten. What might be the length of a sermon of Mr. Prong's no man or woman could foretell, but he never spared himself or his congregation much under an hour.

They all walked home gloomily to their dinner, and ate their cold mutton and potatoes in sorrow and sadness. It seemed as though no sort of conversation was open to them. They could not talk of their usual Sunday subjects. Their minds were full of one matter, and it seemed that that matter was by common consent to be banished from their lips for the day. In the evening, after tea, the two sisters again went up to Cawston church, leaving their mother with her Bible;—but hardly a word was spoken between them, and in the same silence they sat till bed-time. To Mrs. Ray and to Rachel it had been one of the saddest, dreariest days that either of them had ever known. I doubt whether the suffering of Mrs. Prime was so great. She was kept up by the excitement of feeling that some great crisis was at hand. If Rachel were not made amenable to authority she would leave the cottage.

When Rachel had run with hurrying steps from the stile in the churchyard, she left Luke Rowan still standing there. He watched her till she crossed into the lane, and then he turned and again looked out upon the still ruddy line of the horizon. The blaze of light was gone, but there were left, high up in the heavens, those wonderful hues which tinge with softly-changing colour the edges of the clouds when the brightness of some glorious sunset has passed away. He sat himself on the wooden rail, watching till all of it should be over, and thinking, with lazy half-formed thoughts, of Rachel Ray. He did not ask himself what he meant by assuring her of his friendship, and by claiming hers, but he declared to himself that she was very lovely,—more lovely than beautiful, and then smiled inwardly at the prettiness of her perturbed spirit. He remembered well that he had called her Rachel, and that she had allowed his doing so to pass by without notice; but he understood also how and why she had done so. He knew that she had been flurried, and that she had skipped the thing because she had not known the moment at which to make her stand. He gave himself credit for no undue triumph, nor her discredit for any undue easiness. "What a woman she is!" he said to himself; "so womanly in everything." Then his mind rambled away to other subjects, possibly to the practicability of making good beer instead of bad.

He was a young man, by no means of a bad sort, meaning to do well, with high hopes in life, one who had never wronged a woman, or been untrue to a friend, full of energy and hope and pride. But he was conceited, prone to sarcasm, sometimes cynical, and perhaps sometimes affected. It may be that he was not altogether devoid of that Byronic weakness which was so much more prevalent among young men twenty years since than it is now. His two trades had been those of an attorney and a brewer, and yet he dabbled in romance, and probably wrote poetry in his bedroom. Nevertheless, there were worse young men about Baslehurst than Luke Rowan.

"And now for Mr. Tappitt," said he, as he slowly took his legs from off the railing.

CHAPTER V
MR. COMFORT GIVES HIS ADVICE

Mrs. Tappitt was very full of her party. It had grown in her mind as those things do grow, till it had come to assume almost the dimensions of a ball. When Mrs. Tappitt first consulted her husband and obtained his permission for the gathering, it was simply intended that a few of her daughters' friends should be brought together to make the visit cheerful for Miss Rowan; but the mistress of the house had become ambitious; two fiddles, with a German horn, were to be introduced because the piano would be troublesome; the drawing-room carpet was to be taken up, and there was to be a supper in the dining-room. The thing in its altered shape loomed large by degrees upon Mr. Tappitt, and he found himself unable to stop its growth. The word ball would have been fatal; but Mrs. Tappitt was too good a general, and the girls were too judicious as lieutenants, to commit themselves by the presumption of any such term. It was still Mrs. Tappitt's evening tea-party, but it was understood in Baslehurst that Mrs. Tappitt's evening tea-party was to be something considerable.

A great success had attended this lady at the onset of her scheme. Mrs. Butler Cornbury had called at the brewery, and had promised that she would come, and that she would bring some of the Cornbury family. Now Mr. Butler Cornbury was the eldest son of the most puissant squire within five miles of Baslehurst, and was indeed almost as good as Squire himself, his father being a very old man. Mrs. Butler Cornbury had, it is true, not been esteemed as holding any very high rank while shining as a beauty under the name of Patty Comfort; but she had taken kindly to her new honours, and was now reckoned as a considerable magnate in that part of the county. She did not customarily join in the festivities of the town, and held herself aloof from people even of higher standing than the Tappitts. But she was an ambitious woman, and had inspired her lord with the desire of representing Baslehurst in Parliament. There would be an election at Baslehurst in the coming autumn, and Mrs. Cornbury was already preparing for the fight. Hence had arisen her visit at the brewery, and hence also her ready acquiescence in Mrs. Tappitt's half-pronounced request.

The party was to be celebrated on a Tuesday,—Tuesday week after that Sunday which was passed so uncomfortably at Bragg's End; and on the Monday Mrs. Tappitt and her daughters sat conning over the list of their expected guests, and preparing their invitations. It must be understood that the Rowan family had somewhat grown upon them in estimation since Luke had been living with them. They had not known much of him till he came among them, and had been prepared to patronise him; but they found him a young man not to be patronised by any means, and imperceptibly they learned to feel that his mother and sister would have to be esteemed by them rather as great ladies. Luke was in nowise given to boasting, and had no intention of magnifying his mother and sister; but things had been said which made the Tappitts feel that Mrs. Rowan must have the best bedroom, and that Mary Rowan must be provided with the best partners.

"And what shall we do about Rachel Ray?" said Martha, who was sitting with the list before her. Augusta, who was leaning over her sister, puckered up her mouth and said nothing. She had watched from the house door on that Saturday evening, and had been perfectly aware that Luke Rowan had taken Rachel off towards the stile under the trees. She could not bring herself to say anything against Rachel, but she certainly wished that she might be excluded.

"Of course she must be asked," said Cherry. Cherry was sitting opposite to the other girls writing on a lot of envelopes the addresses of the notes which were afterwards to be prepared. "We told her we should ask her." And as she spoke she addressed a cover to "Miss Ray, Bragg's End Cottage, Cawston."

"Stop a moment, my dear," said Mrs. Tappitt from the corner of the sofa on which she was sitting. "Put that aside, Cherry. Rachel Ray is all very well, but considering all things I am not sure that she will quite do for Tuesday night. It's not quite in her line, I think."

"But we have mentioned it to her already, mamma," said Martha.

"Of course we did," said Cherry. "It would be the meanest thing in the world not to ask her now!"

"I am not at all sure that Mrs. Rowan would like it," said Mrs. Tappitt.

"And I don't think that Rachel is quite up to what Mary has been used to," said Augusta.

"If she has half a mind to flirt with Luke already," said Mrs. Tappitt, "I ought not to encourage it."

"That is such nonsense, mamma," said Cherry. "If he likes her he'll find her somewhere if he doesn't find her here."

"My dear, you shouldn't say that what I say is nonsense," said Mrs. Tappitt.

"But, mamma, when we have already asked her!—Besides, she is a lady," said Cherry.

"I can't say that I think Mrs. Butler Cornbury would wish to meet her," said Mrs. Tappitt.

"Mrs. Butler Cornbury's father is their particular friend," said Martha. "Mrs. Ray always goes to Mr. Comfort's parties."

In this way the matter was discussed, and at last Cherry's eagerness and Martha's sense of justice carried the day. The envelope which Cherry had addressed was brought into use, and the note to Rachel was deposited in the post with all those other notes, the destination of which was too far to be reached by the brewery boy without detrimental interference with the brewery work. We will continue our story by following the note which was delivered by the Cawston postman at Bragg's End about seven o'clock on the Tuesday morning. It was delivered into Rachel's own hand, and read by her as she stood by the kitchen dresser before either her mother or Mrs. Prime had come down from their rooms. There still was sadness and gloom at Bragg's End. During all the Monday there had been no comfort in the house, and Rachel had continued to share her mother's bedroom. At intervals, when Rachel had been away, much had been said between Mrs. Ray and Mrs. Prime; but no conclusion had been reached; no line of conduct had received their joint adhesion; and the threat remained that Mrs. Prime would leave the cottage. Mrs. Ray, while listening to her elder daughter's words, still continued to fear that evil spirits were hovering around them; but yet she would not consent to order Rachel to become a devout attendant at the Dorcas meetings. Monday had not been a Dorcas day, and therefore it had been very dull and very tedious.

Rachel stood a while with the note in her hand, fearing that the contest must be brought on again and fought out to an end before she could send her answer to it. She had told her mother that she was to be invited, and Mrs. Ray had lacked the courage at the moment which would have been necessary for an absolute and immediate rejection of the proposition. If Mrs. Prime had not been with them in the house, Rachel little doubted but that she might have gone to the party. If Mrs. Prime had not been there, Rachel, as she was now gradually becoming aware, might have had her own way almost in everything. Without the support which Mrs. Prime gave her, Mrs. Ray would have gradually slid down from that stern code of morals which she had been induced to adopt by the teaching of those around her, and would have entered upon a new school of teaching under Rachel's tutelage. But Mrs. Prime was still there, and Rachel herself was not inclined to fight, if fighting could be avoided. So she put the note into her pocket, and neither answered it or spoke of it till Mrs. Prime had started on her after-dinner walk into Baslehurst. Then she brought it forth and read it to her mother. "I suppose I ought to answer it by the post this evening, mamma?"

"Oh, dear, this evening! that's very short."

"It can be put off till to-morrow if there's any good in putting it off," said Rachel. Mrs. Ray seemed to think that there might be good in putting it off, or rather that there would be harm in doing it at once.

"Do you particularly want to go, my dear?" Mrs. Ray said, after a pause.

"Yes, mamma; I should like to go." Then Mrs. Ray uttered a little sound which betokened uneasiness, and was again silent for a while.

"I can't understand why you want to go to this place,—so particularly. You never used to care about such things. You know your sister won't like it, and I'm not at all sure that you ought to go."

"I'll tell you why I wish it particularly, only—"

"Well, my dear."

"I don't know whether I can make you understand just what I mean."

"If you tell me, I shall understand, I suppose."

Rachel considered her words for a moment or two before she spoke, and then she endeavoured to explain herself. "It isn't that I care for this party especially, mamma, though I own that, after what the girls have said, I should like to be there; but I feel—"

"You feel what, my dear?"

"It is this, mamma. Dolly and I do not agree about these things, and I don't intend to let her manage me just in the way she thinks right."

"Oh, Rachel!"

"Well, mamma, would you wish it? If you could tell me that you really think it wrong to go to parties, I would give them up. Indeed it wouldn't be very much to give up, for I don't often get the chance. But you don't say so. You only say that I had better not go, because Dolly doesn't like it. Now, I won't be ruled by her. Don't look at me in that way, mamma. Is it right that I should be?"

"You have heard what she says about going away."

"I shall be very sorry if she goes, and I hope she won't; but I can't think that her threatening you in that way ought to make any difference. And— I'll tell you more; I do particularly wish to go to Mrs. Tappitt's, because of all that Dolly has said about,—about Mr. Rowan. I wish to show her and you that I am not afraid to meet him. Why should I be afraid of any one?"

"You should be afraid of doing wrong."

"Yes; and if it were wrong to meet any other young man I ought not to go; but there is nothing specially wrong in my meeting him. She has said very unkind things about it, and I intend that she shall know that I will not notice them." As Rachel spoke Mrs. Ray looked up at her, and was surprised by the expression of unrelenting purpose which she saw there. There had come over her face that motion in her eyes and that arching of her brows which Mrs. Ray had seen before, but which hitherto she had hardly construed into their true meaning. Now she was beginning to construe these signs aright, and to understand that there would be difficulty in managing her little family.

The conversation ended in an undertaking on Rachel's part that she would not answer the note till the following day. "Of course that means," said Rachel, "that I am to answer it just as Dolly thinks fit." But she repented of these words as soon as they were spoken, and repented of them almost in ashes when her mother declared, with tears in her eyes, that it was not her intention to be guided by Dorothea in this matter. "You ought not to say such things as that, Rachel," she said. "No, mamma, I ought not; for there is no one so good as you are; and if you'll say that you think I ought not to go, I'll write to Cherry, and explain it to her at once. I don't care a bit about the party,—as far as the party is concerned." But Mrs. Ray would not now pronounce any injunction on the matter. She had made up her mind as to what she would do. She would call upon Mr. Comfort at the parsonage, explain the whole thing to him, and be guided altogether by his counsel.

Not a word was said in the cottage about the invitation when Mrs. Prime came back in the evening, nor was a word said on the following morning. Mrs. Ray had declared her intention of going up to the parsonage, and neither of her daughters had asked her why she was going. Rachel had no need to ask, for she well understood her mother's purpose. As to Mrs. Prime, she was in these days black and full of gloom, asking but few questions, watching the progress of events with the eyes of an evil-singing prophetess, but keeping back her words till the moment should come in which she would be driven by her inner impulses to speak them forth with terrible strength. When the breakfast was over, Mrs. Ray took her bonnet and started forth to the parsonage.

I do not know that a widow, circumstanced as was Mrs. Ray, could do better than go to her clergyman for advice, but nevertheless, when she got to Mr. Comfort's gate she felt that the task of explaining her purpose would not be without difficulty. It would be necessary to tell everything; how Rachel had become suddenly an object of interest to Mr. Luke Rowan, how Dorothea suspected terrible things, and how Rachel was anxious for the world's vanities. The more she thought over it, the more sure she felt that Mr. Comfort would put an embargo upon the party. It seemed but yesterday that he had been telling her, with all his pulpit unction, that the pleasures of this world should never be allowed to creep near the heart. With doubting feet and doubting heart she walked up to the parsonage door, and almost immediately found herself in the presence of her husband's old friend.

Whatever faults there might be in Mr. Comfort's character, he was at any rate good-natured and patient. That he was sincere, too, no one who knew him well had ever doubted,—sincere, that is, as far as his intentions went. When he endeavoured to teach his flock that they should despise money, he thought that he despised it himself. When he told the little children that this world should be as nothing to them, he did not remember that he himself enjoyed keenly the good things of this world. If he had a fault it was perhaps this,—that he was a hard man at a bargain. He liked to have all his temporalities, and make them go as far as they could be stretched. There was the less excuse for this, seeing that his children were well, and even richly, settled in life, and that his wife, should she ever be left a widow, would have ample provision for her few remaining years. He had given his daughter a considerable fortune, without which perhaps the Cornbury Grange people would not have welcomed her so kindly as they had done, and now, as he was still growing rich, it was supposed that he would leave her more.

He listened to Mrs. Ray with the greatest attention, having first begged her to recruit her strength with a glass of wine. As she continued to tell her story he interrupted her from time to time with good-natured little words, and then, when she had done, he asked after Luke Rowan's worldly means. "The young man has got something, I suppose," said he.

"Got something!" repeated Mrs. Ray, not exactly catching his meaning.

"He has some share in the brewery, hasn't he?"

"I believe he has, or is to have. So Rachel told me."

"Yes,—yes; I've heard of him before. If Tappitt doesn't take him into the concern he'll have to give him a very serious bit of money. There's no doubt about the young man having means. Well, Mrs. Ray, I don't suppose Rachel could do better than take him."

"Take him!"

"Yes,—why not? Between you and me, Rachel is growing into a very handsome girl,—a very handsome girl indeed. I'd no idea she'd be so tall, and carry herself so well."

"Oh, Mr. Comfort, good looks are very dangerous for a young woman."

"Well, yes; indeed they are. But still, you know, handsome girls very often do very well; and if this young man fancies Miss Rachel—"

"But, Mr. Comfort, there hasn't been anything of that. I don't suppose he has ever thought of it, and I'm sure she hasn't."

"But young people get to think of it. I shouldn't be disposed to prevent their coming together in a proper sort of way. I don't like night walkings in churchyards, certainly, but I really think that was only an accident."

"I'm sure Rachel didn't mean it."

"I'm quite sure she didn't mean anything improper. And as for him, if he admires her, it was natural enough that he should go after her. If you ask my advice, Mrs. Ray, I should just tell her to be cautious, but I shouldn't be especially careful to separate them. Marriage is the happiest condition for a young woman, and for a young man, too. And how are young people to get married if they are not allowed to see each other?"

"And about the party, Mr. Comfort?"

"Oh, let her go; there'll be no harm. And I'll tell you what, Mrs. Ray; my daughter, Mrs. Cornbury, is going from here, and she shall pick her up and bring her home. It's always well for a young girl to go with a married woman." Then Mrs. Ray did take her glass of sherry, and walked back to Bragg's End, wondering a good deal, and not altogether at ease in her mind as to that great question,—what line of moral conduct might best befit a devout Christian.

Something also had been said at the interview about Mrs. Prime. Mrs. Ray had intimated that Mrs. Prime would separate herself from her mother and her sister unless her views were allowed to prevail in this question regarding the young man from the brewery. But Mr. Comfort, in what few words he had said on this part of the subject, had shown no consideration whatever for Mrs. Prime. "Then she'll behave very wickedly," he had said. "But I'm afraid Mrs. Prime has learned to think too much of her own opinion lately. If that's what she has got by going to Mr. Prong she had better have remained in her own parish." After that, nothing more was said about Mrs. Prime.

"Oh, let her go; there'll be no harm." That had been Mr. Comfort's dictum about the evening party. Such as it was, Mrs. Ray felt herself bound to be guided by it. She had told Rachel that she would ask the clergyman's advice, and take it, whatever it might be. Nevertheless she did not find herself to be easy as she walked home. Mr. Comfort's latter teachings tended to upset all the convictions of her life. According to his teaching, as uttered in the sanctum of his own study, young men were not to be regarded as ravening wolves. And that meeting in the churchyard, which had utterly overwhelmed Dorothea by the weight of its iniquity, and which even to her had been very terrible, was a mere nothing;—a venial accident on Rachel's part, and the most natural proceeding in the world on the part of Luke Rowan! That it was natural enough for a wolf Mrs. Ray could understand; but she was now told that the lamb might go out and meet the wolf without any danger! And then those questions about Rowan's share in the brewery, and Mr. Comfort's ready assertion that the young wolf,—man or wolf, as the case might be,—was well to do in the world! In fact Mrs. Ray's interview with her clergyman had not gone exactly as she had expected, and she was bewildered; and the path into evil,—if it was a path into evil,—was made so easy and pleasant! Mrs. Ray had already considered the difficult question of Rachel's journey to the party, and journey home again; but provision was now made for all that in a way that was indeed very comfortable, but which might make Rachel very vain. She was to be ushered into Mrs. Tappitt's drawing-room under the wing of the most august lady of the neighbourhood. After that, for the remaining half-hour of her walk home, Mrs. Ray gave her mind up to the consideration of what dress Rachel should wear.

When Mrs. Ray reached her own gate, Rachel was in the garden waiting for her. "Well, mamma?" she said. "Is Dorothea at home?" Mrs. Ray asked; and on being informed that Dorothea was at work within, she desired Rachel to follow her up to her bedroom. When there she told her budget of news,—not stinting her child of the gratification which it was sure to give. She said nothing about Luke Rowan and his means, keeping that portion of Mr. Comfort's recommendation to herself; but she declared it out as a fact, that Rachel was to accept the invitation, and to be carried to the party by Mrs. Butler Cornbury. "Oh, mamma! Dear mamma!" said Rachel, who was leaning against the side of the bed. Then she gave a long sigh, and a bright colour came over her face,—almost as though she were blushing. But she said no more at the moment, but allowed her mind to run off and revel in its own thoughts. She had indeed longed to go to this party, though she had taught herself to believe that she could bear being told that she was not to go without disappointment. "And now we must let Dorothea know," said Mrs.

Ray. "Yes,—we must let her know," said Rachel; but her mind was away, straying, I fear, under the churchyard elms with Luke Rowan, and looking at the arm amidst the clouds. He had said that it was stretched out as though to take her; and she had never shaken off from her imagination the idea that it was his arm on which she had been bidden to look,—the arm which had afterwards held her when she strove to go.

It was tea-time before courage was mustered for telling the facts to Mrs. Prime. Mrs. Prime, after dinner, had gone into Baslehurst; but the meeting at Miss Pucker's had not been a regular full gathering, and Mrs. Prime had come back to tea. There was no hot toast, and no clotted cream. It may appear selfish on the part of Mrs. Ray and Rachel that they should have kept such good things for their only little private banquets, but, in truth, such delicacies did not suit Mrs. Prime. Nice things aggravated her spirits and made her fretful. She liked the tea to be stringy and bitter, and she liked the bread to be stale;—as she preferred also that her weeds should be battered and old. She was approaching that stage of discipline at which ashes become pleasant eating, and sackcloth is grateful to the skin. The self-indulgences of the saints in this respect often exceed anything that is done by the sinners.

"Dorothea," said Mrs. Ray, and she looked down upon the dark dingy fluid in her cup as she spoke, "I have been up to Mr. Comfort's to-day."

"Yes; I heard you say you were going there."

"I went to ask him for advice."

"Oh."

"As I was in much doubt, I thought it right to go to the clergyman of my parish."

"I don't think much about parishes myself. Mr. Comfort is an old man now, and I fear he does not give himself up to the Gospel as he used to do. If people were called upon to bind themselves down to parishes, what would those poor creatures do who have over them such a pastor as Dr. Harford?"

"Dr. Harford is a very good man, I believe," said Rachel, "and he keeps two curates."

"I'm afraid, Rachel, you know but little about it. He does keep two curates,—but what are they? They go to cricket-matches, and among young women with bows and arrows! If you had really wanted advice, mamma, I would sooner have heard that you had gone to Mr. Prong."

"But I didn't go to Mr. Prong, my dear;—and I don't mean. Mr. Prong is all very well, I dare say, but I've known Mr. Comfort for nearly thirty years, and I don't like sudden changes." Then Mrs. Ray stirred her tea with rather a quick motion of her hand. Rachel said not a word, but her mother's sharp speech and spirited manner was very pleasant to her. She was quite contented now that Mr. Comfort should be regarded as the family counsellor. She remembered how well she had loved Mr. Comfort always, and thought of days when Patty Comfort had been very good-natured to her as a child.

"Oh, very well," said Mrs. Prime. "Of course, mamma, you must judge for yourself."

"Yes, my dear, I must; or rather, as I didn't wish to trust my own judgment, I went to Mr. Comfort for advice. He says that he sees no harm in Rachel going to this party."

"Party! what party?" almost screamed Mrs. Prime. Mrs. Ray had forgotten that nothing had as yet been said to Dorothea about the invitation.

"Mrs. Tappitt is going to give a party at the brewery," said Rachel, in her very softest voice, "and she has asked me."

"And you are going? You mean to let her go?" Mrs. Prime had asked two questions, and she received two answers. "Yes," said Rachel; "I suppose I shall go, as mamma says so." "Mr. Comfort says there is no harm in it," said Mrs. Ray; "and Mrs. Butler Cornbury is to come from the parsonage to take her up." All question as to Dorcas discipline to be inflicted daily upon Rachel on account of that sin of which she had been guilty in standing under the elms with a young man was utterly lost in this terrible proposition! Instead of being sent to Miss Pucker in her oldest merino dress, Rachel was to be decked in muslin and finery, and sent out to a dancing party at which this young man was to be the hero! It was altogether too much for Dorothea Prime. She slowly wiped the crumbs from off her dingy crape, and with creaking noise pushed back her chair. "Mother," she said, "I couldn't have believed it! I could not have believed it!" Then she withdrew to her own chamber.

Mrs. Ray was much afflicted; but not the less did Rachel look out for the returning postman, on his road into Baslehurst, that she might send her little note to Mrs. Tappitt, signifying her acceptance of that lady's kind invitation.

CHAPTER VI
PREPARATIONS FOR MRS. TAPPITT'S PARTY

I am disposed to think that Mrs. Butler Cornbury did Mrs. Tappitt an injury when she with so much ready goodnature accepted the invitation for the party, and that Mrs. Tappitt was aware of this before the night of the party arrived. She was put on her mettle in a way that was disagreeable to her, and forced into an amount of submissive supplication to Mr. Tappitt for funds, which was vexatious to her spirit. Mrs. Tappitt was a good wife, who never ran her husband into debt, and kept nothing secret from him in the management of her household,—nothing at least which it behoved him to know. But she understood the privileges of her position, and could it have been possible for her to have carried through this party without extra household moneys, or without any violent departure from her usual customs of life, she could have snubbed her husband's objections comfortably, and have put him into the background for the occasion without any inconvenience to herself or power of remonstrance from him. But when Mrs. Butler Cornbury had been gracious, and when the fiddles and horn had become a fact to be accomplished, when Mrs. Rowan and Mary began to loom large on her imagination and a regular supper was projected, then Mrs. Tappitt felt the necessity of superior aid, and found herself called upon to reconcile her lord.

And this work was the more difficult and the more disagreeable to her feelings because she had already pooh-poohed her husband when he asked a question about the party. "Just a few friends got together by the girls," she had said. "Leave it all to them, my dear. It's not very often they see anybody at home."

"I believe I see my friends as often as most people in Baslehurst," Mr. Tappitt had replied indignantly, "and I suppose my friends are their friends." So there had been a little soreness which made the lady's submission the more disagreeable to her.

"Butler Cornbury! He's a puppy. I don't want to see him, and what's more, I won't vote for him."

"You need not tell her so, my dear; and he's not coming. I suppose you like your girls to hold their heads up in the place; and if they show that they've respectable people with them at home, respectable people will be glad to notice them."

"Respectable! If our girls are to be made respectable by giving grand dances, I'd rather not have them respectable. How much is the whole thing to cost?"

"Well, very little, T.; not much more than one of your Christmas dinner-parties. There'll be just the music, and the lights, and a bit of something to eat. What people drink at such times comes to nothing,—just a little negus and lemonade. We might possibly have a bottle or two of champagne at the supper-table, for the look of the thing."

"Champagne!" exclaimed the brewer. He had never yet incurred the cost of a bottle of champagne within his own house, though he thought nothing of it at public dinners. The idea was too much for him; and Mrs. Tappitt, feeling how the ground lay, gave that up,—at any rate for the present. She gave up the champagne; but in abandoning that, she obtained the marital sanction, a quasi sanction which he was too honourable as a husband afterwards to repudiate, for the music and the eatables. Mrs. Tappitt knew that she had done well, and prepared for his dinner that day a beef-steak pie, made with her own hands. Tappitt was not altogether a dull man, and understood these little signs. "Ah," said he, "I wonder how much that pie is to cost me?"

"Oh, T., how can you say such things! As if you didn't have beef-steak pie as often as it's good for you." The pie, however, had its effect, as also did the exceeding "boilishness" of the water which was brought in for his gin-toddy that night; and it was known throughout the establishment that papa was in a good humour, and that mamma had been very clever.

"The girls must have had new dresses anyway before the month was out," Mrs. Tappitt said to her husband the next morning before he had left the conjugal chamber.

"Do you mean to say that they're to have gowns made on purpose for this party?" said the brewer; and it seemed by the tone of his voice that the hot gin and water had lost its kindly effects.

"My dear, they must be dressed, you know. I'm sure no girls in Baslehurst cost less in the way of finery. In the ordinary way they'd have had new frocks almost immediately."

"Bother!" Mr. Tappitt was shaving just at this moment, and dashed aside his razor for a moment to utter this one word. He intended to signify how perfectly well he was aware that a muslin frock prepared for an evening party would not fill the place of a substantial morning dress.

"Well, my dear, I'm sure the girls ain't unreasonable; nor am I. Five-and-thirty shillings apiece for them would do it all. And I shan't want anything myself this year in September." Now Mr. Tappitt, who was a man of sentiment, always gave his wife some costly article of raiment on the 1st of September, calling her his partridge and his bird,—for on that day they had been married. Mrs. Tappitt had frequently offered to intromit the ceremony when calling upon his generosity for other purposes, but the September gift had always been forthcoming.

"Will thirty-five shillings a-piece do it?" said he, turning round with his face all covered with lather. Then again he went to work with his razor just under his right ear.

"Well, yes; I think it will. Two pounds each for the three shall do it anyway."

Mr. Tappitt gave a little jump at this increased demand for fifteen shillings, and not being in a good position for jumping, encountered an unpleasant accident, and uttered a somewhat vehement exclamation. "There," said he, "now I've cut myself, and it's your fault. Oh dear; oh dear! When I cut myself there it never stops. It's no good doing that, Margaret; it only makes it worse. There; now you've got the soap and blood all down inside my shirt."

Mrs. Tappitt on this occasion was subjected to some trouble, for the wound on Mr. Tappitt's cheek-bone declined to be stanched at once; but she gained her object, and got the dresses for her daughters. It was not taken by them as a drawback on their happiness that they had to make the dresses themselves, for they were accustomed to such work; but this necessity joined to all other preparations for the party made them very busy. Till twelve at night on three evenings they sat with their smart new things in their laps and their needles in their hands; but they did not begrudge this, as Mrs. Butler Cornbury was coming to the brewery. They were very anxious to get the heavy part of the work done before the Rowans should arrive, doubting whether they would become sufficiently intimate with Mary to tell her all their little domestic secrets, and do their work in the presence of their new friend during the first day of her sojourn in the house. So they toiled like slaves on the Wednesday and Thursday in order that they might walk about like ladies on the Friday and Saturday.

But the list of their guests gave them more trouble than aught else. Whom should they get to meet Mrs. Butler Cornbury? At one time Mrs. Tappitt had proposed to word certain of her invitations with a special view to this end. Had her idea been carried out people who might not otherwise have come were to be tempted by a notification that they were especially asked to meet Mrs. Butler Cornbury. But Martha had said that this she thought would not do for a dance. "People do do it, my dear," Mrs. Tappitt had pleaded.

"Not for dancing, mamma," said Martha. "Besides, she would be sure to hear of it, and perhaps she might not like it."

"Well, I don't know," said Mrs. Tappitt. "It would show that we appreciated her kindness." The plan, however, was abandoned.

Of the Baslehurst folk there were so few that were fitted to meet Mrs. Butler Cornbury! There was old Miss Harford, the rector's daughter. She was fit to meet anybody in the county, and, as she was good-natured, might probably come. But she was an old maid, and was never very bright in her attire. "Perhaps Captain Gordon's lady would come," Mrs. Tappitt suggested. But at this proposition all the girls shook their heads. Captain Gordon had lately taken a villa close to Baslehurst, but had shown himself averse to any intercourse with the townspeople. Mrs. Tappitt had called on his "lady," and the call had not even been returned, a card having been sent by post in an envelope.

"It would be no good, mamma," said Martha, "and she would only make us uncomfortable if she did come."

"She is always awfully stuck up in church," said Augusta.

"And her nose is red at the end," said Cherry.

Therefore no invitation was sent to Captain Gordon's house.

"If we could only get the Fawcetts," said Augusta. The Fawcetts were a large family living in the centre of Baslehurst, in which there were four daughters, all noted for dancing, and noted also for being the merriest, nicest, and most popular girls in Devonshire. There was a fat good-natured mother, and a thin good-natured father who had once been a banker at Exeter. Everybody desired to know the Fawcetts, and they were the especial favourites of Mrs. Butler Cornbury. But then Mrs. Fawcett did not visit Mrs. Tappitt. The girls and the mothers had a bowing acquaintance, and were always very gracious to each other. Old Fawcett and old Tappitt saw each other in town daily, and knew each other as well as they knew the cross in the butter-market; but none of the two families ever went into each other's houses. It had been tacitly admitted among them that the Fawcetts were above the Tappitts, and so the matter had rested. But now, if anything could be done? "Mrs. Butler Cornbury is all very well, of course," said Augusta, "but it would be so nice for Mary Rowan to see the Miss Fawcetts dancing here."

Martha shook her head, but at last she did write a note in the mothers name. "My girls are having a little dance, to welcome a friend from London, and they would feel so much obliged if your young ladies would come. Mrs. Butler Cornbury has been kind enough to say that she would join us, &c., &c., &c." Mrs. Tappitt and Augusta were in a seventh heaven of happiness when Mrs. Fawcett wrote to say that three of her girls would be delighted to accept the invitation; and even the discreet Martha and the less ambitious Cherry were well pleased.

"I declare I think we've been very fortunate," said Mrs. Tappitt.

"Only the Miss Fawcetts will get all the best partners," said Cherry.

"I'm not so sure of that," said Augusta, holding up her head.

But there had been yet another trouble. It was difficult for them to get people proper to meet Mrs. Butler Cornbury; but what must they do as to those people who must come and who were by no means proper to meet her? There were the Griggses for instance, who lived out of town in a wonderfully red brick house, the family of a retired Baslehurst grocer. They had been asked before Mrs. Cornbury's call had been made, or, I fear, their chance of coming to the party would have been small. There was one young Griggs, a man very terrible in his vulgarity, loud, rampant, conspicuous with villainous jewellery, and odious with the worst abominations of perfumery. He was loathsome even to the Tappitt girls; but then the Griggses and the Tappitts had known each other for half a century, and among their ordinary acquaintances Adolphus Griggs might have been endured. But what should they do when he asked to be introduced to Josceline Fawcett? Of all men he was the most unconscious of his own defects. He had once shown some symptoms of admiration for Cherry, by whom he was hated with an intensity of dislike that had amounted to a passion. She had begged that he might be omitted from the list; but Mrs. Tappitt had been afraid of angering their father.

The Rules also would be much in the way. Old Joshua Rule was a maltster, living in Cawston, and his wife and daughter had been asked before the accession of the Butler Cornbury dignity. Old Rule had supplied the brewery with malt almost ever since it had been a brewery; and no more harmless people than Mrs. Rule and her daughter existed in the neighbourhood;—but they were close neighbours of the Comforts, of Mrs. Cornbury's father and mother, and Mr. Comfort would have as soon asked his sexton to dine with him as the Rules. The Rules never expected such a thing, and therefore lived on very good terms with the clergyman. "I'm afraid she won't like meeting Mrs. Rule," Augusta had said to her mother; and then the mother had shaken her head.

Early in the week, before Rachel had accepted the invitation, Cherry had written to her friend. "Of course you'll come," Cherry had said; "and as you may have some difficulty in getting here and home again, I'll ask old Mrs. Rule to call for you. I know she'll have a place in the fly, and she's very good-natured." In answer to this Rachel had written a separate note to Cherry, telling her friend in the least boastful words which she could use that provision had been already made for her coming and going. "Mamma was up at Mr. Comfort's yesterday," Rachel wrote, "and he was so kind as to say that Mrs. Butler Cornbury would take me and bring me back. I am very much obliged to you all the same, and to Mrs. Rule."

"What do you think?" said Cherry, who had received her note in the midst of one of the family conferences; "Augusta said that Mrs. Butler Cornbury would not like to meet Rachel Ray; but she is going to bring her in her own carriage."

"I never said anything of the kind," said Augusta.

"Oh, but you did, Augusta; or mamma did, or somebody. How nice for Rachel to be chaperoned by Mrs. Butler Cornbury!"

"I wonder what she'll wear," said Mrs. Tappitt, who had on that morning achieved her victory over the wounded brewer in the matter of the three dresses.

On the Friday morning Mrs. Rowan came with her daughter, Luke having met them at Exeter on the Thursday. Mrs. Rowan was a somewhat stately lady, slow in her movements and careful in her speech, so that the girls were at first very glad that they had valiantly worked up their finery before her coming. But Mary was by no means stately; she was younger than them, very willing to be pleased, with pleasant round eager eyes, and a kindly voice. Before she had been three hours in the house Cherry had claimed Mary for her own, had told her all about the party, all about the dresses, all about Mrs. Butler Cornbury and the Miss Fawcetts, and a word or two also about Rachel Ray. "I can tell you somebody that's almost in love with her." "You don't mean Luke?" said Mary. "Yes, but I do," said Cherry; "but of course I'm only in fun." On the Saturday Mary was hard at work herself assisting in the decoration of the drawing-room, and before the all-important Tuesday came even Mrs. Rowan and Mrs. Tappitt were confidential. Mrs. Rowan perceived at once that Mrs. Tappitt was provincial,—as she told her son, but she was a good motherly woman, and on the whole, Mrs. Rowan condescended to be gracious to her.

At Bragg's End the preparations for the party required almost as much thought as did those at the brewery, and involved perhaps deeper care. It may be remembered that Mrs. Prime, when her ears were first astounded by that unexpected revelation, wiped the crumbs from out of her lap and walked off, wounded in spirit, to her own room. On that evening Rachel saw no more of her sister. Mrs. Ray went up to her daughter's bedroom, but stayed there only a minute or two. "What does she say?" asked Rachel, almost in a whisper. "She is very unhappy. She says that unless I can be made to think better of this she must leave the cottage. I told her what Mr. Comfort says, but she only sneers at Mr. Comfort. I'm sure I'm endeavouring to do the best I can."

"It wouldn't do, mamma, to say that she should manage everything, otherwise I'm sure I'd give up the party."

"No, my dear; I don't want you to do that,—not after what Mr. Comfort says." Mrs. Ray had in truth gone to the clergyman feeling sure that he would have given his word against the party, and that, so strengthened, she could have taken a course that would have been offensive to neither of her daughters. She had expected, too, that she would have returned home armed with such clerical thunders against the young man as would have quieted Rachel and have satisfied Dorothea. But in all this she had been,—I may hardly say disappointed,—but dismayed and bewildered by advice the very opposite to that which she had expected. It was perplexing, but she seemed to be aware that she had no alternative now, but to fight the battle on Rachel's side. She had cut herself off from all anchorage except that given by Mr. Comfort, and therefore it behoved her to cling to that with absolute tenacity. Rachel must go to the party, even though Dorothea should carry out her threat. On that night nothing more was said about Dorothea, and Mrs. Ray allowed herself to be gradually drawn into a mild discussion about Rachel's dress.

But there was nearly a week left to them of this sort of life. Early on the following morning Mrs. Prime left the cottage, saying that she should dine with Miss Pucker, and betook herself at once to a small house in a back street of the town, behind the new church, in which lived Mr. Prong. Have I as yet said that Mr. Prong was a bachelor? Such was the fact; and there were not wanting those in Baslehurst who declared that he would amend the fault by marrying Mrs. Prime. But this rumour, if it ever reached her, had no effect upon her. The world would be nothing to her if she were to be debarred by the wickedness of loose tongues from visiting the clergyman of her choice. She went, therefore, in her present difficulty to Mr. Prong.

Mr. Samuel Prong was a little man, over thirty, with scanty, light-brown hair, with a small, rather upturned nose, with eyes by no means deficient in light and expression, but with a mean mouth. His forehead was good, and had it not been for his mouth his face would have been expressive of intellect and of some firmness. But there was about his lips an assumption of character and dignity which his countenance and body generally failed to maintain; and there was a something in the carriage of his head and in the occasional projection of his chin, which was intended to add to his dignity, but which did, I think, only make the failure more palpable. He was a devout, good man; not self-indulgent; perhaps not more self-ambitious than it becomes a man to be; sincere, hard-working, sufficiently intelligent, true in most things to the instincts of his calling, —but deficient in one vital qualification for a clergyman of the Church of England; he was not a gentleman. May I not call it a necessary qualification for a clergyman of any church? He was not a gentleman. I do not mean to say that he was a thief or a liar; nor do I mean hereby to complain that he picked his teeth with his fork and misplaced his "h's." I am by no means prepared to define what I do mean, —thinking, however, that most men and most women will understand me. Nor do I speak of this deficiency in his clerical aptitudes as being injurious to him simply, —or even chiefly, —among folk who are themselves gentle; but that his efficiency for clerical purposes was marred altogether, among high and low, by his misfortune in this respect. It is not the owner of a good coat that sees and admires its beauty. It is not even they who have good coats themselves who recognize the article on the back of another. They who have not good coats themselves have the keenest eyes for the coats of their better-clad neighbours. As it is with coats, so it is with that which we call gentility. It is caught at a word, it is seen at a glance, it is appreciated unconsciously at a touch by those who have none of it themselves. It is the greatest of all aids to the doctor, the lawyer, the member of Parliament, —though in that position a man may perhaps prosper without it, —and to the statesman; but to the clergyman it is a vital necessity. Now Mr. Prong was not a gentleman.

Mrs. Prime told her tale to Mr. Prong, as Mrs. Ray had told hers to Mr. Comfort. It need not be told again here. I fear that she made the most of her sister's imprudence, but she did not do so with intentional injustice. She declared her conviction that Rachel might still be made to go in a straight course, if only she could be guided by a hand sufficiently strict and armed with absolute power. Then she went on to tell Mr. Prong how Mrs. Ray had gone off to Mr. Comfort, as she herself had now come to him. It was hard, —was it not? —for poor Rachel that the story of her few minutes' whispering under the elm tree should thus be bruited about among the ecclesiastical councillors of the locality. Mr. Prong sat with patient face and with mild demeanour while the simple story of Rachel's conduct was being told; but when to this was added the iniquity of Mr. Comfort's advice, the mouth assumed the would-be grandeur, the chin came out, and to any one less infatuated than Mrs. Prime it would have been apparent that the purse was not made of silk, but that a coarser material had come to hand in the manufacture.

"What shall the sheep do," said Mr. Prong, "when the shepherd slumbers in the folds?" Then he shook his head and puckered up his mouth.

"Ah!" said Mrs. Prime; "it is well for the sheep that there are still left a few who do not run from their work, even in the heat of the noonday sun."

Mr. Prong closed his eyes and bowed his head, and then reassumed that peculiarly disagreeable look about his mouth by which he thought to assert his dignity, intending thereby to signify that he would willingly reject the compliment as unnecessary, were he not forced to accept it as being true. He knew himself to be a shepherd who did not fear the noonday heat; but he was wrong in this,—that he suspected all other shepherds of stinting their work. It appeared to him that no sheep could nibble his grass in wholesome content, unless some shepherd were at work at him constantly with his crook. It was for the shepherd, as he thought, to know what tufts of grass were rank, and in what spots the herbage might be bitten down to the bare ground. A shepherd who would allow his flock to feed at large under his eye, merely watching his fences and folding his ewes and lambs at night, was a truant who feared the noonday sun. Such a one had Mr. Comfort become, and therefore Mr. Prong despised him in his heart. All sheep will not endure such ardent shepherding as that practised by Mr. Prong, and therefore he was driven to seek out for himself a peculiar flock. These to him were the elect of Baslehurst, and of his elect, Mrs. Prime was the most elect. Now this fault is not uncommon among young ardent clergymen.

I will not repeat the conversation that took place between the two, because they used holy words and spoke on holy subjects. In doing so they were both sincere, and not, as regarded their language, fairly subject to ridicule. In their judgment I think they were defective. He sustained Mrs. Prime in her resolution to quit the cottage unless she could induce her mother to put a stop to that great iniquity of the brewery. "The Tappitts," he said, "were worldly people,—very worldly people; utterly unfit to be the associates of the sister of his friend. As to the 'young man,' he thought that nothing further should be said at present, but that Rachel should be closely watched,—very closely watched." Mrs. Prime asked him to call upon her mother and explain his views, but he declined to do this. "He would have been most willing,—so willing! but he could not force himself where he would be unwelcome!" Mrs. Prime was, if necessary, to quit the cottage and take up her temporary residence with Miss Pucker; but Mr. Prong was inclined to think, knowing something of Mrs. Ray's customary softness of character, that if Mrs. Prime were firm, things would not be driven to such a pass as that. Mrs. Prime said that she would be firm, and she looked as though she intended to keep her word.

Mr. Prong's manner as he bade adieu to his favourite sheep was certainly of a nature to justify that rumour to which allusion has been made. He pressed Mrs. Prime's hand very closely, and invoked a blessing on her head in a warm whisper. But such signs among such people do not bear the meaning which they have in the outer world. These people are demonstrative and unctuous,—whereas the outer world is reticent and dry. They are perhaps too free with their love, but the fault is better than that other fault of no love at all. Mr. Prong was a little free with his love, but Mrs. Prime took it all in good part, and answered him with an equal fervour. "If I can help you, dear friend,"—and he still held her hand in his,—"come to me always. You never can come too often."

"You can help me, and I will come, always," she said, returning his pressure with mutual warmth. But there was no touch of earthly affection in her pressure; and if there was any in his at its close, there had, at any rate, been none at its commencement.

While Mrs. Prime was thus employed, Rachel and her mother became warm upon the subject of the dress, and when the younger widow returned home to the cottage, the elder widow was actually engaged in Baslehurst on the purchase of trappings and vanities. Her little hoard was opened, and some pretty piece of muslin was purchased by aid of which, with the needful ribbons, Rachel might be made, not fit, indeed, for Mrs. Butler Cornbury's carriage,—no such august fitness was at all contemplated by herself,—but nice and tidy, so that her presence need not be a disgrace. And it was pretty to see how Mrs. Ray revelled in these little gauds for her daughter now that the barrier of her religious awe was broken down, and that the waters of the world had made their way in upon her. She still had a feeling that she was being drowned, but she confessed that such drowning was very pleasant. She almost felt that such drowning was good for her. At any rate it had been ordered by Mr. Comfort, and if things went astray Mr. Comfort must bear the blame. When the bright muslin was laid out on the counter before her, she looked at it with a pleased eye and touched it with a willing hand. She held the ribbon against the muslin, leaning her head on one side, and enjoyed herself. Now and again she would turn her face upon Rachel's figure, and she would almost indulge a wish that this young man might like her child in the new dress. Ah!—that was surely wicked. But if so, how wicked are most mothers in this Christian land!

The morning had gone very comfortably with them during Dorothea's absence. Mrs. Prime had hardly taken her departure before a note came from Mrs. Butler Cornbury, confirming Mr. Comfort's offer as to the carriage. "Oh, papa, what have you done?"—she had said when her father first told her. "Now I must stay there all the night, for of course she'll want to go on to the last dance!" But, like her father, she was good-natured, and therefore, though she would hardly have chosen the task, she resolved, when her first groans were over, to do it well. She wrote a kind note, saying how happy she should be, naming her hour,—and saying that Rachel should name the hour for her return.

"It will be very nice," said Rachel, rejoicing more than she should have done in thinking of the comfortable grandeur of Mrs. Butler Cornbury's carriage.

"And are you determined?" Mrs. Prime asked her mother that evening.

"It is too late to go back now, Dorothea," said Mrs. Ray, almost crying.

"Then I cannot remain in the house," said Dorothea. "I shall go to Miss Pucker's,—but not till that morning; so that if you think better of it, all may be prevented yet."

But Mrs. Ray would not think better of it, and it was thus that the preparations were made for Mrs. Tappitt's—ball. The word "party" had now been dropped by common consent throughout Baslehurst.

CHAPTER VII
AN ACCOUNT OF MRS. TAPPITT'S
BALL—COMMENCED

Mrs. Butler Cornbury was a very pretty woman. She possessed that peculiar prettiness which is so often seen in England, and which is rarely seen anywhere else. She was bright, well-featured, with speaking lustrous eyes, with perfect complexion, and full bust, with head of glorious shape and figure like a Juno;—and yet with all her beauty she had ever about her an air of homeliness which made the sweetness of her womanhood almost more attractive than the loveliness of her personal charms. I have seen in Italy and in America women perhaps as beautiful as any that I have seen in England, but in neither country does it seem that such beauty is intended for domestic use. In Italy the beauty is soft, and of the flesh. In America it is hard, and of the mind. Here it is of the heart, I think, and as such is the happiest of the three. I do not say that Mrs. Butler Cornbury was a woman of very strong feeling; but her strongest feelings were home feelings. She was going to Mrs. Tappitt's party because it might serve her husband's purposes; she was going to burden herself with Rachel Ray because her father had asked her; and her greatest ambition was to improve the worldly position of the squires of Cornbury Grange. She was already calculating whether it might not some day be brought about that her little Butler should sit in Parliament for his county.

At nine o'clock exactly on that much to be remembered Tuesday the Cornbury carriage stopped at the gate of the cottage at Bragg's End, and Rachel, ready dressed, blushing, nervous, but yet happy, came out, and mounting on to the step was almost fearful to take her share of the seat. "Make yourself comfortable, my dear," said Mrs. Cornbury, "you can't crush me. Or rather I always make myself crushable on such occasions as this. I suppose we are going to have a great crowd?" Rachel merely said that she didn't know. She supposed there would be a good many persons. Then she tried to thank Mrs. Cornbury for being so good to her, and of course broke down. "I'm delighted,—quite delighted," said Mrs. Cornbury. "It's so good of you to come with me. Now that I don't dance myself, there's nothing I like so much as taking out girls that do."

"And don't you dance at all?"

"I stand up for a quadrille sometimes. When a woman has five children I don't think she ought to do more than that."

"Oh, I shall not do more than that, Mrs. Cornbury."

"You mean to say you won't waltz?"

"Mamma never said anything about it, but I'm sure she would not like it. Besides—"

"Well—"

"I don't think I know how. I did learn once, when I was very little; but I've forgotten."

"It will soon come again to you if you like to try. I was very fond of waltzing before I was married." And this was the daughter of Mr. Comfort, the clergyman who preached with such strenuous eloquence against worldly vanities! Even Rachel was a little puzzled, and was almost afraid that her head was sinking beneath the waters.

There was a great fuss made when Mrs. Butler Cornbury's carriage drove up to the brewery door, and Rachel almost felt that she could have made her way up to the drawing-room more comfortably under Mrs. Rule's mild protection. All the servants seemed to rush at her, and when she found herself in the hall and was conducted into some inner room, she was not allowed to shake herself into shape without the aid of a maid-servant. Mrs. Cornbury,—who took everything as a matter of course and was ready in a minute,—had turned the maid over to the young lady with a kind idea that the young lady's toilet was more important than that of the married woman. Rachel was losing her head and knew that she was doing so. When she was again taken into the hall she hardly remembered where she was, and when Mrs. Cornbury took her by the arm and began to walk up-stairs with her, her strongest feeling was a wish that she was at home again. On the first landing,—for the dancing-room was upstairs,—they encountered Mr. Tappitt, conspicuous in a blue satin waistcoat; and on the second landing they found Mrs. Tappitt, magnificent in a green Irish poplin. "Oh, Mrs. Cornbury, we are so delighted. The Miss Fawcetts are here; they are just come. How kind of you to bring Rachel Ray. How do you do, Rachel?" Then Mrs. Cornbury moved easily on into the drawing-room, and Rachel still found herself carried with her. She was half afraid that she ought to have slunk away from her magnificent chaperon as soon as she was conveyed safely within the house, and that she was encroaching as she thus went on; but still she could not find the moment in which to take herself off. In the drawing-room,—the room from which the carpets had been taken,—

they were at once encountered by the Tappitt girls, with whom the Fawcett girls on the present occasion were so intermingled that Rachel hardly knew who was who. Mrs. Butler Cornbury was soon surrounded, and a clatter of words went on. Rachel was in the middle of the fray, and some voices were addressed also to her; but her presence of mind was gone, and she never could remember what she said on the occasion.

There had already been a dance,—the commencing operation of the night's work,—a thin quadrille, in which the early comers had taken part without much animation, and to which they had been driven up unwillingly. At its close the Fawcett girls had come in, as had now Mrs. Cornbury, so that it may be said that the evening was beginning again. What had been as yet done was but the tuning of the fiddles before the commencement of the opera. No one likes to be in at the tuning, but there are those who never are able to avoid this annoyance. As it was, Rachel, under Mrs. Cornbury's care, had been brought upon the scene just at the right moment. As soon as the great clatter had ceased, she found herself taken by the hand by Cherry, and led a little on one side. "You must have a card, you know," said Cherry handing her a ticket on which was printed the dances as they were to succeed each other. "That first one is over. Such a dull thing. I danced with Adolphus Griggs, just because I couldn't escape him for one quadrille." Rachel took the card, but never having seen such a thing before did not in the least understand its object. "As you get engaged for the dances you must put down their names in this way, you see,"—and Cherry showed her card, which already bore the designations of several cavaliers, scrawled in hieroglyphics which were intelligible to herself. "Haven't you got a pencil? Well, you can come to me. I have one hanging here, you know." Rachel was beginning to understand, and to think that she should not have very much need for the pencil, when Mrs. Cornbury returned to her, bringing a young man in her wake. "I want to introduce my cousin to you, Walter Cornbury," said she. Mrs. Cornbury was a woman who knew her duty as a chaperon, and who would not neglect it. "He waltzes delightfully," said Mrs. Cornbury, whispering, "and you needn't be afraid of being a little astray with him at first. He always does what I tell him." Then the introduction was made; but Rachel had no opportunity of repeating her fears, or of saying again that she thought she had better not waltz. What to say to Mr. Walter Cornbury she hardly knew; but before she had really said anything he had pricked her down for two dances,—for the first waltz, which was just going to begin, and some not long future quadrille. "She is very pretty," Mrs. Butler Cornbury had said to her cousin, "and I want to be kind to her." "I'll take her in hand and pull her through," said Walter. "What a tribe of people they've got here, haven't they?" "Yes, and you must

dance with them all. Every time you stand up may be as good as a vote."
"Oh," said Walter, "I'm not particular;—I'll dance as long as they keep the house open." Then he went back to Rachel, who had already been at work with Cherry's pencil.

"If there isn't Rachel Ray going to waltz with Walter Cornbury," said Augusta to her mother. Augusta had just refused the odious Griggs, and was about to stand up with a clerk in the brewery, who was almost as odious.

"It's because she came in the carriage," said Mrs. Tappitt; "but I don't think she can waltz." Then she hurried off to welcome other comers.

Rachel had hardly been left alone for a minute, and had been so much bewildered by the lights and crowd and strangeness of everything around her, that she had been unable to turn her thoughts to the one subject on which during the last week her mind had rested constantly. She had not even looked round the room for Luke Rowan. She had just seen Mary Rowan in the crowd, but had not spoken to her. She had only known her from the manner in which Cherry Tappitt had spoken to her, and it must be explained that Rachel had not seen young Rowan since that parting under the elm-trees. Indeed, since then she had seen none of the Tappitt family. Her mother had said no word to her, cautioning her that she had better not seek them in her evening walks; but she had felt herself debarred from going into Baslehurst by all that her sister had said, and in avoiding Luke Rowan she had avoided the whole party from the brewery.

Now the room was partially cleared, the non-dancers being pressed back into a border round the walls, and the music began. Rachel, with her heart in her mouth, was claimed by her partner, and was carried forward towards the ground for dancing, tacitly assenting to her fate because she lacked words in which to explain to Mr. Cornbury how very much she would have preferred to be left in obscurity behind the wall of crinoline.

"Pray wait a minute or two," said she, almost panting.

"Oh, certainly. There's no hurry, only we'll stand where we can get our place when we like it. You need not be a bit afraid of going on with me. Patty has told me all about it, and we'll make it right in a brace of turns." There was something very good-natured in his voice, and she almost felt that she could ask him to let her sit down.

"I don't think I can," she said.

"Oh yes; come, we'll try!" Then he took her by the waist, and away they went. Twice round the room he took her, very gently, as he thought; but her head had gone from her instantly in a whirl of amazement! Of her feet and their movements she had known nothing; though she had followed the music with fair accuracy, she had done so unconsciously, and when he allowed her to stop she did not know which way she had been going, or at which end of the room she stood. And yet she had liked it, and felt some little triumph as a conviction came upon her that she had not conspicuously disgraced herself.

"That's charming," said he. She essayed to speak a word in answer, but her want of breath did not as yet permit it.

"Charming!" he went on. "The music's perhaps a little slow, but we'll hurry them up presently." Slow! It seemed to her that she had been carried round in a vortex, of which the rapidity, though pleasant, had been almost frightful. "Come; we'll have another start," said he; and she was carried away again before she had spoken a word. "I'd no idea that girl could waltz," said Mrs. Tappitt to old Mrs. Rule. "I don't think her mother would like it if she saw it," said Mrs. Rule. "And what would Mrs. Prime say?" said Mrs. Tappitt. However the ice was broken, and Rachel, when she was given to understand that that dance was done, felt herself to be aware that the world of waltzing was open to her, at any rate for that night. Was it very wicked? She had her doubts. If anybody had suggested to her, before Mrs. Cornbury's carriage had called for her, that she would waltz on that evening, she would have repudiated the idea almost with horror. How easy is the path down the shores of the Avernus! but then,—was she going down the shores of the Avernus?

She was still walking through the crowd, leaning on her partner's arm, and answering his good-natured questions almost in monosyllables, when she was gently touched on the arm by a fan, and on turning found herself confronted by Luke Rowan and his sister. "I've been trying to get at you so long," said he, making some sort of half apology to Cornbury, "and haven't been able; though once I very nearly danced you down without your knowing it."

"We're so much obliged to you for letting us escape," said Cornbury; "are we not, Miss Ray?"

"We carried heavy metal, I can tell you," said Rowan. "But I must introduce you to my sister. Where on earth have you been for these ten days?" Then the introduction was made, and young Cornbury, finding that his partner was in the hands of another lady, slipped away.

"I have heard a great deal about you, Miss Ray," said Mary Rowan.

"Have you? I don't know who should say much about me." The words sounded uncivil, but she did not know what words to choose.

"Oh, from Cherry especially;—and—and from my brother."

"I'm very glad to make your acquaintance," said Rachel.

"He told me that you would have been sure to come and walk with us, and we have all been saying that you had disappeared."

"I have been kept at home," said Rachel, who could not help remembering all the words of the churchyard interview, and feeling them down to her finger nails. He must have known why she had not again joined the girls from the brewery in their walks. Or had he forgotten that he had called her Rachel, and held her fast by the hand? Perhaps he did these things so often to other girls that he thought nothing of them!

"You have been keeping yourself up for the ball," said Rowan. "Precious people are right to make themselves scarce. And now what vacancies have you got for me?"

"Vacancies!" said Rachel.

"You don't mean to say you've got none. Look here, I've kept all these on purpose for you, although twenty girls have begged me to dispose of them in their favour."

"Oh, Luke, how can you tell such fibs?" said his sister.

"Well;—here they are," and he showed his card.

"I'm not engaged to anybody," said Rachel; "except for one quadrille to Mr. Cornbury,—that gentleman who just went away."

"Then you've no excuse for not filling up my vacancies,—kept on purpose for you, mind." And immediately her name was put down for she knew not what dances. Then he took her card and scrawled his own name on it in various places. She knew that she was weak to let him thus have his way in everything; but he was strong and she could not hinder him.

She was soon left with Mary Rowan, as Luke went off to fulfil the first of his numerous engagements. "Do you like my brother?" said she. "But of course I don't mean you to answer that question. We all think him so very clever."

"I'm sure he is very clever."

"A great deal too clever to be a brewer. But you mustn't say that I said so. I wanted him to go into the army."

"I shouldn't at all like that for my brother—if I had one."

"And what would you like?"

"Oh, I don't know. I never had a brother;—perhaps to be a clergyman."

"Yes; that would be very nice; but Luke would never be a clergyman. He was going to be an attorney, but he didn't like that at all. He says there's a great deal of poetry in brewing beer, but of course he's only quizzing us. Oh, here's my partner. I do so hope I shall see you very often while I'm at Baslehurst." Then Rachel was alone, but Mrs. Tappitt came up to her in a minute. "My dear," said she, "Mr. Griggs desires the honour of your hand for a quadrille." And thus Rachel found herself standing up with the odious Mr. Griggs. "I do so pity you," said Cherry, coming behind her for a moment. "Remember, you need not do it more than once. I don't mean to do it again."

After that she was allowed to sit still while a polka was being performed. Mrs. Cornbury came to her saying a word or two; but she did not stay with her long, so that Rachel could think about Luke Rowan, and try to make up her mind as to what words she should say to him. She furtively looked down upon her card and found that he had written his own name to five dances, ending with Sir Roger de Coverley at the close of the evening. It was quite impossible that she should dance five dances with him, so she thought that she would mark out two with her nail. The very next was one of them, and during that she would explain to him what she had done. The whole thing loomed large in her thoughts and made her feel anxious. She would have been unhappy if he had not come to her at all, and now she was unhappy because he had thrust himself upon her so violently,—or if not unhappy, she was at any rate uneasy. And what should she say about the elm-trees? Nothing, unless he spoke to her about them. She fancied that he would say something about the arm in the cloud, and if so, she must endeavour to make him understand that—that—that—. She did not know how to fix her thoughts. Would it be possible to make him understand that he ought not to have called her Rachel?

While she was thinking of all this Mr. Tappitt came and sat beside her. "Very pretty; isn't it?" said he. "Very pretty indeed, I call it."

"Oh yes, very pretty. I had no idea it would be so nice." To Mr. Tappitt in his blue waistcoat she could speak without hesitation. Ah me! It is the young men who receive all the reverence that the world has to pay;—all the reverence that is worth receiving. When a man is turned forty and has become fat, anybody can speak to him without awe!

"Yes, it is nice," said Mr. Tappitt, who, however, was not quite easy in his mind. He had been into the supper room, and had found the waiter handling long-necked bottles, arranging them in rows, apparently by the dozen. "What's that?" said he, sharply. "The champagne, sir! there should have been ice, sir, but I suppose they forgot it." Where had Mrs. T. procured all that wine? It was very plain to him that she had got the better of him by some deceit. He would smile, and smile, and smile during the evening; but he would have it out with Mrs. Tappitt before he would allow that lady to have any rest. He lingered in the room, pretending that he was overlooking the arrangements, but in truth he was counting the bottles. After all there was but a dozen. He knew that at Griggs's they sold it for sixty shillings. "Three pounds!" he said to himself. "Three pounds more; dear, dear!"

"Yes, it is nice!" he said to Rachel. "Mind you get a glass of champagne when you go in to supper. By-the-by, shall I get a partner for you? Here, Buckett, come and dance the next dance with Miss Ray." Buckett was the clerk in the brewery. Rachel had nothing to say for herself; so Buckett's name was put down on the card, though she would rather not have danced with Buckett. A week or two ago, before she had been taken up into Mrs. Cornbury's carriage, or had waltzed with Mrs. Cornbury's cousin, or had looked at the setting sun with Luke Rowan, she would have been sufficiently contented to dance with Mr. Buckett,—if in those days she had ever dreamed of dancing with any one. Then Mrs. Cornbury came to her again, bringing other cavaliers, and Rachel's card began to be filled. "The quadrille before supper you dance with me," said Walter Cornbury. "That's settled, you know." Oh, what a new world it was, and so different from the Dorcas meetings at Miss Pucker's rooms!

Then came the moment of the evening which, of all the moments, was the most trying to her. Luke Rowan came to claim her hand for the next quadrille. She had already spoken to him,—or rather he to her; but that had been in the presence of a third person, when, of course, nothing could be said about the sunset and the clouds,—nothing about that promise of friendship. But now she would have to stand again with him in solitude,—a solitude of another kind,—in a solitude which was authorized, during which he might whisper what words he pleased to her, and from which she could not even run away. It had been thought to be a great sin on her part to have remained a moment with him by the stile; but now she was to stand up with him beneath the glare of the lights, dressed in her best, on purpose that he might whisper to her what words he pleased. But she was sure—she thought that she was sure, that he would utter no words so sweet, so full of meaning, as those in which he bade her watch the arm in the clouds.

Till the first figure was over for them he hardly spoke to her. "Tell me," said he then, "why has nobody seen you since Saturday week last?"

"I have been at home."

"Ah; but tell me the truth. Remember what we said as we parted,—about being friends. One tells one's friend the real truth. But I suppose you do not remember what we said?"

"I don't think I said anything, Mr. Rowan."

"Did you not? Then I must have been dreaming. I thought you promised me your friendship." He paused for her answer, but she said nothing. She could not declare to him that she would not be his friend. "But you have not told me yet why it was that you remained at home. Come;—answer me a fair question fairly. Had I offended you?" Again she paused and made him no reply. It seemed to her that the room was going round her, and that the music made her dizzy. If she told him that he had not offended her would she not thereby justify him in having called her Rachel?

"Then I did offend you?" said he.

"Oh, Mr. Rowan,—never mind now; you must go on with the figure," and thus for a moment she was saved from her difficulty. When he had done his work of dancing, she began hers, and as she placed both her hands in his to make the final turn, she flattered herself that he would not go back to the subject.

Nor did he while the quadrille lasted. As they continued to dance he said very little to her, and before the last figure was over she had almost settled down to enjoyment. He merely spoke a word or two about Mrs. Cornbury's dress, and another word about the singular arrangement of Mr. Griggs' jewellery, at which word she almost laughed outright, and then a third word laudatory of the Tappitt girls. "As for Cherry," said he "I'm quite in love with her for her pure good-nature and hearty manners; and of all living female human beings Martha is the most honest and just."

"Oh! I'll tell her that," said Rachel. "She will so like it."

"No, you mustn't. You mustn't repeat any of the things I tell you in confidence." That word confidence again silenced her, and nothing more was said till he had offered her his arm at the end of the dance.

"Come away and have some negus on the stairs," he said. "The reason I like these sort of parties is, that one is allowed to go into such queer places. You see that little room with the door open. That's where Mr. Tappitt keeps his old boots and the whip with which he drives his grey horse. There are four men playing cards there now, and one is seated on the end of an upturned portmanteau."

"And where are the old boots?"

"Packed away on the top of Mrs. Tappitt's bed. I helped to put them there. Some are stuck under the grate because there are no fires now. Look here; there's a seat in the window." Then he placed her in the inclosure of an old window on the staircase landing, and brought her lemonade, and when she had drunk it he sat down beside her.

"Hadn't we better go back to the dancing?"

"They won't begin for a few minutes. They're only tuning up again. You should always escape from the hot air for a moment or two. Besides, you must answer me that question. Did I offend you?"

"Please don't talk of it. Please don't. It's all over now."

"Ah, but it is not all over. I knew you were angry with me because,— shall I say why?"

"No, Mr. Rowan, don't say anything about it."

"At any rate, I may think that you have forgiven me. But what if I offend in the same way again? What if I ask permission to do it, so that it may be no offence? Only think; if I am to live here in Baslehurst all my life, is it not reasonable that I should wish you to be my friend? Are you going to separate yourself from Cherry Tappitt because you are afraid of me?"

"Oh, no."

"But is not that what you have done during the last week, Miss Ray;—if it must be Miss Ray?" Then he paused, but still she said nothing. "Rachel is such a pretty name."

"Oh, I think it so ugly."

"It's the prettiest name in the Bible, and the name most fit for poetic use. Who does not remember Rachel weeping for her children?"

"That's the idea, and not the name. Ruth is twice prettier, and Mary the sweetest of all."

"I never knew anybody before called Rachel," said he.

"And I never knew anybody called Luke."

"That's a coincidence, is it not?—a coincidence that ought to make us friends. I may call you Rachel then?"

"Oh, no; please don't. What would people think?"

"Perhaps they would think the truth," said he. "Perhaps they would imagine that I called you so because I liked you. But perhaps they might think also that you let me do so because you liked me. People do make such mistakes."

At this moment up came to them, with flushed face, Mr. Buckett. "I have been looking for you everywhere," said he to Rachel. "It's nearly over now."

"I am so sorry," said Rachel, "but I quite forgot."

"So I presume," said Mr. Buckett angrily, but at the same time he gave his arm to Rachel and led her away. The fag end of some waltz remained, and he might get a turn with her. People in his hearing had spoken of her as the belle of the room, and he did not like to lose his chance. "Oh, Mr. Rowan," said Rachel, looking back as she was being led away. "I must speak one word to Mr. Rowan." Then she separated herself, and returning a step or two almost whispered to her late partner—"You have put me down for ever so many dances. You must scratch out two or three of them."

"Not one," said he. "An engagement is an engagement."

"Oh, but I really can't."

"Of course I cannot make you, but I will scratch out nothing,—and forget nothing."

Then she rejoined Mr. Buckett, and was told by him that young Rowan was not liked in the brewery at all. "We think him conceited, you know. He pretends to know more than anybody else."

CHAPTER VIII
AN ACCOUNT OF MRS. TAPPITT'S BALL—CONCLUDED

It came to be voted by public acclamation that Rachel Ray was the belle of the evening. I think this was brought about quite as much by Mrs. Butler Cornbury's powerful influence as by Rachel's beauty. Mrs. Butler Cornbury having begun the work of chaperon carried it on heartily, and talked her young friend up to the top of the tree. Long before supper her card was quite full, but filled in a manner that was not comfortable to herself,—for she knew that she had made mistakes. As to those spaces on which the letter R was written, she kept them very sacred. She was quite resolved that she would not stand up with him on all those occasions,—that she would omit at any rate two; but she would accept no one else for those two dances, not choosing to select any special period for throwing him over. She endeavoured to explain this when she waltzed with him, shortly before supper; but her explanation did not come easy, and she wanted all her attention for the immediate work she had in hand. "If you'd only give yourself to it a little more eagerly," he said, "you'd waltz beautifully."

"I shall never do it well," she answered. "I don't suppose I shall ever try again."

"But you like it?"

"Oh yes; I like it excessively. But one can't do everything that one likes."

"No; I can't. You won't let me do what I like."

"Don't talk in that way, Mr. Rowan. If you do you'll destroy all my pleasure. You should let me enjoy it while it lasts." In this way she was becoming intimate with him.

"How very nicely your house does for a dance," said Mrs. Cornbury to Mrs. Tappitt.

"Oh dear,—I don't think so. Our rooms are so small. But it's very kind of you to say so. Indeed, I never can be sufficiently obliged—"

"By-the-by," said Mrs. Cornbury, "what a nice girl Rachel Ray has grown."

"Yes, indeed," said Mrs. Tappitt.

"And dances so well! I'd no idea of it. The young men seem rather taken with her. Don't you think so?"

"I declare I think they are. I always fancy that is rather a misfortune to a young girl,—particularly when it must mean nothing, as of course it can't with poor Rachel."

"I don't see that at all."

"Her mother, you know, Mrs. Cornbury;—they are not in the way of seeing any company. It was so kind of you to bring her here, and really she does look very nice. My girls are very good-natured to her. I only hope her head won't be turned. Here's Mr. Tappitt. You must go down Mrs. Cornbury, and eat a little bit of supper." Then Mr. Tappitt in his blue waistcoat led Mrs. Cornbury away.

"I am a very bad hand at supper," said the lady.

"You must take just one glass of champagne," said the gentleman. Now that the wine was there, Mr. Tappitt appreciated the importance of the occasion.

For the last dance before supper,—or that which was intended to be the last,—Rachel had by long agreement been the partner of Walter Cornbury. But now that it was over, the majority of the performers could not go into the supper-room because of the crowd. Young Cornbury therefore proposed that they should loiter about till their time came. He was very well inclined for such loitering with Rachel.

"You're flirting with that girl, Master Walter," said Mrs. Cornbury.

"I suppose that's what she came for," said the cousin.

"By no means, and she's under my care; therefore I beg you'll talk no nonsense to her."

Walter Cornbury probably did talk a little nonsense to her, but it was very innocent nonsense. Most of such flirtations if they were done out loud would be very innocent. Young men are not nearly so pointed in their compliments as their elders, and generally confine themselves to remarks of which neither mothers nor grandmothers could disapprove if they heard them. The romance lies rather in the thoughts than in the words of those concerned. Walter Cornbury believed that he was flirting and felt himself to be happy, but he had uttered nothing warmer to Rachel than a hope that he might meet her at the next Torquay ball.

"I never go to public balls," said Rachel.

"But why not, Miss Ray?" said Walter.

"I never went to a dance of any description before this."

"But now that you've begun of course you'll go on." Mr. Cornbury's flirtation never reached a higher pitch than that.

When he had got as far as that Luke Rowan played him a trick,—an inhospitable trick, seeing that he, Rowan, was in some sort at home, and that the people about him were bound to obey him. He desired the musicians to strike up again while the elders were eating their supper,—and then claimed Rachel's hand, so that he might have the pleasure of serving her with cold chicken and champagne.

"Miss Ray is going into supper with me," said Cornbury.

"But supper is not ready," said Rowan, "and Miss Ray is engaged to dance with me."

"Quite a mistake on your part," said Cornbury.

"No mistake at all," said Rowan.

"Indeed it is. Come, Miss Ray, we'll take a turn down into the hall, and see if places are ready for us." Cornbury rather despised Rowan, as being a brewer and mechanical; and probably he showed that he did so.

"Places are not ready, so you need not trouble Miss Ray to go down as yet. But a couple is wanted for a quadrille, and therefore I'm sure she'll stand up."

"Come along, Rachel," said Cherry. "We just want you. This will be the nicest of all, because we shall have room."

Rachel had become unhappy seeing that the two men were in earnest. Had not Cherry spoken she would have remained with Mr. Cornbury, thinking that to be her safer conduct; but Cherry's voice had overpowered her, and she gave her arm to young Rowan, moving away with slow, hesitating step.

"Of course Miss Ray will do as she pleases," said Cornbury.

"Of course she will," said Rowan.

"I am so sorry," said Rachel, "but I was engaged, and it seems I am really wanted." Walter Cornbury bowed very stiffly, and there was an end of his flirtation. "That's the sort of thing that always happens when a fellow comes among this sort of people!" It was thus he consoled himself as he went down solitary to his supper.

"That's all right," said Rowan; "now we've Cherry for our vis-à-vis, and after that we'll go down to supper comfortably."

"But I said I'd go with him."

"You can't now, for he has gone without you. What a brick Cherry is! Do you know what she said of you?"

"No; do tell me."

"I won't. It will make you vain."

"Oh, dear no; but I want Cherry to like me, because I am so fond of her."

"She says you're by far— But I won't tell you. I hate compliments, and that would look like one. Come, who's forgetting the figure now? I shouldn't wonder if young Cornbury went into the brewery and drowned himself in one of the vats."

It was very nice,—very nice indeed. This was her third dance with Luke Rowan, and she was beginning to think that the other two might perhaps come off without any marked impropriety on her part. She was a little unhappy about Mr. Cornbury,—on his cousin's account rather than on his own. Mrs. Cornbury had been so kind to her that she ought to have remained with Walter when he desired it. So she told herself;—but yet she liked being taken down to supper by Luke Rowan. She had one other cause of uneasiness. She constantly caught Mrs. Tappitt's eye fixed upon herself, and whenever she did so Mrs. Tappitt's eye seemed to look unkindly at her. She had also an instinctive feeling that Augusta did not regard her with favour, and that this disfavour arose from Mr. Rowan's attentions. It was all very nice; but still she felt that there was danger around her, and sometimes she would pause a moment in her happiness, and almost tremble as she thought of things. She was dividing herself poles asunder from Mrs. Prime.

"And now we'll go to supper," said Rowan. "Come, Cherry; do you and Boyd go on first." Boyd was a friend of Rowan's. "Do you know, I've done such a clever trick. This is my second descent among the eatables. As I belong in a manner to the house I took down Miss Harford, and hovered about her for five minutes. Then I managed to lose myself in the crowd, and coming up here got the music up. The fellows were just going off. We've plenty of time now, because they're in the kitchen eating and drinking. I contrived all that dodge that I might give you this glass of wine with my own hands."

"Oh, Mr. Rowan, it was very wrong!"

"And that's my reward! I don't care about its being wrong as long as it's pleasant."

"What shocking morality!"

"All is fair in— Well, never mind, you'll own it is pleasant."

"Oh, yes; it's very pleasant."

"Then I'm contented, and will leave the moral of it for Mr. Cornbury. I'll tell you something further if you'll let me."

"Pray don't tell me anything that you ought not."

"I've done all I could to get up this party on purpose that we might have you here."

"Nonsense."

"But I have. I have cared about it just because it would enable me to say one word to you;—and now I'm afraid to say it."

She was sitting there close to him, and she couldn't go away. She couldn't run as she had done from the stile. She couldn't show any feeling of offence before all those who were around her; and yet,—was it not her duty to do something to stop him? "Pray don't say such things," she whispered.

"I tell you that I'm afraid to say it. Here; give me some wine. You'll take some more. No? Well; shall we go? I am afraid to say it." They were now out in the hall, standing idly there, with their backs to another door. "I wonder what answer you would make me!"

"We had better go up-stairs. Indeed we had."

"Stop a moment, Miss Ray. Why is it that you are so unwilling even to stay a moment with me?"

"I'm not unwilling. Only we had better go now."

"Do you remember when I held your arm at the stile?"

"No; I don't remember anything about it. You ought not to have done it. Do you know, I think you are very cruel." As she made the accusation, she looked down upon the floor, and spoke in a low, trembling voice that almost convinced him that she was in earnest.

"Cruel!" said he. "That's hard too."

"Or you wouldn't prevent me enjoying myself while I am here, by saying things which you ought to know I don't like."

"I have hardly thought whether you would like what I say or not; but I know this; I would give anything in the world to make myself sure that you would ever look back upon this evening as a happy one."

"I will if you'll come up-stairs, and—"

"And what?"

"And go on without,—without seeming to mind me so much."

"Ah, but I do mind you. Rachel—no; you shall not go for a minute. Listen to me for one moment." Then he tried to stand before her, but she was off from him, and ran up-stairs by herself. What was it that he wished to say to her? She knew that she would have liked to have heard it;—nay, that she was longing to hear it. But she was startled and afraid of him, and as she gently crept in at the door of the dancing-room, she determined that she would tell Mrs. Cornbury that she was quite ready for the carriage. It was impossible that she should go through those other two dances with Luke Rowan; and as for her other engagements, they must be allowed to shift for themselves. One had been made early in the evening with Mr. Griggs. It would be a great thing to escape dancing with Mr. Griggs. She would ask Cherry to make her apologies to everybody. As she entered the room she felt ashamed of herself, and unable to take any place. She was oppressed by an idea that she ought not to be walking about without some gentleman with her, and that people would observe her. She was still very near the door when she perceived that Mr. Rowan was also coming in. She determined to avoid him if she could, feeling sure that she could not stop him in anything that he might say, while so many people would be close around them. And yet she felt almost disappointment when she heard his voice as he talked merrily with some one at the door. At that moment Mrs. Cornbury came up to her, walking across the room on purpose to join her.

"What, all alone! I thought your hand was promised for every dance up to five o'clock."

"I believe I'm engaged to some one now, but I declare I don't know who it is. I dare say he has forgotten."

"Ah, yes; people do get confused a little just about this time. Will you come and sit down?"

"Thank you, I should like that. But, Mrs. Cornbury, when you're ready to go away, I am,—quite ready."

"Go away! Why I thought you intended to dance at least for the next two hours."

In answer to this, Rachel declared that she was tired. "And, Mrs. Cornbury, I want to avoid that man," and she pointed out Mr. Griggs by a glance of her eye. "I think he'll say I'm engaged to him for the next waltz, and—I don't like him."

"Poor man; he doesn't look very nice, certainly; but if that's all I'll get you out of the scrape without running away." Then Mr. Griggs came up, and, with a very low bow, struck out the point of his elbow towards Rachel, expecting her immediately to put her hand within it.

"I'm afraid, sir, you must excuse Miss Ray just at present. She's too tired to dance immediately."

Mr. Griggs looked at his card, then looked at Rachel, then looked at Mrs. Cornbury, and stood twiddling the bunch of little gilt playthings that hung from his chain. "That is too hard," said he; "deuced hard."

"I'm very sorry," said Rachel.

"So shall I be,—uncommon. Really, Mrs. Cornbury, I think a turn or two would do her good. Don't you?"

"I can't say I do. She says she would rather not, and of course you won't press her."

"I don't see it in that light,—I really don't. A gentleman has his rights you know, Mrs. Cornbury. Miss Ray won't deny—"

"Miss Ray will deny that she intends to stand up for this dance. And one of the rights of a gentleman is to take a lady at her word."

"Really, Mrs. Cornbury, you are down upon one so hard."

"Rachel," said she, "would you mind coming across the room with me? There are seats on the sofa on the other side." Then Mrs. Cornbury sailed across the floor, and Rachel crept after her more dismayed than ever. Mr. Griggs the while stood transfixed to his place, stroking his mustaches with his hand, and showing plainly by his countenance that he didn't know what he ought to do next. "Well, that's cool," said he; "confounded cool!"

"Anything wrong, Griggs, my boy?" said a bank clerk, slapping him on the back.

"I call it very wrong; very wrong, indeed," said Griggs; "but people do give themselves such airs! Miss Cherry, may I have the honour of waltzing with you?"

"Certainly not," said Cherry, who was passing by. Then Mr. Griggs made his way back to the door.

Rachel felt that things were going wrong with her. It had so happened that she had parted on bad terms with three gentlemen. She had offended Mr. Cornbury and Mr. Griggs, and had done her best to make Mr. Rowan understand that he had offended her! She conceived that all the room would know of it, and that Mrs. Cornbury would become ashamed of her. That Mrs.

Tappitt was already very angry with her she was quite sure. She wished she had not come to the ball, and began to think that perhaps her sister might be right. It almost seemed to herself that she had not known how to behave herself. For a short time she had been happy,—very happy; but she feared that she had in some way committed herself during the moments of her happiness. "I hope you are not angry with me," she said, "about Mr. Griggs?" appealing to her friend in a plaintive voice.

"Angry!—oh dear, no. Why should I be angry with you? I should be angry with that man, only I'm a person that never gets angry with anybody. You were quite right not to dance with him. Never be made to dance with any man you don't like; and remember that a young lady should always have her own way in a ball-room. She doesn't get much of it anywhere else; does she, my dear? And now I'll go whenever you like it, but I'm not the least in a hurry. You're the young lady, and you're to have your own way. If you're quite in earnest, I'll get some one to order the carriage."—Rachel said that she was quite in earnest, and then Walter was called. "So you're going, are you?" said he. "Miss Ray has ill-treated me so dreadfully that I can't express my regret." "Ill-treated you, too, has she? Upon my word, my dear, you've shown yourself quite great upon the occasion. When I was a girl, there was nothing I liked so much as offending all my partners." But Rachel was red with dismay, and wretched that such an accusation should be made against her. "Oh, Mrs. Cornbury, I didn't mean to offend him! I'll explain it all in the carriage. What will you think of me?" "Think, my dear?—why, I shall think that you are going to turn all the young men's heads in Baslehurst. But I shall hear all about it from Walter to-morrow. He tells me of all his loves and all his disappointments."

While the carriage was being brought round, Rachel kept close to her chaperon; but every now and again her eyes, in spite of herself, would wander away to Mr. Rowan. Was he in any way affected by her leaving him, or was it all a joke to him? He was dancing now with Cherry Tappitt, and Rachel was sure that all of it was a joke. But it was a cruel joke,—cruel because it exposed her to so much ill-natured remark. With him she would quarrel,— quarrel really. She would let him know that he should not call her by her Christian name just when it suited him to do so, and then take himself off to play with others in the same way. She would tell Cherry, and make Cherry understand that all walks and visiting and friendly intercommunications must be abandoned because this young man would take advantage of her position to annoy her! He should be made to understand that she was not in his power! Then, as she thought of this, she caught his eye as he made a sudden stop in the dance close to her, and all her hard thoughts died away. Ah, dear, what was it that she wanted of him?

At that moment they got up to go away. Such a person as Mrs. Butler Cornbury could not, of course, escape without a parade of adieux. Mr. Tappitt was searched up from the little room in which the card-party held their meeting in order that he might hand the guest that had honoured him down to her carriage; and Mrs. Tappitt fluttered about, profuse in her acknowledgments for the favour done to them. "And we do so hope Mr. Cornbury will be successful," she said, as she bade her last farewell. This was spoken close to Mr. Tappitt's ear; and Mrs. Cornbury flattered herself that after that Mr. Tappitt's vote would be secure. Mr. Tappitt said nothing about his vote, but handed the lady down stairs in solemn silence.

The Tappitt girls came and clustered about Rachel as she was going. "I can't conceive why you are off so early," said Martha. "No, indeed," said Mrs. Tappitt; "only of course it would be very wrong to keep Mrs. Cornbury waiting when she has been so excessively kind to you." "The naughty girl! It isn't that at all," said Cherry. "It's she that is hurrying Mrs. Cornbury away." "Good night," said Augusta very coldly. "And Rachel," said Cherry, "mind you come up to-morrow and talk it all over; we shall have so much to say." Then Rachel turned to go, and found Luke Rowan at her elbow waiting to take her down. She had no alternative;—she must take his arm; and thus they walked down stairs into the hall together.

"You'll come up here to-morrow," said he.

"No, no; tell Cherry that I shall not come."

"Then I shall go to Bragg's End. Will your mother let me call?"

"No, don't come. Pray don't."

"I certainly shall;—certainly, certainly! What things have you got? Let me put your shawl on for you. If you do not come up to the girls, I shall certainly go down to you. Now, good-night. Good-night, Mrs. Cornbury." And Luke, getting hold of Rachel's reluctant hand, pressed it with all his warmth.

"I don't want to ask indiscreet questions," said Mrs. Cornbury; "but that young man seems rather smitten, I think."

"Oh, no," said Rachel, not knowing what to say.

"But I say,—oh, yes; a nice good-looking man he is too, and a gentleman, which is more than I can say for all of them there. What an escape you had of Mr. Griggs, my dear!"

"Yes, I had. But I was so sorry that you should have to speak to him."

"Of course I spoke to him. I was there to fight your battles for you. That's why married ladies go to balls. You were quite right not to dance with him. A girl should always avoid any intimacy with such men as that. It is not that he would have done you any harm; but they stand in the way of your satisfaction and contentment. Balls are given specially for young ladies; and it is my theory that they are to make themselves happy while they are there, and not sacrifice themselves to men whom they don't wish to know. You can't always refuse when you're asked, but you can always get out of an engagement afterwards if you know what you're about. That was my way when I was a girl." And this was the daughter of Mr. Comfort, whose somewhat melancholy discourses against the world's pleasures and vanities had so often filled Rachel's bosom with awe!

Rachel sat silent, thinking of what had occurred at Mrs. Tappitt's; and thinking also that she ought to make some little speech to her friend, thanking her for all that she had done. Ought she not also to apologise in some way for her own conduct? "What was that between you and my cousin Walter?" Mrs. Cornbury asked, after a few moments.

"I hope I wasn't to blame," said Rachel. "But—"

"But what? Of course you weren't to blame;—unless it was in being run after by so many gentlemen at once."

"He was going to take me down to supper,—and it was so kind of him. And then while we were waiting because the room down-stairs was full, there was another quadrille, and I was engaged to Mr. Rowan."

"Ah, yes; I understand. And so Master Walter got thrown once. His wrath in such matters never lasts very long. Here we are at Bragg's End. I've been so glad to have you with me; and I hope I may take you again with me somewhere before long. Remember me kindly to your mother. There she is at the door waiting for you." Then Rachel jumped out of the carriage, and ran across the little gravel-path into the house.

Mrs. Ray had been waiting up for her daughter, and had been listening eagerly for the wheels of the carriage. It was not yet two o'clock, and by ball-going people the hour of Rachel's return would have been considered early; but to Mrs. Ray anything after midnight was very late. She was not, however, angry, or even vexed, but simply pleased that her girl had at last come back to her. "Oh, mamma, I'm afraid it has been very hard upon you, waiting for me!" said Rachel; "but I did come away as soon as I could." Mrs. Ray declared that she had not found it all hard, and then,—with a laudable curiosity, seeing how little she had known about balls,—desired to have an immediate account of Rachel's doings.

"And did you get anybody to dance with you?" asked the mother, feeling a mother's ambition that her daughter should have been "respectit like the lave."

"Oh, yes; plenty of people asked me to dance."

"And did you find it come easy?"

"Quite easy. I was frightened about the waltzing, at first."

"Do you mean that you waltzed, Rachel?"

"Yes, mamma. Everybody did it. Mrs. Cornbury said she always waltzed when she was a girl; and as the things turned out I could not help myself. I began with her cousin. I didn't mean to do it, but I got so ashamed of myself that I couldn't refuse."

Mrs. Ray still was not angry; but she was surprised, and perhaps a little dismayed. "And did you like it?"

"Yes, mamma."

"Were they all kind to you?"

"Yes, mamma."

"You seem to have very little to say about it; but I suppose you're tired."

"I am tired, but it isn't that. It seems that there is so much to think about. I'll tell you everything to-morrow, when I get quiet again. Not that there is much to tell."

"Then I'll wish you good-night, dear."

"Good-night, mamma. Mrs. Cornbury was so kind,—you can have no idea how good-natured she is."

"She always was a good creature."

"If I'd been her sister she couldn't have done more for me. I feel as though I were really quite fond of her. But she isn't a bit like what I expected. She chooses to have her own way; but then she is so good-humoured! And when I got into any little trouble she—"

"Well, what else did she do; and what trouble had you?"

"I can't quite describe what I mean. She seemed to make so much of me;—just as she might have done if I'd been some grand young lady down from London, or any, any;—you know what I mean."

Mrs. Ray sat with her candle in her hand, receiving great comfort from the knowledge that her daughter had been "respectit." She knew well what Rachel meant, and reflected, with perhaps a pardonable pride, that she herself had "come of decent people." The Tappitts were higher than her in the world, and so were the Griggses. But she knew that her forbears had been gentlefolk, when there were, so to speak, no Griggses and no Tappitts in existence. It was pleasant to her to think that her daughter had been treated as a lady.

"And she did do me such a kindness. That horrid Mr. Griggs was going to dance with me, and she wouldn't let him."

"I don't like that young man at all."

"Poor Cherry! you should hear her talk of him! And she would have stayed ever so much longer if I had not pressed her to go; and then she has such a nice way of saying things."

"She always had that, when she was quite a young girl."

"I declare I feel that I quite love her. And there was such a grand supper. Champagne!"

"No!"

"I got some cold turkey. Mr. Rowan took me down to supper." These last words were spoken very mildly, and Rachel, as she uttered them, did not dare to look into her mother's face.

"Did you dance with him?"

"Yes, mamma, three times. I should have stayed later only I was engaged to dance with him twice more; and I didn't choose to do so."

"Was he—? Did he—?"

"Oh, mamma; I can't tell you. I don't know how to tell you. I wish you knew it all without my saying anything. He says he shall come here to-morrow if I don't go up to the brewery; and I can't possibly go there now, after that."

"Did he say anything more than that, Rachel?"

"He calls me Rachel, and speaks—I can't tell you how he speaks. If you think it wrong, mamma, I won't ever see him again."

Mrs. Ray didn't know whether she ought to think it wrong or not. She was inclined to wish that it was right and to believe that it was wrong. A few minutes ago Rachel was unable to open her mouth, and was anxious to escape to bed; but, now that the ice was broken between her and her mother, they sat up for more than an hour talking about Luke Rowan.

"I wonder whether he will really come?" Rachel said to herself, as she laid her head upon her pillow—"and why does he want to come?"

CHAPTER IX
MR. PRONG AT HOME

Mrs. Tappitt's ball was celebrated on a Tuesday, and on the preceding Monday Mrs. Prime moved herself off, bag and baggage, to Miss Pucker's lodgings. Miss Pucker had been elated with a dismal joy when the proposition was first made to her. "Oh, yes; it was very dreadful. She would do anything;—of course she would give up the front bedroom up-stairs to Mrs. Prime, and get a stretcher for herself in the little room behind, which looked out on the tiles of Griggs' sugar warehouse. She hadn't thought such a thing would have been possible; she really had not. A ball! Mrs. Prime couldn't help coming away;—of course not. And there would be plenty of room for all her boxes in the small room behind the shop. Mrs. Ray's daughter go to a ball!" And then some threatening words were said as to the destiny of wicked people, which shall not be repeated here.

That flitting had been a very dismal affair. An old man out of Baslehurst had come for Mrs. Prime's things with a donkey-cart, and the old man, assisted by the girl, had carried them out together. Rachel had remained secluded in her mother's room. The two sisters had met at the same table at breakfast, but had not spoken over their tea and bread and butter. As Rachel was taking the cloth away Mrs. Prime had asked her solemnly whether she still persisted in bringing perdition upon herself and her mother. "You have no right to ask me such a question," Rachel had answered, and taking herself up-stairs had secluded herself till the old man with the donkey, followed by Mrs. Prime, had taken himself away from Bragg's End. Mrs. Ray, as her eldest daughter was leaving her, stood at the door of her house with her handkerchief to her eyes. "It makes me very unhappy, Dorothea; so it does." "And it makes me very unhappy, too, mother. Perhaps my sorrow in the matter is deeper than yours. But I must do my duty." Then the two widows kissed each other with a cold unloving kiss, and Mrs. Prime had taken her departure from Bragg's End Cottage. "It will make a great difference in the housekeeping," Mrs. Ray said to Rachel, and then she went to work at her little accounts.

It was Dorcas-day at Miss Pucker's, and as the work of the meeting began soon after Mrs. Prime had unpacked her boxes in the front bedroom and had made her little domestic arrangements with her friend, that first day passed by without much tedium. Mrs. Prime was used to Miss Pucker, and was not therefore grievously troubled by the ways and habits of that lady, much as they were unlike those to which she had been accustomed at Bragg's End; but on the next morning, as she was sitting with her companion after breakfast, an idea did come into her head that Miss Pucker would not be a pleasant companion for life. She would talk incessantly of the wickednesses of the cottage, and ask repeated questions about Rachel and the young man. Mrs. Prime was undoubtedly very angry with her mother, and much shocked at her sister, but she did not relish the outspoken sympathy of her confidential friend. "He'll never marry her, you know. He don't think of such a thing," said Miss Pucker over and over again. Mrs. Prime did not find this pleasant when spoken of her sister. "And the young men I'm told goes on anyhow, as they pleases at them dances," said Miss Pucker, who in the warmth of her intimacy forgot some of those little restrictions in speech with which she had burdened herself when first striving to acquire the friendship of Mrs. Prime. Before dinner was over Mrs. Prime had made up her mind that she must soon move her staff again, and establish herself somewhere in solitude.

After tea she took herself out for a walk, having managed to decline Miss Pucker's attendance, and as she walked she thought of Mr. Prong. Would it not be well for her to go to him and ask his further advice? He would tell her in what way she had better live. He would tell her also whether it was impossible that she should ever return to the cottage, for already her heart was becoming somewhat more soft than was its wont. And as she walked she met Mr. Prong himself, intent on his pastoral business. "I was thinking of coming to you to-morrow," she said, after their first salutation was over.

"Do," said he; "do; come early,—before the toil of the day's work commences. I also am specially anxious to see you. Will nine be too early,— or, if you have not concluded your morning meal by that time, half-past nine?"

Mrs. Prime assured him that her morning meal was always concluded before nine o'clock, and promised to be with him by that hour. Then as she slowly paced up the High Street to the Cawston Bridge and back again, she wondered within herself as to the matter on which Mr. Prong could specially want to see her. He might probably desire to claim her services for some woman's work in his sheepfold. He should have them willingly, for she had begun to feel that she would sooner co-operate with Mr. Prong than with Miss Pucker. As she returned down the High Street, and came near to her own door, she saw the cause of all her family troubles standing at the entrance to Griggs's wine-store. He was talking to the shopman within, and as she passed she frowned grimly beneath her widow's bonnet. "Send them to the brewery at once," said Luke Rowan to the man. "They are wanted this evening."

"I understand," said the man.

"And tell your fellow to take them round to the back door."

"All right," said the man, winking with one eye. He understood very well that young Rowan was ordering the champagne for Mrs. Tappitt's supper, and that it was thought desirable that Mr. Tappitt shouldn't see the bottles going into the house.

Miss Pucker possessed at any rate the virtue of being early, so that Mrs. Prime had no difficulty in concluding her "morning meal," and being at Mr. Prong's house punctually at nine o'clock. Mr. Prong, it seemed, had not been quite so steadfast to his purpose, for his teapot was still upon the table, together with the debris of a large dish of shrimps, the eating of small shellfish being an innocent enjoyment to which he was much addicted.

"Dear me; so it is; just nine. We'll have these things away in a minute. Mrs. Mudge; Mrs. Mudge!" Whereupon Mrs. Mudge came forth, and between the three the table was soon cleared. "I wish you hadn't caught me so late," said Mr. Prong; "it looks as though I hadn't been thinking of you." Then he picked up the stray shell of a shrimp, and in order that he might get rid of it, put it into his mouth. Mrs. Prime said she hoped she didn't trouble him, and that of course she didn't expect him to be thinking about her particularly. Then Mr. Prong looked at her in a way that was very particular out of the corner of his eyes, and assured her that he had been thinking of her all night. After that Mrs. Prime sat down on a horsehair-seated chair, and Mr. Prong sat on another opposite to her, leaning back, with his eyes nearly closed, and his hands folded upon his lap.

"I don't think Miss Pucker's will quite do for me," said Mrs. Prime, beginning her story first.

"I never thought it would, my friend," said Mr. Prong, with his eyes still nearly closed.

"She's a very good woman,—an excellent woman, and her heart is full of love and charity. But—"

"I quite understand it, my friend. She is not in all things the companion you desire."

"I am not quite sure that I shall want any companion."

"Ah!" sighed Mr. Prong, shaking his head, but still keeping his eyes closed.

"I think I would rather be alone, if I do not return to them at the cottage. I would fain return if only they—"

"If only they would return too. Yes! That would be a glorious end to the struggle you have made, if you can bring them back with you from following after the Evil One! But you cannot return to them now, if you are to countenance by your presence dancings and love-makings in the open air,"—why worse in the open air than in a close little parlour in a back street, Mr. Prong did not say,—"and loud revellings, and the absence of all good works, and rebellion against the Spirit." Mr. Prong was becoming energetic in his language, and at one time had raised himself in his chair, and opened his eyes. But he closed them at once, and again fell back. "No, my friend," said he, "no. It must not be so. They must be rescued from the burning; but not so,—not so." After that for a minute or two they both sat still in silence.

"I think I shall get two small rooms for myself in one of the quiet streets, near the new church," said she.

"Ah, yes, perhaps so,—for a time."

"Till I may be able to go back to mother. It's a sad thing families being divided, Mr. Prong."

"Yes, it is sad;—unless it tends to the doing of the Lord's work."

"But I hope;—I do hope, that all this may be changed. Rachel I know is obstinate, but mother means well, Mr. Prong. She means to do her duty, if only she had good teaching near her."

"I hope she may, I hope she may. I trust that they may both be brought to see the true light. We will wrestle for them,—you and me. We will wrestle for them,—together. Mrs. Prime, my friend, if you are prepared to hear me with attention, I have a proposition to make which I think you will acknowledge to be one of importance." Then suddenly he sat bolt upright, opened his eyes wide, and dressed his mouth with all the solemn dignity of which he was the master. "Are you prepared to listen to me, Mrs. Prime?"

Mrs. Prime, who was somewhat astonished, said in a low voice that she was prepared to listen.

"Because I must beg you to hear me out. I shall fail altogether in reaching your intelligence,—whatever effect I might possibly have upon your heart,—unless you will hear me to the end."

"I will hear you certainly, Mr. Prong."

"Yes, my friend, for it will be necessary. If I could convey to your mind all that is now passing through my own, without any spoken word, how glad should I be! The words of men, when taken at the best, how weak they are! They often tell a tale quite different from that which the creature means who uses them. Every minister has felt that in addressing his flock from the pulpit. I feel it myself sadly, but I never felt it so sadly as I do now."

Mrs. Prime did not quite understand him, but she assured him again that she would give his words her best attention, and that she would endeavour to gather from them no other meaning than that which seemed to be his. "Ah,—seemed!" said he. "There is so much of seeming in this deceitful world. But you will believe this of me, that whatever I do, I do as tending to the strengthening of my hands in the ministry." Mrs. Prime said that she would believe so much; and then as she looked into her companion's face, she became aware that there was something of weakness displayed in that assuming mouth. She did not argue about it within her own mind, but the fact had in some way become revealed to her.

"My friend," said he,—and as he spoke he drew his chair across the rug, so as to bring it very near to that on which Mrs. Prime was sitting—"our destinies in this world, yours and mine, are in many things alike. We are both alone. We both of us have our hands full of work, and of work which in many respects is the same. We are devoted to the same cause: is it not so?" Mrs. Prime, who had been told that she was to listen and not to speak, did not at first make any answer. But she was pressed by a repetition of the question. "Is it not so, Mrs. Prime?"

"I can never make my work equal to that of a minister of the Gospel," said she.

"But you can share the work of such a minister. You understand me now. And let me assure you of this; that in making this proposition to you, I am not self-seeking. It is not my own worldly comfort and happiness to which I am chiefly looking."

"Ah," said Mrs. Prime, "I suppose not." Perhaps there was in her voice the slightest touch of soreness.

"No;—not chiefly to that. I want assistance, confidential intercourse, sympathy, a congenial mind, support when I am like to faint, counsel when I am pressing on, aid when the toil is too heavy for me, a kind word when the day's work is over. And you,—do you not desire the same? Are we not alike in that, and would it not be well that we should come together?" Mr. Prong as he spoke had put out his hand, and rested it on the table with the palm upwards, as though expecting that she would put hers within it; and he had tilted his chair so as to bring his body closer to hers, and had dropped from his face his assumed look of dignity. He was quite in earnest, and being so had fallen away into his natural dispositions of body.

"I do not quite understand you," said Mrs. Prime. She did however understand him perfectly, but thought it expedient that he should be required to speak a little further before she answered him. She wanted time also to arrange her reply. As yet she had not made up her mind whether she would say yes or no.

"Mrs. Prime, I am offering to make you my wife. I have said nothing of love, of that human affection which one of God's creatures entertains for another;—not, I can assure you, because I do not feel it, but because I think that you and I should be governed in our conduct by a sense of duty, rather than by the poor creature-longings of the heart."

"The heart is very deceitful," said Mrs. Prime.

"That is true,—very true; but my heart, in this matter, is not deceitful. I entertain for you all that deep love which a man should feel for her who is to be the wife of his bosom."

"But Mr. Prong—"

"Let me finish before you give me your answer. I have thought much of this, as you may believe; and by only one consideration have I been made to doubt the propriety of taking this step. People will say that I am marrying you for,—for your money, in short. It is an insinuation which would give me much pain, but I have resolved within my own mind, that it is my duty to bear it. If my motives are pure,"—here he paused a moment for a word or two of encouragement, but received none,—"and if the thing itself be good, I ought not to be deterred by any fear of what the wicked may say. Do you not agree with me in that?"

Mrs. Prime still did not answer. She felt that any word of assent, though given by her to a minor proposition, might be taken as involving some amount of assent towards the major proposition. Mr. Prong had enjoyed the advantage of thinking over his matrimonial prospects in undisturbed solitude, but she had as yet possessed no such advantage. As the idea had never before presented itself to her, she did not feel inclined to commit herself hastily.

"And as regards money," he continued.

"Well," said Mrs. Prime, looking down demurely upon the ground, for Mr. Prong had not at once gone on to say what were his ideas about money.

"And as regards money,—need I hardly declare that my motives are pure and disinterested? I am aware that in worldly affairs you are at present better off than I am. My professional income from the pew-rents is about a hundred and thirty pounds a year."—It must be admitted that it was very hard work. By this time Mr. Prong had withdrawn his hand from the table, finding that attempt to be hopeless, and had re-settled his chair upon its four feet. He had commenced by requesting Mrs. Prime to hear him patiently, but he had probably not calculated that she would have listened with a patience so cruel and unrelenting. She did not even speak a word when he communicated to her the amount of his income. "That is what I receive here," he continued, "and you are probably aware that I have no private means of my own."

"I didn't know," said Mrs. Prime.

"No; none. But what then?"

"Oh, dear no."

"Money is but dross. Who feels that more strongly than you do?"

Mr. Prong in all that he was saying intended to be honest, and in asserting that money was dross, he believed that he spoke his true mind. He thought also that he was passing a just eulogium on Mrs. Prime, in declaring that she was of the same opinion. But he was not quite correct in this, either as regarded himself, or as regarded her. He did not covet money, but he valued it very highly; and as for Mrs. Prime, she had an almost unbounded satisfaction in her own independence. She had, after all, but two hundred a year, out of which she gave very much in charity. But this giving in charity was her luxury. Fine raiment and dainty food tempted her not at all; but nevertheless she was not free from temptations, and did not perhaps always resist them. To be mistress of her money, and to superintend the gifts, not only of herself but of others; to be great among the poor, and esteemed as a personage in her district,—that was her ambition. When Mr. Prong told her that money in her sight was dross, she merely shook her head. Why was it that she wrote those terribly caustic notes to the agent in Exeter if her quarterly payments were ever late by a single week? "Defend me from a lone widow," the agent used to say, "and especially if she's evangelical." Mrs. Prime delighted in the sight of the bit of paper which conveyed to her the possession of her periodical wealth. To her money certainly was not dross, and I doubt if it was truly so regarded by Mr. Prong himself.

"Any arrangements that you choose as to settlements or the like of that, could of course be made." Mr. Prong when he began, or rather when he made up his mind to begin, had determined that he would use all his best power of language in pressing his suit; but the work had been so hard that his fine language had got itself lost in the struggle. I doubt whether this made much difference with Mrs. Prime; or it may be, that he had sustained the propriety of his words as long as such propriety was needful and salutary to his purpose. Had he spoken of the "like of that" at the opening of the negotiation, he might have shocked his hearer; but now she was too deeply engaged in solid serious considerations to care much for the words which were used. "A hundred and thirty from pew-rents," she said to herself, as he endeavoured, unsuccessfully, to look under her bonnet into her face.

"I think I have said it all now," he continued. "If you will trust yourself into my keeping I will endeavour, with God's assistance, to do my duty by you. I have said but little personally of myself or of my feelings, hoping that it might be unnecessary."

"Oh, quite so," said she.

"I have spoken rather of those duties which we should undertake together in sweet companionship, if you will consent to—to—to be Mrs. Prong, in short." Then he waited for an answer.

As she sat in her widow's weeds, there was not, to the eye, the promise in her of much sweet companionship. Her old crape bonnet had been lugged and battered about—not out of all shape, as hats and bonnets are sometimes battered by young ladies, in which guise, if the young ladies themselves be pretty, the battered hats and bonnets are often more becoming than ever they were in their proper shapes—but so as closely to fit her head, and almost hide her face. Her dress was so made, and so put on, as to give to her the appearance of almost greater age than her mother's. She had studied to divest herself of all outward show of sweet companionship; but perhaps she was not the less, on that account, gratified to find that she had not altogether succeeded.

"I have done with the world, and all the world's vanities and cares," she said, shaking her head.

"No one can have done with the world as long as there is work in it for him or her to do. The monks and nuns tried that, and you know what they came to."

"But I am a widow."

"Yes, my friend; and have shown yourself, as such, very willing to do your part. But do you not know that you could be more active and more useful as a clergyman's wife than you can be as a solitary woman?"

"But my heart is buried, Mr. Prong."

"No; not so. While the body remains in this vale of tears, the heart must remain with it." Mrs. Prime shook her head; but in an anatomical point of view, Mr. Prong was no doubt strictly correct. "Other hopes will arise,—and perhaps, too, other cares, but they will be sources of gentle happiness."

Mrs. Prime understood him as alluding to a small family, and again shook her head at the allusion.

"What I have said may probably have taken you by surprise."

"Yes, it has, Mr. Prong;—very much."

"And if so, it may be that you would wish time for consideration before you give me an answer."

"Perhaps that will be best, Mr. Prong."

"Let it be so. On what day shall we say? Will Friday suit you? If I come to you on Friday morning, perhaps Miss Pucker will be there."

"Yes, she will."

"And in the afternoon."

"We shall be at the Dorcas meeting."

"I don't like to trouble you to come here again."

Mrs. Prime herself felt that there was a difficulty. Hitherto she had entertained no objection to calling on Mr. Prong at his own house. His little sitting-room had been as holy ground to her,—almost as part of the church, and she had taken herself there without scruple. But things had now been put on a different footing. It might be that that room would become her own peculiar property, but she could never again regard it in a simply clerical light. It had become as it were a bower of love, and she could not take her steps thither with the express object of assenting to the proposition made to her,—or even with that of dissenting from it. "Perhaps," said she, "you could call at ten on Saturday. Miss Pucker will be out marketing." To this Mr. Prong agreed, and then Mrs. Prime got up and took her leave. How fearfully wicked would Rachel have been in her eyes, had Rachel made an appointment with a young man at some hour and some place in which she might be found alone! But then it is so easy to trust oneself, and so easy also to distrust others.

"Good-morning," said Mrs. Prime; and as she went she gave her hand as a matter of course to her lover.

"Good-bye," said he; "and think well of this if you can do so. If you believe that you will be more useful as my wife than you can be in your present position,—then—"

"You think it would be my duty to—"

"Well, I will leave that for you to decide. I merely wish to put the matter before you. But, pray, understand this; money need be no hindrance." Then, having said that last word, he let her go.

She walked away very slowly, and did not return by the most direct road to Miss Pucker's rooms. There was much to be considered in the offer that had been made to her. Her lot in life would be very lonely if this separation from her mother and sister should become permanent. She had already made up her mind that a continued residence with Miss Pucker would not suit her; and although, on that very morning, she had felt that there would be much comfort in living by herself, now, as she looked forward to that loneliness, it had for her very little attraction. Might it not be true, also, that she could do more good as a clergyman's wife than could possibly come within her reach as a single woman? She had tried that life once already, but then she had been very young. As that memory came upon her, she looked back to her early life, and thought of the hopes which had been hers as she stood at the altar, now so many years ago. How different had been everything with her then! She remembered the sort of love she had felt in her heart, and told herself that there could be no repetition of such love on Mr. Prong's behalf. She had come round in her walk to that very churchyard stile at which she had seen Rachel standing with Luke Rowan, and as she remembered some passages in her own girlish days, she almost felt inclined to forgive her sister. But then, on a sudden, she drew herself up almost with a gasp, and went on quickly with her walk. Had she not herself in those days walked in darkness, and had it not since that been vouchsafed to her to see the light? In her few months of married happiness it had been given to her to do but little of that work which might now be possible to her. Then she had been married in the flesh; now she would be married in the spirit;— she would be married in the spirit, if it should, on final consideration, seem good to her to accept Mr. Prong's offer in that light. Then unconsciously, she began to reflect on the rights of a married woman with regard to money,— and also on the wrongs. She was not sure as to the law, and asked herself whether it would be possible for her to consult an attorney. Finally, she thought it would not be practicable to do so before giving her answer to Mr. Prong.

And she could not even ask her mother. As to that, too, she questioned herself, and resolved that she could not so far lower herself under existing circumstances. There was no one to whom she could go for advice. But we may say this of her,—let her have asked whom she would, she would have at least been guided by her own judgment. If only she could have obtained some slight amount of legal information, how useful it would have been!

CHAPTER X
LUKE ROWAN DECLARES HIS
PLANS AS TO THE BREWERY

"The truth is, T., there was some joking among the young people about the wine, and then Rowan went and ordered it." This was Mrs. Tappitt's explanation about the champagne, made to her husband on the night of the ball, before she was allowed to go to sleep. But this by no means satisfied him. He did not choose, as he declared, that any young man should order whatever he might think necessary for his house. Then Mrs. Tappitt made it worse. "To tell the truth, T., I think it was intended as a present to the girls. We are doing a great deal to make him comfortable, you know, and I fancy he thought it right to make them this little return." She should have known her husband better. It was true that he grudged the cost of the wine; but he would have preferred to endure that to the feeling that his table had been supplied by another man,—by a young man whom he wished to regard as subject to himself, but who would not be subject, and at whom he was beginning to look with very unfavourable eyes. "A present to the girls? I tell you I won't have such presents. And if it was so, I think he has been very impertinent,—very impertinent indeed. I shall tell him so,—and I shall insist on paying for the wine. And I must say, you ought not to have taken it."

"Oh, dear T., I have been working so hard all night; and I do think you ought to let me go to sleep now, instead of scolding me."

On the following morning the party was of course discussed in the Tappitt family under various circumstances. At the breakfast-table Mrs. Rowan, with her son and daughter, were present; and then a song of triumph was sung. Everything had gone off with honour and glory, and the brewery had been immortalized for years to come. Mrs. Butler Cornbury's praises were spoken,—with some little drawback of a sneer on them, because "she had made such a fuss with that girl Rachel Ray;" and then the girls had told of their partners, and Luke had declared it all to have been superb. But when the Rowans' backs were turned, and the Tappitts were alone together, others besides old Tappitt himself had words to say in dispraise of

Luke. Mrs. Tappitt had been much inclined to make little of her husband's objections to the young man while she hoped that he might possibly become her son-in-law. He might have been a thorn in the brewery, among the vats, but he would have been a flourishing young bay-tree in the outer world of Baslehurst. She had, however, no wish to encourage the growth of a thorn within her own premises, in order that Rachel Ray, or such as she, might have the advantage of the bay-tree. Luke Rowan had behaved very badly at her party. Not only had he failed to distinguish either of her own girls, but he had, as Mrs. Tappitt said, made himself so conspicuous with that foolish girl, that all the world had been remarking it.

"Mrs. Butler Cornbury seemed to think it all right," said Cherry.

"Mrs. Butler Cornbury is not everybody," said Mrs. Tappitt. "I didn't think it right, I can assure you;—and what's more, your papa didn't think it right."

"And he was going on all the evening as though he were quite master in the house," said Augusta. "He was ordering the musicians to do this and that all the evening."

"He'll find that he's not master. Your papa is going to speak to him this very day."

"What!—about Rachel?" asked Cherry, in dismay.

"About things in general," said Mrs. Tappitt. Then Mary Rowan returned to the room, and they all went back upon the glories of the ball. "I think it was nice," said Mrs. Tappitt, simpering. "I'm sure there was no trouble spared,—nor yet expense." She knew that she ought not to have uttered that last word, and she would have refrained if it had been possible to her;—but it was not possible. The man who tells you how much his wine costs a dozen, knows that he is wrong while the words are in his mouth; but they are in his mouth, and he cannot restrain them.

Mr. Tappitt was not about to lecture Luke Rowan as to his conduct in regard to Rachel Ray. He found some difficulty in speaking to his would-be partner, even on matters of business, in a proper tone, and with becoming authority. As he was so much the senior, and Rowan so much the junior, some such tone of superiority was, as he thought, indispensable. But he had great difficulty in assuming it. Rowan had a way with him that was not exactly a way of submission, and Tappitt would certainly not have dared to encounter him on any such matter as his behaviour in a drawing-room. When the time came he had not even the courage to allude to those champagne bottles; and it may be as well explained that Rowan paid the little bill at Griggs's, without further reference to the matter. But the question of the brewery management was a matter vital to Tappitt. There, among the vats, he had reigned supreme since Bungall ceased to be king, and for continual mastery there it was worth his while to make a fight. That he was under difficulties even in that fight he had already begun to know. He could not talk Luke Rowan down, and make him go about his work in an orderly, every-day, business-like fashion. Luke Rowan would not be talked down, nor would he be orderly,—not according to Mr. Tappitt's orders. No doubt Mr. Tappitt, under these circumstances, could decline the partnership; and this he was disposed to do; but he had been consulting lawyers, consulting papers, and looking into old accounts, and he had reason to fear, that under Bungall's will, Luke Rowan would have the power of exacting from him much more than he was inclined to give.

"You'd better take him into the concern," the lawyer had said. "A young head is always useful."

"Not when the young head wants to be master," Tappitt had answered. "If I'm to do that the whole thing will go to the dogs." He did not exactly explain to the lawyer that Rowan had carried his infatuation so far as to be desirous of brewing good beer, but he did make it very clear that such a partner would, in his eyes, be anything but desirable.

"Then, upon my word, I think you'll have to give him the ten thousand pounds. I don't even know but what the demand is moderate."

This was very bad news to Tappitt. "But suppose I haven't got ten thousand pounds!" Now it was very well known that the property and the business were worth money, and the lawyer suggested that Rowan might take steps to have the whole concern sold. "Probably he might buy it himself and undertake to pay you so much a year," suggested the lawyer. But this view of the matter was not at all in accordance with Mr. Tappitt's ideas. He had been brewer in Baslehurst for nearly thirty years, and still wished to remain so. Mrs. Tappitt had been of opinion that all difficulties might be overcome if only Luke would fall in love with one of her girls. Mrs. Rowan had been invited to Baslehurst specially with a view to some such arrangement. But Luke Rowan, as it seemed to them both now, was an obstinate young man, who, in matters of beer as well as in matters of love, would not be guided by those who best knew how to guide him. Mrs. Tappitt had watched him closely at the ball, and had now given him up altogether. He had danced only once with Augusta, and then had left her the moment the dance was over. "I should offer him a hundred and fifty pounds a year out of the concern, and if he didn't like that let him lump it," said Mrs. Tappitt. "Lump it!" said Mr. Tappitt. "That means going to a London lawyer." He felt the difficulties of his position as he prepared to speak his mind to young Rowan on the morning after the party; but on that occasion his strongest feeling was in favour of expelling the intruder. Any lot in life would be preferable to working in the brewery with such a partner as Luke Rowan.

"I suppose your head's hardly cool enough for business," he said, as Luke came in and took a stool in his office. Tappitt was sitting in his customary chair, with his arm resting on a large old-fashioned leather-covered table, which was strewed with his papers, and which had never been reduced to cleanliness or order within the memory of any one connected with the establishment. He had turned his chair round from its accustomed place so as to face Rowan, who had perched himself on a stool which was commonly occupied by a boy whom Tappitt employed in his own office.

"My head not cool!" said Rowan. "It's as cool as a cucumber. I wasn't drinking last night."

"I thought you might be tired with the dancing." Then Tappitt's mind flew off to the champagne, and he determined that the young man before him was too disagreeable to be endured.

"Oh, dear, no. Those things never tire me. I was across here with the men before eight this morning. Do you know, I'm sure we could save a third of the fuel by altering the flues. I never saw such contrivances. They must have been put in by the coal-merchants, for the sake of wasting coal."

"If you please, we won't mind the flues at present."

"I only tell you; it's for your sake much more than my own. If you won't believe me, do you ask Newman to look at them the first time you see him in Baslehurst."

"I don't care a straw for Newman."

"He's got the best concerns in Devonshire, and knows what he's about better than any man in these parts."

"I dare say. But now, if you please, we won't mind him. The concerns, as I have managed them, have done very well for me for the last thirty years;—very well I may say also for your uncle, who understood what he was doing. I'm not very keen for so many changes. They cost a great deal of money, and as far as I can see don't often lead to much profit."

"If we don't go on with the world," said Rowan, "the world will leave us behind. Look at the new machinery they're introducing everywhere. People don't do it because they like to spend their money. It's competition; and there's competition in beer as well as in other things."

For a minute or two Mr. Tappitt sat in silence collecting his thoughts, and then he began his speech. "I'll tell you what it is, Rowan, I don't like these new-fangled ways. They're very well for you, I dare say. You are young, and perhaps you may see your way. I'm old, and I don't see mine among all these changes. It's clear to me that you and I could not go on together as partners in the same concern. I should expect to have my own way,—first because I've a deal of experience, and next because my share in the concern would be so much the greatest."

"Stop a moment, Mr. Tappitt; I'm not quite sure that it would be much the greatest. I don't want to say anything about that now; only if I were to let your remark pass without notice it would seem that I had assented."

"Ah; very well. I can only say that I hope you'll find yourself mistaken. I've been over thirty years in the concern, and it would be odd if I with my large family were to find myself only equal to you, who have never been in the business at all, and ain't even married yet."

"I don't see what being married has to do with it."

"Don't you? You'll find that's the way we look at these things down in these parts. You're not in London here, Mr. Rowan."

"Certainly not; but I suppose the laws are the same. This is an affair of capital."

"Capital!" said Mr. Tappitt. "I don't know that you've brought in any capital."

"Bungall did, and I'm here as his representative. But you'd better let that pass by just at present. If we can agree as to the management of the business, you won't find me a hard man to deal with as to our relative shares." Hereupon Tappitt scratched his head, and tried to think. "But I don't see how we are to agree about the management," he continued. "You won't be led by anybody."

"I don't know about that. I certainly want to improve the concern."

"Ah, yes; and so ruin it. Whereas I've been making money out of it these thirty years. You and I won't do together; that's the long of it and the short of it."

"It would be a putting of new wine into old bottles, you think?" suggested Rowan.

"I'm not saying anything about wine; but I do think that I ought to know something about beer."

"And I'm to understand," said Rowan, "that you have definitively determined not to carry on the old concern in conjunction with me as your partner."

"Yes; I think I have."

"But it will be as well to be sure. One can't allow one's self to depend upon thinking."

"Well, I am sure; I've made up my mind. I've no doubt you're a very clever young man, but I am quite sure we should not do together; and to tell you the truth, Rowan, I don't think you'll ever make your fortune by brewing."

"You think not?"

"No; never."

"I'm sorry for that."

"I don't know that you need be sorry. You'll have a nice income for a single man to begin the world with, and there's other businesses besides brewing,—and a deal better."

"Ah! But I've made up my mind to be a brewer. I like it. There's opportunity for chemical experiments, and room for philosophical inquiry, which gives the trade a charm in my eyes. I dare say it seems odd to you, but I like being a brewer."

Tappitt only scratched his head, and stared at him. "I do indeed," continued Rowan. "Now a man can't do anything to improve his own trade as a lawyer. A great deal will be done; but I've made up my mind that all that must come from the outside. All trades want improving; but I like a trade in which I can do the improvements myself,—from the inside. Do you understand me, Mr. Tappitt?" Mr. Tappitt did not understand him,—was very far indeed from understanding him.

"With such ideas as those I don't think Baslehurst is the ground for you," said Mr. Tappitt.

"The very ground!" said Rowan. "That's just it;—it's the very place I want. Brewing, as I take it, is at a lower ebb here than in any other part of England,"—this at any rate was not complimentary to the brewer of thirty years' standing—"than in any other part of England. The people swill themselves with the nasty juice of the apple because sound malt and hops have never been brought within their reach. I think Devonshire is the very county for a man who means to work hard, and who wishes to do good; and in all Devonshire I don't think there's a more fitting town than Baslehurst."

Mr. Tappitt was dumbfounded. Did this young man mean him to understand that it was his intention to open a rival establishment under his nose; to set up with Bungall's money another brewery in opposition to Bungall's brewery? Could such ingratitude as that be in the mind of any one? "Oh," said Tappitt; "I don't quite understand, but I don't doubt but what you say is all very fine."

"I don't think that it's fine at all, Mr. Tappitt, but I believe that it's true. I represent Mr. Bungall's interest here in Baslehurst, and I intend to carry on Mr. Bungall's business in the town in which he established it."

"This is Mr. Bungall's business;—this here, where I'm sitting, and it is in my hands."

"The use of these premises depends on you certainly."

"Yes; and the name of the firm, and the—the—the—. In point of fact, this is the old establishment. I never heard of such a thing in all my life."

"Quite true; it is the old establishment; and if I should set up another brewery here, as I think it probable I may, I shall not make use of Bungall's name. In the first place it would hardly be fair; and in the next place, by all accounts, he brewed such very bad beer that it would not be a credit to me. If you'll tell me what your plan is, then I'll tell you mine. You'll find that everything shall be above-board, Mr. Tappitt."

"My plan? I've got no plan. I mean to go on here as I've always done."

"But I suppose you intend to come to some arrangement with me. My claims are these: I will either come into this establishment on an equal footing with yourself, as regards share and management, or else I shall look to you to give me the sum of money to which my lawyers tell me I am entitled. In fact, you must either take me in or buy me out."

"I was thinking of a settled income."

"No; it wouldn't suit me. I have told you what are my intentions, and to carry them out I must either have a concern of my own, or a share in a concern. A settled income would do me no good."

"Two hundred a-year," suggested Tappitt.

"Psha! Three per cent. would give me three hundred."

"Ten thousand pounds is out of the question, you know."

"Very well, Mr. Tappitt. I can't say anything fairer than I have done. It will suit my own views much the best to start alone, but I do not wish to oppose you if I can help it. Start alone I certainly will, if I cannot come in here on my own terms."

After that there was nothing more said. Tappitt turned round, pretending to read his letters, and Rowan descending from his seat walked out into the yard of the brewery. His intention had been, ever since he had looked around him in Baslehurst, to be master of that place, or if not of that, to be master of some other. "It would break my heart to be sending out such stuff as that all my life," he said to himself, as he watched the muddy stream run out of the shallow coolers. He had resolved that he would brew good beer. As to that ambition of putting down the consumption of cider, I myself am inclined to think that the habits of the country would be too strong for him. At the present moment he lighted a cigar and sauntered about the yard. He had now, for the first time, spoken openly of his purpose to Mr. Tappitt; but, having done so, he resolved that there should be no more delay. "I'll give him till Saturday for an answer," he said. "If he isn't ready with one by that time I'll manage it through the lawyers." After that he turned his mind to Rachel Ray and the events of the past evening. He had told Rachel that he would go out to Bragg's End if she did not come into town, and he was quite resolved that he would do so. He knew well that she would not come in, understanding exactly those feelings of hers which would prevent it. Therefore his walk to Bragg's End on that afternoon was a settled thing with him. They were to dine at the brewery at three, and he would go almost immediately after dinner. But what would he say to her when he got there, and what would he say to her mother? He had not even yet made up his mind that he would positively ask her on that day to be his wife, and yet he felt that if he found her at home he would undoubtedly do so. "I'll arrange it all," said he, "as I'm walking over." Then he threw away the end of his cigar, and wandered about for the next half-hour among the vats and tubs and furnaces.

Mr. Tappitt took himself into the house as soon as he found himself able to do so without being seen by young Rowan. He took himself into the house in order that he might consult with his wife as to this unexpected revelation that had been made to him; or rather that he might have an opportunity of saying to some one all the hard things which were now crowding themselves upon his mind with reference to this outrageous young man. Had anything ever been known, or heard, or told, equal in enormity to this wickedness! He was to be called upon to find capital for the establishment of a rival in his own town, or else he was to bind himself in a partnership with a youth who knew nothing of his business, but was nevertheless resolved to constitute himself the chief manager of it! He who had been so true to Bungall in his young days was now to be sacrificed in his old age to Bungall's audacious representative! In the first glow of his anger he declared to his wife that he would pay no money and admit of no partnership. If Rowan did not choose to take his income as old Mrs. Bungall had taken hers he might seek what redress the law would give him. It was in vain that Mrs. Tappitt suggested that they would all be ruined. "Then we will be ruined," said Tappitt, hot with indignation; "but all Baslehurst,—all Devonshire shall know why." Pernicious young man! He could not explain,—he could not even quite understand in what the atrocity of Rowan's proposed scheme consisted, but he was possessed by a full conviction that it was atrocious. He had admitted this man into his house; he was even now entertaining as his guests the man's mother and sister; he had allowed him to have the run of the brewery, so that he had seen both the nakedness and the fat of the land; and this was to be his reward! "If I were to tell it at the reading-room," said Tappitt, "he would never be able to show himself again in the High Street."

Mrs. Tappitt, who was anxious but not enraged, did not see the matter quite in the same light, but she was not able to oppose her husband in his indignation. When she suggested that it might be well for them to raise money and pay off their enemy's claim, merely stipulating that a rival brewery should not be established in Baslehurst, he swore an oath that he would raise no money for such a purpose. He would have no dealings with so foul a traitor except through his lawyer, Honyman. "But Honyman thinks you'd better settle with him," pleaded Mrs. T. "Then I'll go to another lawyer," said Tappitt. "If Honyman won't stand to me I'll go to Sharpit and Longfite. They won't give way as long as there's a leg to stand on." For the time Mrs. Tappitt let this pass. She knew how useless it would be to tell her husband at the present moment that Sharpit and Longfite would be the only winners in such a contest as that of which he spoke. At the present moment Mr. Tappitt felt a pride in his anger, and was almost happy in the fury of his wrath; but Mrs. Tappitt was very wretched. If that nasty girl, Rachel Ray, had not come in the way all might have been well.

"He shan't eat another meal in this house," said Tappitt. "I don't care," he went on, when his wife pleaded that Luke Rowan must be admitted to their table because of Mrs. Rowan and Mary. "You can say what you like to them. They're welcome to stay if they like it, or welcome to go; but he shan't put his feet under my mahogany again." On this point, however, he was brought to relent before the hour of dinner. Baslehurst, his wife told him, would be against him if he turned his guests away from his house hungry. If a fight was necessary for them, it would be everything to them that Baslehurst should be with them in the fight. It was therefore arranged that Mrs. Tappitt should have a conversation with Mrs. Rowan after dinner, while the young people were out in the evening. "He shan't sleep in this house to-morrow," said Tappitt, riveting his assertion with very strong language; and Mrs. Tappitt understood that her communications were to be carried on upon that basis.

At three o'clock the Tappitts and Rowans all sat down to dinner. Mr. Tappitt ate his meal in absolute silence; but the young people were full of the ball, and the elder ladies were very gracious to each other. At such entertainments Paterfamilias is simply required to find the provender and to carve it. If he does that satisfactorily, silence on his part is not regarded as a great evil. Mrs. Tappitt knew that her husband's mood was not happy, and Martha may have remarked that all was not right with her father. To the others I am inclined to think his ill humour was a matter of indifference.

CHAPTER XI
LUKE ROWAN TAKES HIS TEA
QUITE LIKE A STEADY YOUNG MAN

It was the custom of the Miss Tappitts, during these long midsummer days, to start upon their evening walk at about seven o'clock, the hour for the family gathering round the tea-table being fixed at six. But, in accordance with the same custom, dinner at the brewery was usually eaten at one. At this immediate time with which we are now dealing, dinner had been postponed till three, out of compliment to Mrs. Rowan, Mrs. Tappitt considering three o'clock more fashionable than one; and consequently the afternoon habits of the family were disarranged. Half-past seven, it was thought, would be a becoming hour for tea, and therefore the young ladies were driven to go out at five o'clock, while the sun was still hot in the heavens.

"No," said Luke, in answer to his sister's invitation; "I don't think I will mind walking to-day: you are all going so early." He was sitting at the moment after dinner with his glass of brewery port wine before him.

"The young ladies must be very unhappy that their hours can't be made to suit you," said Mrs. Tappitt, and the tone of her voice was sarcastic and acid.

"I think we can do without him," said Cherry, laughing.

"Of course we can," said Augusta, who was not laughing.

"But you might as well come all the same," said Mary.

"There's metal more attractive somewhere else," said Augusta.

"I cannot bear to see so much fuss made with the young men," said Mrs. Tappitt. "We never did it when I was young. Did we, Mrs. Rowan?"

"I don't think there's much change," said Mrs. Rowan; "we used to be very glad to get the young men when we could, and to do without them when we couldn't."

"And that's just the way with us," said Cherry.

"Speak for yourself," said Augusta.

During all this time Mr. Tappitt spoke never a word. He also sipped his glass of wine, and as he sipped it he brooded over his wrath. Who were these Rowans that they should have come about his house and premises, and forced everything out of its proper shape and position? The young man sat there as though he were lord of everything,—so Tappitt declared to himself; and his own wife was snubbed in her own parlour as soon as she opened her mouth. There was an uncomfortable atmosphere of discord in the room, which gradually pervaded them all, and made even the girls feel that things were going wrong.

Mrs. Tappitt rose from her chair, and made a stiff bow across the table to her guest, understanding that that was the proper way in which to effect a retreat into the drawing-room; whereupon Luke opened the door, and the ladies went. "Thank you, sir," said Mrs. Tappitt very solemnly as she passed by him. Mrs. Rowan, going first, had given him a loving little nod of recognition, and Mary had pinched his arm. Martha uttered a word of thanks, intended for conciliation; Augusta passed him in silence with her nose in the air; and Cherry, as she went by, turned upon him a look of dismay. He returned Cherry's look with a shake of his head, and both of them understood that things were going wrong.

"I don't think I'll take any more wine, sir," said Rowan.

"Do as you like," said Tappitt. "It's there if you choose to take it."

"It seems to me, Mr. Tappitt, that you want to quarrel with me," said Luke.

"You can form your own opinion about that. I'm not bound to tell my mind to everybody."

"Oh, no; certainly not. But it's very unpleasant going on in that way in the same house. I'm thinking particularly of Mrs. Tappitt and the girls."

"You needn't trouble yourself about them at all. You may leave me to take care of them."

Luke had not sat down since the ladies left the room, and now determined that he had better not do so. "I think I'll say good afternoon," said Rowan.

"Good day to you," said Tappitt, with his face turned away, and his eyes fixed upon one of the open windows.

"Well, Mr. Tappitt, if I have to say good-bye to you in that way in your own house, of course it must be for the last time. I have not meant to offend you, and I don't think I've given you ground for offence."

"You don't, don't you?"

"Certainly not. If, unfortunately, there must be any disagreement between us about matters of business, I don't see why that should be brought into private life."

"Look here, young man," said Tappitt, turning upon him. "You lectured me in my counting-house this morning, and I don't intend that you shall lecture me here also. I'm drinking my own wine in my own parlour, and choose to drink it in peace and quietness."

"Very well, sir; I will not disturb you much longer. Perhaps you will make my apologies to Mrs. Tappitt, and tell her how much obliged I am by her hospitality, but that I will not trespass upon it any longer. I'll get a bed at the Dragon, and I'll write a line to my mother or sister." Then Luke left the room, took his hat up from the hall, and made his way out of the house.

He had much to occupy his mind at the present moment. He felt that he was being turned out of Mr. Tappitt's house, but would not much have regarded that if no one was concerned in it but Mr. Tappitt himself. He had, however, been on very intimate terms with all the ladies of the family; even for Mrs. Tappitt he had felt a friendship; and for the girls—especially for Cherry—he had learned to entertain an easy brotherly affection, which had not weighed much with him as it grew, but which it was not in his nature to throw off without annoyance. He had acknowledged to himself, as soon as he found himself among them, that the Tappitts did not possess, in their ways and habits of life, quite all that he should desire in his dearest and most intimate friends. I do not know that he had thought much of this; but he had felt it. Nevertheless he had determined that he would like them. He intended to make his way in life as a tradesman, and boldly resolved that he would not be above his trade. His mother sometimes reminded him, with perhaps not the truest pride, that he was a gentleman. In answer to this he had once or twice begged her to define the word, and then there had been some slight, very slight, disagreement between them. In the end the mother always gave way to the son; as to whom she believed that the sun shone with more special brilliancy for him than for any other of God's creatures. Now, as he left the brewery house, he remembered how intimate he had been with them all but a few hours since, arranging matters for their ball, and giving orders about the place as though he had belonged to the family. He had allowed himself to be at home with them, and to be one of them. He was by nature impulsive, and had thus fallen instantly into the intimacy which had been permitted to him. Now he was turned out of the house; and as he walked across the churchyard to bespeak a bed for himself at the inn, and write the necessary note to his sister, he was melancholy and almost unhappy. He felt sure that he was right in his views regarding the business, and could not accuse himself of any fault in his manner of making them known to Mr. Tappitt; but, nevertheless, he was ill at ease with himself in that he had given offence. And with all these thoughts were mingled other thoughts as to Rachel Ray. He did not in the least imagine that any of the anger felt towards him at the brewery had been caused by his open admiration of Rachel. It had never occurred to him that Mrs. Tappitt had regarded him as a possible son-in-law, or that, having so regarded him, she could hold him in displeasure because he had failed to fall into her views. He had never regarded himself as being of value as a possible future husband, or entertained the idea that he was a prize. He had taken hold in good faith of the Tappitt right hand which had been stretched out to him, and was now grieved that that hand should be suddenly withdrawn.

But as he was impulsive, so also was he light-hearted, and when he had chosen his bedroom and written the note to Mary, in which he desired her to pack up his belongings and send them to him, he was almost at ease as regarded that matter. Old Tappitt was, as he said to himself, an old ass, and if he chose to make that brewery business a cause of quarrel no one could help it. Mary was bidden in the note to say very civil things to Mrs. Tappitt; but, at the same time, to speak out the truth boldly. "Tell her," said he, "that I am constrained to leave the house because Mr. Tappitt and I cannot agree at the present moment about matters of business." When this was done he looked at his watch, and started off on his walk to Bragg's End.

It has been said that Rowan had not made up his mind to ask Rachel to be his wife, — that he had not made up his mind on this matter, although he was going to Bragg's End in a mood which would very probably bring him to such a conclusion. It will, I fear, be thought from this that he was light in purpose as well as light in heart; but I am not sure that he was open to any special animadversion of that nature. It is the way of men to carry on such affairs without any complete arrangement of their own plans or even wishes. He knew that he admired Rachel and liked her. I doubt whether he had ever yet declared to himself that he loved her. I doubt whether he had done so when he started on that walk, — thinking it probable, however, that he had persuaded himself of the fact before he reached the cottage door. He had already, as we know, said words to Rachel which he should not have said unless he intended to seek her as his wife; — he had spoken words and done things of that nature, being by no means perfect in all his ways. But he had so spoken and so acted without premeditation, and now was about to follow up those little words and little acts to their natural consequence, — also without much premeditation.

Rachel had told her mother, on her return from the ball, that Luke Rowan had promised to call; and had offered to take herself off from the cottage for the whole afternoon, if her mother thought it wrong that she should see him. Mrs. Ray had never felt herself to be in greater difficulty.

"I don't know that you ought to run away from him," said she: "and besides, where are you to go to?"

Rachel said at once that if her absence were desirable she would find whither to betake herself. "I'd stay upstairs in my bedroom, for the matter of that, mamma."

"He'd be sure to know it," said Mrs. Rowan, speaking of the young man as though he were much to be feared;—as indeed he was much feared by her.

"If you don't think I ought to go, perhaps it would be best that I should stay," said Rachel, at last, speaking in a very low tone, but still with some firmness in her voice.

"I'm sure I don't know what I'm to say to him," said Mrs. Ray.

"That must depend upon what he says to you, mamma," said Rachel.

After that there was no further talk of running away; but the morning did not pass with them lightly or pleasantly. They made an effort to sit quietly at their work, and to talk over the doings at Mrs. Tappitt's ball; but this coming of the young man threw its shadow, more or less, over everything. They could not talk, or even look at each other, as they would have talked and looked had no such advent been expected. They dined at one, as was their custom, and after dinner I think it probable that each of them stood before her glass with more care than she would have done on ordinary days. It was no ordinary day, and Mrs. Ray certainly put on a clean cap.

"Will that collar do?" she said to Rachel.

"Oh, yes, mamma," said Rachel, almost angrily. She also had taken her little precautions, but she could not endure to have such precautions acknowledged, even by a word.

The afternoon was very tedious. I don't know why Luke should have been expected exactly at three; but Mrs. Ray had, I think, made up her mind that he might be looked for at that time with the greatest certainty. But at three he was sitting down to dinner, and even at half-past five had not as yet left his room at the "Dragon."

"I suppose that we can't have tea till he's been," said Mrs. Ray, just at that hour; "that is, if he does come at all."

Rachel felt that her mother was vexed, because she suspected that Mr. Rowan was not about to keep his word.

"Don't let his coming make any difference, mamma," said Rachel. "I will go and get tea."

"Wait a few minutes longer, my dear," said Mrs. Ray.

It was all very well for Rachel to beg that it might make "no difference." It did make a very great deal of difference.

"I think I'll go over and see Mrs. Sturt for a few minutes," said Rachel, getting up.

"Pray don't, my dear,—pray don't; I should never know what to say to him if he should come while you were away."

So Rachel again sat down.

She had just, for the second time, declared her intention of getting tea, having now resolved that no weakness on her mother's part should hinder her, when Mrs. Ray, from her seat near the window, saw the young man coming over the green. He was walking very slowly, swinging a big stick as he came, and had taken himself altogether away from the road, almost to the verge of Mrs. Sturt's farmyard. "There he is," said Mrs. Ray, with a little start. Rachel, who was struggling hard to retain her composure, could not resist her impulse to jump up and look out upon the green from behind her mother's shoulder. But she did this from some little distance inside the room, so that no one might possibly see her from the green. "Yes; there he is, certainly," and, having thus identified their visitor, she immediately sat down again. "He's talking to Farmer Sturt's ploughboy," said Mrs. Ray. "He's asking where we live," said Rachel. "He's never been here before."

Rowan, having completed his conversation with the ploughboy, which by the way seemed to Mrs. Ray to have been longer than was necessary for its alleged purpose, came boldly across the green, and without pausing for a moment made his way through the cottage gate. Mrs. Ray caught her breath, and could not keep herself quite steady in her chair. Rachel, feeling that something must be done, got up from her seat and went quickly out into the passage. She knew that the front door was open, and she was prepared to meet Rowan in the hall.

"I told you I should call," said he. "I hope you'll let me come in."

"Mamma will be very glad to see you," she said. Then she brought him up and introduced him. Mrs. Ray rose from her chair and curtseyed, muttering something as to its being a long way for him to walk out there to the cottage.

"I said I should come, Mrs. Ray, if Miss Ray did not make her appearance at the brewery in the morning. We had such a nice party, and of course one wants to talk it over."

"I hope Mrs. Tappitt is quite well after it,—and the girls," said Rachel.

"Oh, yes. You know we kept it up two hours after you were gone. I can't say Mr. Tappitt is quite right this morning."

"Is he ill?" asked Mrs. Ray.

"Well, no; not ill, I think, but I fancy that the party put him out a little. Middle-aged gentlemen don't like to have all their things poked away anywhere. Ladies don't mind it, I fancy."

"Ladies know where to find them, as it is they who do the poking away," said Rachel. "But I'm sorry about Mr. Tappitt."

"I'm sorry, too, for he's a good-natured sort of a man when he's not put out. I say, Mrs. Ray, what a very pretty place you have got here."

"We think so because we're proud of our flowers."

"I do almost all the gardening myself," said Rachel.

"There's nothing I like so much as a garden, only I never can remember the names of the flowers. They've got such grand names down here. When I was a boy, in Warwickshire, they used to have nothing but roses and sweetwilliams. One could remember them."

"We haven't got anything very grand here," said Rachel. Soon after that they were sauntering out among the little paths and Rachel was picking flowers for him. She felt no difficulty in doing it, as her mother stood by her, though she would not for worlds have given him even a rose if they'd been alone.

"I wonder whether Mr. Rowan would come in and have some tea," said Mrs. Ray.

"Oh, wouldn't I," said Rowan, "if I were asked?"

Rachel was highly delighted with her mother, not so much on account of her courtesy to their guest, as that she had shown herself equal to the occasion, and had behaved, in an unabashed manner, as a mistress of a house should do. Mrs. Ray had been in such dread of the young man's coming, that Rachel had feared she would be speechless. Now the ice was broken, and she would do very well. The merit, however, did not belong to Mrs. Ray, but to Rowan. He had the gift of making himself at home with people, and had done much towards winning the widow's heart, when, after an interval of ten minutes, they two followed Rachel into the house. Rachel then had her hat on, and was about to go over the green to the farmer's house. "Mamma, I'll just run over to Mrs. Sturt's for some cream," said she.

"Mayn't I go with you?" said Rowan.

"Certainly not," said Rachel. "You'd frighten Mrs. Sturt out of all her composure, and we should never get the cream." Then Rachel went off, and Rowan was again left with her mother.

He had seated himself at her request in an arm-chair, and there for a minute or two he sat silent. Mrs. Ray was busy with the tea-things, but she suddenly felt that she was oppressed by the stranger's presence. While Rachel had been there, and even when they had been walking among the flower-beds, she had been quite comfortable; but now the knowledge that he was there, in the room with her, as he sat silent in the chair, was becoming alarming. Had she been right to ask him to stay for tea? He looked and spoke like a sheep; but then, was it not known to all the world that wolves dressed themselves often in that guise, so that they might carry out their wicked purposes? Had she not been imprudent? And then there was the immediate trouble of his silence. What was she to say to him to break it? That trouble, however, was soon brought to an end by Rowan himself. "Mrs. Ray," said he, "I think your daughter is the nicest girl I ever saw in my life."

Mrs. Ray instantly put down the tea-caddy which she had in her hand, and started, with a slight gasp in her throat, as though cold water had been thrown over her. At the instant she said nothing. What was she to say in answer to so violent a proposition?

"Upon my word I do," said Luke, who was too closely engaged with his own thoughts and his own feelings to pay much immediate attention to Mrs. Ray. "It isn't only that she's good-looking, but there's something,—I don't know what it is,—but she's just the sort of person I like. I told her I should come to-day, and I have come on purpose to say this to you. I hope you won't be angry with me."

"Pray, sir, don't say anything to her to turn her head."

"If I understand her, Mrs. Ray, it wouldn't be very easy to turn her head. But suppose she has turned mine?"

"Ah, no. Young gentlemen like you are in no danger of that sort of thing. But for a poor girl—"

"I don't think you quite understand me, Mrs. Ray. I didn't mean anything about danger. My danger would be that she shouldn't care twopence for me; and I don't suppose she ever will. But what I want to know is whether you would object to my coming over here and seeing her. I don't doubt but she might do much better."

"Oh dear no," said Mrs. Ray.

"But I should like to have my chance."

"You've not said anything to her yet, Mr. Rowan?"

"Well, no; I can't say I have. I meant to do so last night at the party, but she wouldn't stay and hear me. I don't think she cares very much about me, but I'll take my chance if you'll let me."

"Here she is," said Mrs. Ray. Then she again went to work with the tea-caddy, so that Rachel might be led to believe that nothing special had occurred in her absence. Nevertheless, had Rowan been away, every word would have been told to her.

"I hope you like clotted cream," said Rachel, taking off her hat. Luke declared that it was the one thing in all the world that he liked best, and that he had come into Devonshire with the express object of feasting upon it all his life. "Other Devonshire dainties were not," he said, "so much to his taste. He had another object in life. He intended to put down cider."

"I beg you won't do anything of the kind," said Mrs. Ray, "for I always drink it at dinner." Then Rowan explained how that he was a brewer, and that he looked upon it as his duty to put down so poor a beverage as cider. The people of Devonshire, he averred, knew nothing of beer, and it was his ambition to teach them. Mrs. Ray grew eager in the defence of cider, and then they again became comfortable and happy. "I never heard of such a thing in my life," said Mrs. Ray. "What are the farmers to do with all their apple trees? It would be the ruin of the whole country."

"I don't suppose it can be done all at once," said Luke.

"Not even by Mr. Rowan," said Rachel.

He sat there for an hour after their tea, and Mrs. Ray had in truth become fond of him. When he spoke to Rachel he did so with the utmost respect, and he seemed to be much more intimate with the mother than with the daughter. Mrs. Ray's mind was laden with the burden of what he had said in Rachel's absence, and with the knowledge that she would have to discuss it when Rowan was gone; but she felt herself to be happy while he remained, and had begun to hope that he would not go quite yet. Rachel also was perfectly happy. She said very little, but thought much of her different meetings with him, — of the arm in the clouds, of the promise of his friendship, of her first dance, of the little fraud by which he had secured her company at supper, and then of those words he had spoken when he detained her after supper in the hall. She knew that she liked him well, but had feared that such liking might not be encouraged. But what could be nicer than this,—to sit and listen to him in her mother's presence? Now she was not afraid of him. Now she feared no one's eyes. Now she was disturbed by no dread lest she might be sinning against rules of propriety. There was no Mrs. Tappitt by, to rebuke her with an angry look.

"Oh, Mr. Rowan, I'm sure you need not go yet," she said, when he got up and sought his hat.

"Mr. Rowan, my dear, has got other things to do besides talking to us."

"Oh no, he has not. He can't go and brew after eight o'clock."

"When my brewery is really going, I mean to brew all night; but just at present I'm the idlest man in Baslehurst. When I go away I shall sit upon Cawston Bridge and smoke for an hour, till some of the Briggses of the town come and drive me away. But I won't trouble you any longer. Good night, Mrs. Ray."

"Good night, Mr. Rowan."

"And I may come and see you again?"

Mrs. Ray was silent. "I'm sure mamma will be very happy," said Rachel.

"I want to hear her say so herself," said Luke.

Poor woman! She felt that she was driven into a position from which any safe escape was quite impossible. She could not tell her guest that he would not be welcome. She could not even pretend to speak to him with cold words after having chatted with him so pleasantly, and with such cordial good humour; and yet, were she to tell him that he might come, she would be granting him permission to appear there as Rachel's lover. If Rachel had been away, she would have appealed to his mercy, and have thrown herself, in the spirit, on her knees before him. But she could not do this in Rachel's presence.

"I suppose business will prevent your coming so far out of town again very soon."

It was a foolish subterfuge; a vain, silly attempt.

"Oh dear no," said he; "I always walk somewhere every day, and you shall see me again before long." Then he turned to Rachel. "Shall you be at Mr. Tappitt's to-morrow?"

"I don't quite know," said Rachel.

"I suppose I might as well tell you the truth and have done with it," said Luke, laughing. "I hate secrets among friends. The fact is Mr. Tappitt has turned me out of his house."

"Turned you out?" said Mrs. Ray.

"Oh, Mr. Rowan!" said Rachel.

"That's the truth," said Rowan. "It's about that horrid brewery. He means to be honest, and so do I. But in such matters it is so hard to know what the right of each party really is. I fear we shall have to go to law. But there's a lady coming in, so I'll tell you the rest of it to-morrow. I want you to know it all, Mrs. Ray, and to understand it too."

"A lady!" said Mrs. Ray, looking out through the open window. "Oh dear, if here isn't Dorothea!"

Then Rowan shook hands with them both, pressing Rachel's very warmly, close under her mother's eyes; and as he went out of the house into the garden, he passed Mrs. Prime on the walk, and took off his hat to her with great composure.

CHAPTER XII
RACHEL RAY THINKS "SHE DOES LIKE HIM"

Luke Rowan's appearance at Mrs. Ray's tea-table, as described in the last chapter, took place on Wednesday evening, and it may be remembered that on the morning of that same day Mrs. Prime had been closeted with Mr. Prong in that gentleman's parlour. She had promised to give Mr. Prong an answer to his proposal on Saturday, and had consequently settled herself down steadily to think of all that was good and all that might be evil in such an arrangement as that suggested to her. She wished much for legal advice, but she made up her mind that that was beyond her reach, was beyond her reach as a preliminary assistance. She knew enough of the laws of her country to enable her to be sure that, though she might accept the offer, her own money could be so tied up on her behalf that her husband could not touch the principal of her wealth; but she did not know whether things could be so settled that she might have in her own hands the spending of her income. By three o'clock on that day she thought that she would accept Mr. Prong, if she could be satisfied on that head. Her position as a clergyman's wife,—a minister's wife she called it,—would be unexceptionable. The company of Miss Pucker was distasteful. Solitude was not charming to her. And then, could she not work harder as a married woman than in the position which she now held? and also, could she not so work with increased power and increased perseverance? At three o'clock she had almost made up her mind, but still she was sadly in need of counsel and information. Then it occurred to her that her mother might have some knowledge in this matter. In most respects her mother was not a woman of the world; but it was just possible that in this difficulty her mother might assist her. Her mother might at any rate ask of others, and there was no one else whom she could trust to seek such information for her. And if she did this thing she must tell her mother. It is true that she had quarrelled with them both at Bragg's End; but there are affairs in life which will ride over family quarrels and trample them out, unless they be deeper and of longer standing than that between Mrs. Prime and Mrs. Ray. Therefore it was that she appeared at the cottage at Bragg's End just as Luke Rowan was leaving it.

She had entered upon the green with something of the olive-branch in her spirit, and before she reached the gate had determined that, as far as was within her power, all unkindness should be buried on the present occasion; but when she saw Luke Rowan coming out of her mother's door, she was startled out of all her good feeling. She had taught herself to look on Rowan as the personification of mischief, as the very mischief itself in regard to Rachel. She had lifted up her voice against him. She had left her home and torn herself from her family because it was not compatible with the rigour of her principles that any one known to her should be known to him also! But she had hardly left her mother's house when this most pernicious cause of war was admitted to all the freedom of family intercourse! It almost seemed to her that her mother must be a hypocrite. It was but the other day that Mrs. Ray could not hear Luke Rowan's name mentioned without wholesome horror. But where was that wholesome horror now? On Monday, Mrs. Prime had left the cottage; on Tuesday, Rachel had gone to a ball, expressly to meet the young man! and on Wednesday the young man was drinking tea at Bragg's End cottage! Mrs. Prime would have gone away without speaking a word to her mother or sister, had such retreat been possible.

Stately and solemn was the recognition which she accorded to Luke's salutation, and then she walked on into the house.

"Oh, Dorothea!" said her mother, and there was a tone almost of shame in Mrs. Ray's voice.

"We're so glad to see you, Dolly," said Rachel, and in Rachel's voice there was no tone of shame. It was all just as it should not be!

"I did not mean to disturb you, mother, while you were entertaining company."

Mrs. Ray said nothing,—nothing at the moment; but Rachel took upon herself to answer her sister. "You wouldn't have disturbed us at all, even if you had come a little sooner. But you are not too late for tea, if you'll have some."

"I've taken tea, thank you, two hours ago;" and she spoke as though there were much virtue in the distance of time at which she had eaten and drunk, as compared with the existing rakish and dissipated appearance of her mother's tea-table. Tea-things about at eight o'clock! It was all of a piece together.

"We are very glad to see you, at any rate," said Mrs. Ray; "I was afraid you would not have come out to us at all."

"Perhaps it would have been better if I had not come."

"I don't see that," said Rachel. "I think it's much better. I hate quarrelling, and I hope you're going to stay now you are here."

"No, Rachel, I'm not going to stay. Mother, it is impossible I should see that young man walking out of your house in that way without speaking of it; although I'm well aware that my voice here goes for nothing now."

"That was Mr. Luke Rowan," said Mrs. Ray.

"I know very well who it was," said Mrs. Prime, shaking her head. "Rachel will remember that I've seen him before."

"And you'll be likely to see him again if you stay here, Dolly," said Rachel. This she said out of pure mischief,—that sort of mischief which her sister's rebuke was sure to engender.

"I dare say," said Mrs. Prime; "whenever he pleases, no doubt. But I shall not see him. If you approve of it, mother, of course I can say nothing further,—nothing further than this, that I don't approve of such things."

"But what ails him that he shouldn't be a very good young man?" says Mrs. Ray. "And if it was so that he was growing fond of Rachel, why shouldn't he? And if Rachel was to like him, I don't see why she shouldn't like somebody some day as well as other girls." Mrs. Ray had been a little put beside herself or she would hardly have said so much in Rachel's presence. She had forgotten, probably, that Rachel had not as yet been made acquainted with the nature of Rowan's proposal.

"Mamma, don't talk in that way. There's nothing of that kind," said Rachel.

"I don't believe there is," said Mrs. Prime.

"I say there is then," said Mrs. Ray; "and it's very ill-natured in you, Dorothea, to speak and think in that way of your sister."

"Oh, very well. I see that I had better go back to Baslehurst at once."

"So it is very ill-natured. I can't bear to have these sort of quarrels; but I must speak out for her. I believe he's a very good young man, with nothing bad about him at all, and he is welcome to come here whenever he pleases. And as for Rachel, I believe she knows how to mind herself as well as you did when you were her age; only poor Mr. Prime was come and gone at that time. And as for his not intending, he came out here just because he did intend, and only to ask my permission. I didn't at first tell him he might because Rachel was over at the farm getting the cream, and I thought she ought to be consulted first; and if that's not straightforward and proper, I'm sure I don't know what is; and he having a business of his own, too, and able to maintain a wife to-morrow! And if a young man isn't to be allowed to ask leave to see a young woman when he thinks he likes her, I for one don't know how young people are to get married at all." Then Mrs. Ray sat down, put her apron up to her eyes, and had a great cry.

It was a most eloquent speech, and I cannot say which of her daughters was the most surprised by it. As to Rachel, it must be remembered that very much was communicated to her of which she had hitherto known nothing. Very much indeed, we may say, so much that it was of a nature to alter the whole tone and tenor of her life. This young man of whom she had thought so much, and of whom she had been so much in dread,—fearing that her many thoughts of him were becoming dangerous,—this young man who had interested her so warmly, had come out to Bragg's End simply to get her mother's leave to pay his court to her. And he had done this without saying a word to herself! There was something in this infinitely sweeter to her than would have been any number of pretty speeches from himself. She had hitherto been angry with him, though liking him well; she had been angry with though almost loving him. She had not known why it was so, but the cause had been this,—that he had seemed in their intercourse together, to have been deficient in that respect which she had a right to claim. But now all that sin was washed away by such a deed as this. As the meaning of her mother's words sank into her heart, and as she came to understand her mother's declaration that Luke Rowan should be welcome to the cottage as her lover, her eyes became full of tears, and the spirit of her animosity against her sister was quenched by the waters of her happiness.

And Mrs. Prime was almost equally surprised, but was by no means equally delighted. Had the whole thing fallen out in a different way, she would probably have looked on a marriage with Luke Rowan as good and salutary for her sister. At any rate, seeing that the world is as it is, and that all men cannot be hard-working ministers of the Gospel, nor all women the wives of such or their assistants in godly ministrations, she would not have taken upon herself to oppose such a marriage. But as it was, she had resolved that Luke Rowan was a black sheep; that he was pitch, not to be touched without defilement; that he was, in short, a man to be regarded by religious people as anathema,—a thing accursed; and of that idea she was not able to divest herself suddenly. Why had the young man walked about under the churchyard elms at night? Why, if he were not wicked and abandoned, did he wear that jaunty look,—that look which was so worldly? And, moreover, he went to balls, and tempted others to do the like! In a word, he was a young man manifestly of that class which was esteemed by Mrs. Prime more dangerous than roaring lions. It was not possible that she should give up her opinion merely because this roaring lion had come out to her mother with a plausible story. Upon her at that moment fell the necessity of forming a judgment to which it would be necessary that she should hereafter abide. She must either at once give in her adherence to the Rowan alliance; or else, if she opposed it, she must be prepared to cling to that opposition. She was aware that some such decision was now required, and paused for a moment before she declared herself. But that moment only strengthened her verdict against Rachel's lover. Could any serious young man have taken off his hat with the flippancy which had marked that action on his part? Would not any serious young man, properly intent on matrimonial prospects, have been subdued at such a moment to a more solemn deportment? Mrs. Prime's verdict was still against him, and that verdict she proceeded to pronounce.

"Oh, very well; then of course I shall interfere no further. I shouldn't have thought that Rachel's seeing him twice, in such a way as that, too—hiding under the churchyard trees!"

"I wasn't hiding," said Rachel, "and you've no business to say so." Her tears, however, prevented her from fighting her own battle manfully, or with her usual courage.

"It looked very much like it, Rachel, at any rate. I should have thought that mother would have wished you to have known a great deal more about any young man before she encouraged you to regard him in that way, than you can possibly know of Mr. Rowan."

"But how are they to know each other, Dorothea, if they mustn't see one another?" said Mrs. Ray.

"I have no doubt he knows how to dance very cleverly. As Rachel is being taught to live now, that may perhaps be the chief thing necessary."

This blow did reach poor Mrs. Ray, who a week or two since would certainly have agreed with her elder daughter in thinking that dancing was sinful. Into this difficulty, however, she had been brought by Mr. Comfort's advice. "But what else can she know of him?" continued Mrs. Prime. "He is able to maintain a wife you say,—and is that all that is necessary to consider in the choice of a husband, or is that the chief thing? Oh, mother, you should think of your responsibility at such a time as this. It may be very pleasant for Rachel to have this young man as her lover, very pleasant while it lasts. But what—what—what?" Then Mrs. Prime was so much oppressed by the black weight of her own thoughts, that she was unable further to express them.

"I do think about it," said Mrs. Ray. "I think about it more than anything else."

"And have you concluded that in this way you can best secure Rachel's welfare? Oh, mother!"

"He always goes to church on Sundays," said Rachel. "I don't know why you are to make him out so bad." This she said with her eyes fixed upon her mother, for it seemed to her that her mother was almost about to yield.

A good deal might be said in excuse for Mrs. Prime. She was not only acting for the best in accordance with her own lights, but the doctrine which she now preached was the doctrine which had been held by the inhabitants of the cottage at Bragg's End. The fault, if fault there was, had been in the teaching under which had lived both Mrs. Prime and her mother. In their desire to live in accordance with that teaching, they had agreed to regard all the outer world, that is all the world except their world, as wicked and dangerous. They had never conceived that in forming this judgment they were deficient in charity; nor, indeed, were they conscious that they had formed any such judgment. In works of charity they had striven to be abundant, but had taken simply the Dorcas view of that virtue. The younger and more energetic woman had become sour in her temper under the *régime* of this life, while the elder and weaker had retained her own sweetness partly because of her weakness. But who can say that either of them were other than good women,—good according to such lights as had been lit for their guidance? But now the younger was stanch to her old lessons while the elder was leaving them. The elder was leaving them, not by force of her own reason, but under the necessity of coming in contact with the world which was brought upon her by the vitality and instincts of her younger child. This difficulty she had sought to master, once and for ever, by a reference to her clergyman. What had been the result of that reference the reader already knows.

"Mother," said Mrs. Prime, very solemnly, "is this young man such a one as you would have chosen for Rachel's husband six months ago?"

"I never wished to choose any man for her husband," said Mrs. Ray. "I don't think you ought to talk to me in that way, Dorothea."

"I don't know in what other way to talk to you. I cannot be indifferent on such a subject as this. When you tell me, and that before Rachel herself, that you have given this young man leave to come and see her whenever he pleases."

"I never said anything of the kind, Dorothea."

"Did you not, mother? I am sure I understood you so."

"I said he had come to ask leave, and that I should be glad to see him when he did come, but I didn't say anything of having told him so. I didn't tell him anything of the kind; did I, Rachel? But I know he will come, and I don't see why he shouldn't. And if he does, I can't turn him out. He took his tea here quite like a steady young man. He drank three large cups; and if, as Rachel says, he always goes to church regularly, I don't know why we are to judge him and say that he's anything out of the way."

"I have not judged him, mother."

Then Rachel spoke out, and we may say that it was needful that she should do so. This offering of her heart had been discussed in her presence in a manner that had been very painful to her, though the persons discussing it had been her own mother and her own sister. But in truth she had been so much affected by what had been said, there had been so much in it that was first joyful and then painful to her, that she had not hitherto been able to repress her emotions so as to acquire the power of much speech. But she had struggled, and now so far succeeded as to be able to come to her mother's support.

"I don't know, mamma, why anybody should judge him yet; and as to what he has said to me, I'm sure no one has a right to judge him unkindly. Dolly has been very angry with me because she saw me speaking to him in the churchyard, and has said that I was—hiding."

"I meant that he was hiding."

"Neither of us were hiding, and it was an unkind word, not like a sister. I have never had to hide from anybody. And as for—for—for liking Mr. Rowan after such words as that, I will not say anything about it to anybody, except to mamma. If he were to ask me to be—his wife, I don't know what answer I should make,—not yet. But I shall never listen to any one while mamma lives, if she wishes me not." Then she turned to her mother, and Mrs. Ray, who had before been driven to doubt by Mrs. Prime's words, now again became strong in her resolution to cherish Rachel's lover.

"I don't believe she'll ever do anything to make me think that I oughtn't to have trusted her," said Mrs. Ray, embracing Rachel and speaking with her own eyes full of tears.

It now seemed to Mrs. Prime that there was nothing left for her but to go. In her eagerness about her sister's affairs, she had for a while forgotten her own; and now, as she again remembered the cause that had brought her on the present occasion to Bragg's End, she felt that she must return without accomplishing her object. After having said so much in reprobation of her sister's love-affair, it was hardly possible that she should tell the tale of her own. And yet her need was urgent. She had pledged herself to give Mr. Prong an answer on Friday, and she could hardly bring herself to accept that gentleman's offer without first communicating with her mother on the subject. Any such communication at the present moment was quite out of the question.

"Perhaps it would be better that I should go and leave you," she said. "If I can do no good, I certainly don't want to do any harm. I wish that Rachel would have taken to what I think a better course of life."

"Why, what have I done?" said Rachel, turning round sharply.

"I mean about the Dorcas meetings."

"I don't like the women there;—that's why I haven't gone."

"I believe them to be good, praiseworthy, godly women. But it is useless to talk about that now. Good-night, Rachel," and she gave her hand coldly to her sister. "Good-night, mother; I wish I could see you alone to-morrow."

"Come here for your dinner," said Mrs. Ray.

"No;—but if you would come to me in the morning I should take it kindly." This Mrs. Ray promised to do, and then Mrs. Prime walked back to Baslehurst.

Rachel, when her sister was gone, felt that there was much to be said between her and her mother. Mrs. Ray herself was so inconsequent in her mental workings, so shandy-pated if I may say so, that it did not occur to her that an entirely new view of Luke Rowan's purposes had been exposed to Rachel during this visit of Mrs. Prime's, or that anything had been said, which made a further explanation necessary. She had, as it were, authorized Rachel to regard Rowan as her lover, and yet was not aware that she had done so. But Rachel had remembered every word. She had resolved that she would permit herself to form no special intimacy with Luke Rowan without her mother's leave; but she was also beginning to resolve that with her mother's leave, such intimacy would be very pleasant. Of this she was quite sure within her own heart,—that it should not be abandoned at her sister's instigation.

"Mamma," she said, "I did not know that he had spoken to you in that way."

"In what way, Rachel?" Mrs. Ray's voice was not quite pleasant. Now that Mrs. Prime was gone, she would have been glad to have had the dangerous subject abandoned for a while.

"That he had asked you to let him come here, and that he had said that about me."

"He did then,—while you were away at Mrs. Sturt's."

"And what answer did you give him?"

"I didn't give him any answer. You came back, and I'm sure I was very glad that you did, for I shouldn't have known what to say to him."

"But what was it that he did say, mamma?—that is, if you don't think it wrong to tell me."

"I hardly know; but I don't suppose it can be wrong, for no young man could have spoken nicer; and it made me happy to hear him,—so it did, for the moment."

"Oh, mamma, do tell me!" and Rachel kneeled down before her.

"Well;—he said you were the nicest girl he had ever seen."

"Did he, mamma?" And the girl clung closer to her mother as she heard the pleasant words.

"But I oughtn't to tell you such nonsense as that; and then he said that he wanted to come out here and see you, and—and—and—; it is simply this, that he meant to ask you to be his sweetheart, if I would let him."

"And what did you say, mamma?"

"I couldn't say anything because you came back."

"But you told Dolly that you would be glad to see him whenever he might choose to come here."

"Did I?"

"Yes; you said he was welcome to come whenever he pleased, and that you believed him to be a very good young man."

"And so I do. Why should he be anything else?"

"I don't say that he's anything else; but, mamma—"

"Well, my dear."

"What shall I say to him if he does ask me that question? He has called me by my name two or three times, and spoken to me as though he wanted me to like him. If he does say anything to me like that, what shall I answer?"

"If you think you don't like him well enough, you must tell him so, of course."

"Yes, of course I must." Then Rachel was silent for a minute or two. She had not as yet received the full answer which she desired. In such an alternative as that which her mother had suggested, we may say that she would have known how to frame her answer to the young man without any advice from her mother. But there was another alternative as to which she thought it well that she should have her mother's judgment and opinion. "But, mamma, I think I do like him," said Rachel, burying her face.

"I'm sure I don't wonder at it," said Mrs. Ray, "for I like him very much. He has a way with him so much nicer than most of the young men now; and then, he's very well off, which, after all, must count for something. A young woman should never fall in love with a man who can't earn his bread, not if he was ever so religious or steady. And he's very good-looking, too. Good looks are only skin-deep I know, and they won't bring much comfort when sorrow comes; but I do own I love to look on a young fellow with a sonsy face and a quick lively step. Mr. Comfort seemed to think it would do very well if there was to be any such thing; and if he's not able to tell, I'm sure I don't know who ought to be. And nothing could be fairer than his coming out here and telling me first. There's so many of them are sly; but there was nothing sly about that."

In this way, with many more rambling words, with many kisses also, and with some tears, Rachel Ray received from her mother permission to regard Luke Rowan as her lover.

CHAPTER XIII
MR. TAPPITT IN HIS COUNTING-HOUSE

Luke Rowan, when he left the cottage, walked quickly back across the green towards Baslehurst. He had sauntered out slowly on his road from the brewery to Bragg's End, being in doubt as to what he would do when he reached his destination; but there was no longer room for doubt now; he had said that to Rachel's mother which made any further doubt impossible, and he was resolved that he would ask Rachel to be his wife. He had spoken to Mrs. Ray of his intention in that respect as though he thought that such an offer on his part might probably be rejected, and in so speaking had at the time spoken the truth; but he was eager, sanguine, and self-confident by nature, and though he was by no means disposed to regard himself as a conquering hero by whom any young lady would only be too happy to find herself beloved, he did not at the present moment look forward to his future fate with despair. He walked quickly home along the dusty road, picturing to himself a happy prosperous future in Baslehurst, with Rachel as his wife, and the Tappitts living in some neighbouring villa on an income paid to old Tappitt by him out of the proceeds of the brewery. That was his present solution of the brewery difficulty. Tappitt was growing old, and it might be quite as well not only for himself, but for the cause of humanity in Devonshire, that he should pass the remainder of his life in that dignity which comfortable retirement from business affords. He did not desire Tappitt for a partner any more than Tappitt desired him. Nevertheless he was determined to brew beer, and was anxious to do so if possible on the spot where his great-uncle Bungall had commenced operations in that line.

It may be well to explain here that Rowan was not without good standing-ground in his dispute with Tappitt. Old Bungall's will had somewhat confused matters, as it is in the nature of wills to do; but it had been Bungall's desire that his full share in the brewery should go to his nephew after his widow's death, should he on dying leave a widow. Now it had happened that he had left a widow, and that the widow had contrived to live longer than the nephew. She had drawn an income of five hundred a year from the concern, by agreement between her and her lawyer and Tappitt and his lawyer; and Tappitt, when the elder Rowan, Bungall's nephew, died, had taught himself to believe that all the affairs of the brewery must now remain for ever in his own hands, unless he himself might choose to make other provision. He knew that some property in the concern would pass away from him when the old lady died, but he had not acknowledged to himself that young Rowan would inherit from his father all the rights which old Rowan would have possessed had he lived. Luke's father had gone into other walks of life, and had lived prosperously, leaving behind him money for his widow, and money also for his children; and Tappitt, when he found that there was a young man with a claim to a partnership in his business, had been not only much annoyed, but surprised also. He had been, as we have seen, persuaded to hold out the right hand of friendship, and the left hand of the partnership to the young man. He had thought that he might manage a young man from London who knew nothing of beer; and his wife had thought that the young man might probably like to take a wife as well as an income out of the concern; but, as we have seen, they had both been wrong in their hopes. Luke chose to manage the brewery instead of being managed; and had foolishly fallen in love with Rachel Ray instead of taking Augusta Tappitt to himself as he should have done.

There was much certainly of harshness and cruelty in that idea of an opposition brewery in Baslehurst to be established in enmity to Bungall and Tappitt, and to be so established with Bungall's money, and by Bungall's heir. But Luke, as he walked back to Baslehurst, thinking now of his beer and now of his love, declared to himself that he wanted only his own. Let Tappitt deal justly with him in that matter of the partnership, and he would deal even generously with Tappitt. The concern gave an income of some fifteen hundred pounds, out of which Mrs. Bungall, as taking no share of the responsibility or work, had been allowed to have a third. He was informed by his lawyer that he was entitled to claim one-half of the whole concern. If Tappitt would give in his adhesion to that villa arrangement, he should still have his thousand a year for life, and Mrs. Tappitt afterwards should have due provision, and the girls should have all that could fairly be claimed for them. Or, if the villa scheme could not be carried out quite at present, he, Rowan, would do two shares of the work, and allow Tappitt to take two shares of the pay; but then, in that case, he must be allowed scope for his improvements. Good beer should be brewed for the people of Baslehurst, and the eyes of Devonshire should be opened. Pondering over all this, and resolving that he would speak out his mind openly to Rachel on the morrow, Luke Rowan reached his inn.

"There's a lady, sir, up-stairs, as wishes to speak to you," said the waiter.

"A lady?"

"Quite elderly, sir," said the waiter, intending to put an end to any excitement on Rowan's part.

"It's the gentleman's own mother," said the chambermaid, in a tone of reproof, "and she's in number two sitting-room, private." So Luke went to number two sitting-room, private, and there he found his mother waiting for him.

"This is very sad," she said, when their first greetings were over.

"About old Tappitt? yes, it is; but what could I do, mother? He's a stupid old man, and pig-headed. He would quarrel with me, so that I was obliged to leave the house. If you and Mary like to come into lodgings while you stay here, I can get rooms for you."

But Mrs. Rowan explained that she herself did not wish to come to any absolute or immediate rupture with Mrs. Tappitt. Of course their visit would be shortened, but Mrs. Tappitt was disposed to be very civil, as were the girls. Then Mrs. Rowan suggested whether there might not be a reconciliation between Luke and the brewery family.

"But, mother, I have not quarrelled with the family."

"It comes to the same thing, Luke; does it not? Don't you think you could say something civil to Mr. Tappitt, so as to—to bring him round again? He's older than you are, you know, Luke."

Rowan perceived at once that his mother was ranging herself on the Tappitt side in the contest, and was therefore ready to fight with so much the more vigour. He was accustomed to yield to his mother in all little things, Mrs. Rowan being a woman who liked such yieldings; but for some time past he had held his own against her in all greater matters. Now and again, for an hour or so, she would show that she was vexed; but her admiration for him was so genuine, and her love so strong, that this vexation never endured, and Luke had been taught to think that his judgment was to be held supreme in all their joint concerns. "Yes, mother, he is older than I am; but I do not know that I can say anything particularly civil to him,—that is, more civil than what I have said. The civility which he wants is the surrender of my rights. I can't be so civil as that."

"No, Luke, I should be the last to ask you to surrender any of your rights; you must be sure of that. But—oh, Luke, if what I hear is true I shall be so unhappy!"

"And what have you heard, mother?"

"I am afraid all this is not about the brewery altogether."

"But it is about the brewery altogether;—about that and about nothing else to any smallest extent. I don't at all know what you mean."

"Luke, is there no young lady in the case?"

"Young lady! in what case;—in the case of my quarrel with old Tappitt;—whether he and I have had a difference about a young lady?"

"No, Luke; you know I don't mean that."

"But what do you mean, mother?"

"I'm afraid that you know too well. Is there not a young lady whom you've met at Mrs. Tappitt's, and whom you—you pretend to admire?"

"And suppose there is,—for the sake of the argument,—what has that to do with my difference with Mr. Tappitt?" As Rowan asked this question some slight conception of the truth flashed across his mind; some faint idea came home to him of the connecting link between his admiration for Rachel Ray and Mr. Tappitt's animosity.

"But is it so, Luke?" asked the anxious mother. "I care much more about that than I do about all the brewery put together. Nothing would make me so wretched as to see you make a marriage that was beneath you."

"I don't think I shall ever make you wretched in that way."

"And you tell me that there is nothing in this that I have heard;—nothing at all."

"No, by heavens!—I tell you no such thing. I do not know what you may have heard. That you have heard falsehood and calumny I guess by your speaking of a marriage that would be beneath me. But, as you think it right to ask me, I will not deceive you by any subterfuge. It is my purpose to ask a girl here in Baslehurst to be my wife."

"Then you have not asked her yet."

"You are cross-examining me very closely, mother. If I have not asked her I am bound to do so; not that any binding is necessary,—for without being bound I certainly should do so."

"And it is Miss Ray?"

"Yes, it is Miss Ray."

"Oh, Luke, then indeed I shall be very wretched."

"Why so, mother? Have you heard anything against her?"

"Against her! well; I will not say that, for I do not wish to say anything against any young woman. But do you know who she is, Luke; and who her mother is? They are quite poor people."

"And is that against them?"

"Not against their moral character certainly, but it is against them in considering the expediency of a connection with them. You would hardly wish to marry out of your own station. I am told that the mother lives in a little cottage, quite in a humble sphere, and that the sister—"

"I intend to marry neither the mother nor the sister; but Rachel Ray I do intend to marry,—if she will have me. If I had been left to myself I should not have told you of this till I had found myself to be successful; as you have asked me I have not liked to deceive you. But, mother, do not speak against her if you can say nothing worse of her than that she is poor."

"You misunderstand me, Luke."

"I hope so. I do not like to think that that objection should be made by you."

"Of course it is an objection, but it is not the one which I meant to make. There may be many a young lady whom it would be quite fitting that you should wish to marry even though she had not got a shilling. It would be much pleasanter of course that the lady should have something, though I should never think of making any serious objection about that. But what I should chiefly look to would be the young lady herself, and her position in life."

"The young lady herself would certainly be the main thing," said Luke.

"That's what I say;—the young lady herself and her position in life. Have you made any inquiries?"

"Yes, I have;—and am almost ashamed of myself for doing so."

"I have no doubt Mrs. Ray is very respectable, but the sort of people who are her friends are not your friends. Their most particular friends are the farmer's family that lives near them."

"How was it then that Mrs. Cornbury took her to the party?"

"Ah, yes; I can explain that. And Mrs. Tappitt has told me how sorry she is that people should have been deceived by what has occurred." Luke Rowan's brow grew black as Mrs. Tappitt's name was mentioned, but he said nothing and his mother continued her speech. "Her girls have been very kind to Miss Ray, inviting her to walk with them and all that sort of thing, because of her being so much alone without any companions of her own."

"Oh, that has been it, has it? I thought she had the farmer's family out near where she lived."

"If you choose to listen to me, Luke, I shall be obliged to you, but if you take me up at every word in that way, of course I must leave you." Then she paused, but as Luke said nothing she went on with her discourse. "It was in that way that she came to know the Miss Tappitts, and then one of them, the youngest I think, asked her to come to the party. It was very indiscreet; but Mrs. Tappitt did not like to go back from her daughter's word, and so the girl was allowed to come."

"And to make the blunder pass off easily, Mrs. Cornbury was induced to take her?"

"Mrs. Cornbury happened to be staying with her father, in whose parish they had lived for many years, and it certainly was very kind of her. But it has been an unfortunate mistake altogether. The poor girl has for a moment been lifted out of her proper sphere, and, — as you must have seen yourself, — hardly knew how to behave herself. It made Mrs. Tappitt very unhappy."

This was more than Luke Rowan was able to bear. His anger was not against his own mother, but against the mistress of the brewery. It was manifest that she had been maligning Rachel, and instigating his mother to take up the cudgels against her. And he was vexed also that his mother had not perceived that Rachel held, or was entitled to hold, among women a much higher position than could be fairly accorded to Mrs. Tappitt. "I do not care one straw for Mrs. Tappitt's unhappiness," he said; "and as to Miss Ray's conduct at her house, I do not think that there was anything in it that did not become her. I do not know what you mean, the least in the world; and I think you would have no such idea yourself, if Mrs. Tappitt had not put it into your head."

"You should not speak in that way to your mother, Luke."

"I must speak strongly when I am defending my wife, — as I hope she will be. I never heard of anything in my life so little as this woman's conduct! It is mean, paltry jealousy, and nothing else. You, as my mother, may think it better that I should not marry."

"But, my dear, I want you to marry."

"Then I will do as you want. Or you may think that I should find some one with money, or with grand friends, or with a better connection. It is natural that you should think like this. But why should she want to belittle a young girl like Rachel Ray, — a girl that her own daughters call their friend? I'll tell you why, mother. Because Rachel Ray was admired and they were not."

"Is there anybody in Baslehurst that will say that she is your equal?"

"I am not disposed to ask any one in Baslehurst just at present; and I would not advise any one in Baslehurst to volunteer an opinion to me on the subject. I intend that she shall be my equal,—my equal in every respect, if I can make her so. I shall certainly ask her to be my wife; and, mother, as my mind is positively made up on that point,—as nothing on earth will alter me,—I hope you will teach yourself to think kindly of her. I should be very unhappy if my house could not be your home when you may choose to make it so."

But Mrs. Rowan, much as she was accustomed to yield to her son, could not bring herself to yield in this matter,—or, at least, not to yield with grace. She felt that the truth and wisdom all lay on her side in the argument, though she knew that she had lacked words in which to carry it on. She declared to herself that she was not at all inclined to despise anybody for living in a small cottage, or for being poor. She would have been delighted to be very civil to Mrs. Ray herself, and could have patronized Rachel quite as kindly, though perhaps not so graciously, as Mrs. Cornbury had done. But it was a different thing when her son came to think of making this young woman his wife! Old Mrs. Cornbury would have been very sorry to see either of her sons make such an alliance. When anything so serious as marriage was to be considered, it was only proper to remember that Mrs. Ray lived in a cottage, and that farmer Sturt was her friend and neighbour. But to all this prudence and wisdom Luke would not listen at all, and at last Mrs. Rowan left him in dudgeon. Foolish and hasty as he was, he could, as she felt, talk better than she could; and therefore she retreated, feeling that she had been worsted. "I have done my duty," said she, going away. "I have warned you. Of course you are your own master and can do as you please." Then she left him, refusing his escort, and in the last fading light of the long summer evening, made her way back to the brewery.

Luke's first impulse was to start off instantly to the cottage, and settle the matter out of hand; but before he had taken up his hat for this purpose he remembered that he could not very well call at Bragg's End on such a mission at eleven o'clock at night; so he threw himself back on the hotel sofa, and gave vent to his feelings against the Tappitt family. He would make them understand that they were not going to master him. He had come down there disposed to do them all manner of kindness,—to the extent even of greatly improving their fortunes by improving the brewing business,—and they had taken upon themselves to treat him as though he were a dependent. He did not tell himself that a plot had been made to catch him for one of the girls; but he accused them of jealousy, meanness, selfishness, and all those sins and abominations by which such a plot would be engendered. When, about an hour afterwards, he took himself off to bed, he was full of wrath, and determined to display his wrath early on the morrow. As he prayed for forgiveness on condition that he forgave others, his conscience troubled him; but he gulped it down, and went on with his angry feelings till sleep came upon him.

But in the morning some of this bitterness had worn away. His last resolve overnight had been to go to the brewery before breakfast, at which period of the day Mr. Tappitt was always to be found for half an hour in his counting-house, and curtly tell the brewer that all further negotiations between them must be made by their respective lawyers; but as he was dressing, he reflected that Mr. Tappitt's position was certainly one of difficulty, that amicable arrangements would still be best if amicable arrangements were possible, and that something was due to the man who had for so many years been his uncle's partner. Mr. Tappitt, moreover, was not responsible for any of those evil things which had been said about Rachel by Mrs. Tappitt. Therefore, priding himself somewhat on his charity, he entered Mr. Tappitt's office without the display of any anger on his face.

The brewer was standing with his back to the empty fireplace, with his hands behind the tails of his coat, and his eyes fixed upon a letter which he had just read, and which lay open upon his desk. Rowan advanced with his hand out, and Tappitt, hesitating a little as he obeyed the summons, put out his own and just touched that of his visitor; then hastily he resumed his position, with his arm behind his coat-tail.

"I have come down," said Rowan, "because I thought it might be well to have a little chat with you before breakfast."

The letter which lay open on the desk was from Rowan's lawyer in London, and contained that offer on Rowan's part of a thousand a year and retirement, to which Luke still looked as the most comfortable termination of all their difficulties. Luke had almost forgotten that he had, ten days since, absolutely instructed his lawyer to make the offer; but there was the offer made, and lying on Tappitt's table. Tappitt had been considering it for the last five minutes, and every additional moment had added to the enmity which he felt against Rowan. Rowan, at twenty-five, no doubt regarded Tappitt, who was nearer sixty than fifty, as a very old man; but men of fifty-five do not like to be so regarded, and are not anxious to be laid upon shelves by their juniors. And, moreover, where was Tappitt to find his security for the thousand a year,—as he had not failed to remark to himself on his first glance over the lawyer's letter. Buy him out, indeed, and lay him on one side! He hated Rowan with all his heart;—and his hatred was much more bitter in its nature than that which Rowan was capable of feeling for him. He remembered the champagne; he remembered the young man's busy calling for things in his own house; he remembered the sneers against the beer, and the want of respect with which his experience in the craft had been treated. Buy him out! No; not as long as he had a five-pound note to spend, or a leg to stand upon. He was strong in his resolution now, and capable of strength, for Mrs. Tappitt was also on his side. Mrs. Rowan had not quite kept her secret as to what had transpired at the inn, and Mrs. Tappitt was certain that Rachel Ray had succeeded. When Tappitt declared that morning that he would fight it out to the last, Mrs. T. applauded his courage.

"Oh! a little chat, is it?" said Tappitt. "About this letter that I've just got, I suppose;" and he gave a contemptuous poke to the epistle with one of his hands.

"What letter?" asked Rowan.

"Come now, young man, don't let us have any humbug and trickery, whatever we may do. If there's anything I do hate, it's deceit."

All Rowan's wrath returned upon him instantly, redoubled and trebled in its energy. "What do you mean, sir?" said he. "Who is trying to deceive anybody? How dare you speak to me in such language as that?"

"Now, look here, Mr. Rowan. This letter comes from your man in Craven Street, as of course you know very well. You have chosen to put our business in the hands of the lawyers, and in the hands of the lawyers it shall remain. I have been very wrong in attempting to have any dealings with you. I should have known what sort of a man you were before I let you put your foot in the concern. But I know enough of you now, and, if you please, you'll keep yourself on the other side of those gates for the future. D'ye hear me? Unless you wish to be turned out by the men, don't you put your feet inside the brewery premises any more." And Tappitt's face as he uttered these words was a face very unpleasant to behold.

Luke was so astounded that he could not bethink himself at the moment of the most becoming words in which to answer his enemy. His first idea had prompted him to repudiate all present knowledge of the lawyer's letter, seeing that the lawyer's letter had been the ground of that charge against him of deceit. But having been thus kicked out,—kicked out as far as words could kick him, and threatened with personal violence should those words not be obeyed, he found himself unable to go back to the lawyer's letter. "I should like to see any one of your men dare to touch me," said he.

"You shall see it very soon if you don't take yourself off," said Tappitt. Luckily the men were gone to breakfast, and opportunity for violence was wanting.

Luke looked round, and then remembered that he and Tappitt were probably alone in the place. "Mr. Tappitt," said he, "you're a very foolish man."

"I dare say," said Tappitt; "very foolish not to give up my own bread, and my wife's and children's bread, to an adventurer like you."

"I have endeavoured to treat you with kindness and also with honesty, and because you differ from me, as of course you have a right to do, you think it best to insult me with all the Billingsgate you can muster."

"If you don't go out of my counting-house, young man, I'll see if I can't put you out myself;" and Tappitt, in spite of his fifty-five years, absolutely put his hand down upon the poker.

There is no personal encounter in which a young man is so sure to come by the worst as in that with a much older man. This is so surely the case that it ought to be considered cowardly in an old man to attack a young one. If an old man hit a young man over the head with a walking-stick, what can the young man do, except run away to avoid a second blow? Then the old man, if he be a wicked old man, as so many are, tells all his friends that he has licked the young man. Tappitt would certainly have acted in this way if the weapon in his hand had been a stick instead of a poker. But Tappitt, when he saw his own poker in his own hand, was afraid of it. If a woman attack a man with a knife, the man will be held to have fought fairly, though he shall have knocked her down in the encounter. And so also with an old man, if he take a poker instead of a stick, the world will refuse to him the advantage of his gray hairs. Some such an idea as this came upon Tappitt — by instinct, and thus, though he still held the poker, he refrained his hand.

"The man must be mad this morning," said Rowan, standing firmly before him, with his two hands fixed upon his hips.

"Am I to send for the police?" said Tappitt.

"For a mad-doctor, I should think," said Rowan. Then Tappitt turned round and rang a bell very violently. But as the bell was intended to summon some brewery servant who was now away at his breakfast, it produced no result.

"But I have no intention of staying here against your wish, Mr. Tappitt, whether you're mad or only foolish. This matter must of course be settled by the lawyers now, and I shall not again come on to these premises unless I acquire a legal right to do so as the owner of them." And then, having so spoken, Luke Rowan walked off.

Growling inwardly Tappitt deposited the poker within the upright fender, and thrusting his hands into his trousers pockets stood scowling at the door through which his enemy had gone. He knew that he had been wrong; he knew that he had been very foolish. He was a man who had made his way upwards through the world with fair success, and had walked his way not without prudence. He had not been a man of violence, or prone to an illicit use of pokers. He had never been in difficulty for an assault; and had on his conscience not even the blood of a bloody nose, or the crime of a blackened eye. He was hard-working and peaceable; had been churchwarden three times, and mayor of Baslehurst once. He was poor-law guardian and way-warden, and filled customarily the various offices of a steady good citizen. What had he to do with pokers, unless it were to extract heat from his coals? He was ashamed of himself as he stood scowling at the door. One fault he perhaps had; and of that fault he had been ruthlessly told by lips that should have been sealed for ever on such a subject. He brewed bad beer; and by whom had this been thrown in his teeth? By Bungall's nephew,—by Bungall's heir,—by him who claimed to stand in Bungall's shoes within that establishment! Who had taught him to brew beer—bad or good? Had it not been Bungall? And now, because in his old age he would not change these things, and ruin himself in a vain attempt to make some beverage that should look bright to the eye, he was to be turned out of his place by this chip from the Bungall block, this stave out of one of Bungall's vats! "*Ruat cœlum, fiat justitia,*" he said, as he walked forth to his own breakfast. He spoke to himself in other language, indeed, though the Roman's sentiment was his own. "I'll stand on my rights, though I have to go into the poor-house."

CHAPTER XIV
LUKE ROWAN PAYS A SECOND VISIT TO BRAGG'S END

Early after breakfast on that morning,—that morning on which Tappitt had for a moment thought of braining Luke Rowan with the poker,—Mrs. Ray started from the cottage on her mission into Baslehurst. She was going to see her daughter, Mrs. Prime, at Miss Pucker's lodgings, and felt sure that the object of her visit was to be a further discourse on the danger of admitting that wolf Rowan into the sheepfold at Bragg's End. She would willingly have avoided the conference had she been able to do so, knowing well that Mrs. Prime would get the better of her in words when called upon to talk without having Rachel at her back. And indeed she was not happy in her mind. It had been conceded at the cottage as an understood thing that Rachel was to have this man as her lover; but what, if after all, the man didn't mean to be a lover in the proper sense; and what, if so meaning, he should still turn out to be a lover of a bad sort,—a worldly, good-for-nothing, rakish lover? "I wonder," says the wicked man in the play, "I wonder any man alive would ever rear a daughter!" Mrs. Ray knew nothing of the play, and had she done so, she would not have repeated such a line. But the hardness of the task which Providence had allotted to her struck her very forcibly on this morning. Rachel was dearer to her than aught else in the world. For Rachel's happiness she would have made any sacrifice. In Rachel's presence, and sweet smile, and winning caresses was the chief delight of her existence. Nevertheless, in these days the possession of Rachel was hardly a blessing to her. The responsibility was so great; and, worse than that as regarded her own comfort, the doubts were so numerous; and then, they recurred over and over again, as often as they were settled!

"I'm sure I don't know what she can have to say to me." Mrs. Ray, as she spoke, was tying on her bonnet, and Rachel was standing close to her with her light summer shawl.

"It will be the old story, mamma, I'm afraid; my terrible iniquity and backslidings, because I went to the ball, and because I won't go to Miss

Pucker's. She'll want you to say that I shall go, or else be sent to bed without my supper."

"That's nonsense, Rachel. Dorothea knows very well that I can't make you go." Mrs. Ray was wont to become mildly petulant when things went against her.

"But, mamma, you don't want me to go?"

"I don't suppose it's about Miss Pucker at all. It's about that other thing."

"You mean Mr. Rowan."

"Yes, my dear. I'm sure I don't know what's for the best. When she gets me to herself she does say such terrible things to me that it quite puts me in a heat to have to go to her. I don't think anybody ought to say those sort of things to me except a clergyman, or a person's parents, or a schoolmaster, or masters and mistresses, or such like." Rachel thought so too,—thought that at any rate a daughter should not so speak to such a mother as was her mother; but on that subject she said nothing.

"And I don't like going to that Miss Pucker's house," continued Mrs. Ray. "I'm sure I don't want her to come here. I wouldn't go, only I said that I would."

"I would go now, if I were you, mamma."

"Of course I shall go; haven't I got myself ready?"

"But I would not let her go on in that way."

"That's very easy said, Rachel; but how am I to help it? I can't tell her to hold her tongue; and if I did, she wouldn't. If I am to go I might as well start. I suppose there's cold lamb enough for dinner?"

"Plenty, I should think."

"And if I find poultry cheap, I can bring a chicken home in my basket, can't I?" And so saying, with her mind full of various cares, Mrs. Ray walked off to Baslehurst.

"I wonder when he'll come." Rachel, as she said or thought these words, stood at the open door of the cottage looking after her mother as she made her way across the green. It was a delicious midsummer day, warm with the heat of the morning sun, but not yet oppressed with the full blaze of its noonday rays. The air was alive with the notes of birds, and the flowers were in their brightest beauty. "I wonder when he'll come." None of those doubts which so harassed her mother troubled her mind. Other doubts there were. Could it be possible that he would like her well enough to wish to make her his own? Could it be that any one so bright, so prosperous in the world, so clever, so much above herself in all worldly advantages, should come and seek her as his wife,—take her from their little cottage and lowly ways of life? When he had first said that he would come to Bragg's End, she declared to herself that it would be well that he should see in how humble a way they lived. He would not call her Rachel after that, she said to herself; or, if he did, he should learn from her that she knew how to rebuke a man who dared to take advantage of the humility of her position. He had come, and he had not called her Rachel. He had come, and taking advantage of her momentary absence, had spoken of her behind her back as a lover speaks, and had told his love honestly to her mother. In Rachel's view of the matter no lover could have carried himself with better decorum or with a sweeter grace; but because he had so done, she would not hold him to be bound to her. He had been carried away by his feelings too rapidly, and had not as yet known how poor and lowly they were. He should still have opened to him a clear path backwards. Then if the path backwards were not to his mind, then in that case—. I am not sure that Rachel ever declared to herself in plain terms what in such case would happen; but she stood at the door as though she was minded to stand there till he should appear upon the green.

"I wonder when he'll come." She had watched her mother's figure disappear along the lane, and had plucked a flower or two to pieces before she returned within the house. He will not come till the evening, she determined,—till the evening, when his day's work in the brewery would be over. Then she thought of the quarrel between him and Tappitt, and wondered what it might be. She was quite sure that Tappitt was wrong, and thought of him at once as an obstinate, foolish, pigheaded old man. Yes; he would come to her, and she would take care to be provided in that article of cream which he pretended to love so well. She would not have to run away again. But how lucky on that previous evening had been that necessity, seeing that it had given opportunity for that great display of a lover's excellence on Rowan's part. Having settled all this in her mind, she went into the house, and was beginning to think of her household work, when she heard a man's steps in the passage. She went at once out from the sitting-room, and encountered Luke Rowan at the door.

"How d'ye do?" said he. "Is Mrs. Ray at home?"

"Mamma?—no. You must have met her on the road if you've come from Baslehurst."

"But I could not meet her on the road, because I've come across the fields."

"Oh!—that accounts for it."

"And she's away in Baslehurst, is she?"

"She's gone in to see my sister, Mrs. Prime." Rachel, still standing at the door of the sitting-room, made no attempt of asking Rowan into the parlour.

"And mayn't I come in?" he said. Rachel was absolutely ignorant whether, under such circumstances, she ought to allow him to enter. But there he was, in the house, and at any rate she could not turn him out.

"I'm afraid you'll have to wait a long time if you wait for mamma," she said, slightly making way, so that he obtained admittance. Was she not a hypocrite? Did she not know that Mrs. Ray's absence would be esteemed by him as a great gain, and not a loss? Why did she thus falsely talk of his waiting a long time? Dogs fight with their teeth, and horses with their heels; swans with their wings, and cats with their claws;—so also do women use such weapons as nature has provided for them.

"I came specially to see you," said he; "not but what I should be very glad to see your mother, too, if she comes back before I am gone. But I don't suppose she will, for you won't let me stay so long as that."

"Well, now you mention it, I don't think I shall, for I have got ever so many things to do;—the dinner to get ready, and the house to look after." This she did by way of making him acquainted with her mode of life,—according to the plan which she had arranged for her own guidance.

He had come into the room, had put down his hat, and had got himself up to the window, so that his back was turned to her. "Rachel," he said, turning round quickly, and speaking almost suddenly. Now he had called her Rachel again, but she could find at the moment no better way of answering him than by the same plaintive objection which she had made before. "You shouldn't call me by my name in that way, Mr. Rowan; you know you shouldn't."

"Did your mother tell you what I said to her yesterday?" he asked.

"What you said yesterday?"

"Yes, when you were away across the green."

"What you said to mamma?"

"Yes; I know she told you. I see it in your face. And I am glad she did so. May I not call you Rachel now?"

As they were placed the table was still between them, so that he was debarred from making any outward sign of his presence as a lover. He could not take her hand and press it. She stood perfectly silent, looking down upon the table on which she leaned, and gave no answer to his question. "May I not call you Rachel now?" he said, repeating the question.

I hope it will be understood that Rachel was quite a novice at this piece of work which she now had in hand. It must be the case that very many girls are not novices. A young lady who has rejected the first half-dozen suitors who have asked for her love, must probably feel herself mistress of the occasion when she rejects the seventh, and will not be quite astray when she accepts the eighth. There are, moreover, young ladies who, though they may have rejected and accepted none, have had so wide an advantage in society as to be able, when the moment comes, to have their wits about them. But Rachel had known nothing of what is called society, and had never before known either the trouble or the joy of being loved. So when the question was pressed upon her, she trembled, and felt that her breath was failing her. She had filled herself full of resolutions as to what she would do when this moment came,—as to how she would behave and what words she would utter. But all that was gone from her now. She could only stand still and tremble. Of course he might call her Rachel;—might call her what he pleased. To him, with his wider experience, that now became manifest enough.

"You must give me leave for more than that, Rachel, if you would not send me away wretched. You must let me call you my own." Then he moved round the table towards her; and as he moved, though she retreated from him, she did not retreat with a step as rapid as his own. "Rachel,"—and he put out his hand to her—"I want you to be my wife." She allowed the tips of her fingers to turn themselves toward him, as though unable altogether to refuse the greeting which he offered her, but as she did so she turned away from him, and bent down her head. She had heard all she wanted to hear. Why did he not go away, and leave her to think of it? He had named to her the word so sacred between man and woman. He had said that he sought her for his wife. What need was there that he should stay longer?

He got her hand in his, and then passed his arm round her waist. "Say, love; say, Rachel;—shall it be so? Nay, but I will have an answer from you. You shall look it to me, if you will not speak it;" and he got his head round over her shoulder, as though to look into her eyes.

"Oh, Mr. Rowan; pray don't;—pray don't pull me."

"But, dearest, say a word to me. You must say some word. Can you learn to love me, Rachel?"

Learn to love him! The lesson had come to her very easily. How was it possible, she had once thought, not to love him.

"Say a word to me," said Rowan, still struggling to look into her face; "one word, and then I will let you go."

"What word?"

"Say to me, 'Dear Luke, I will be your wife.'"

She remained for a moment quite passive in his hands, trying to say it, but the words would not come. Of course she would be his wife. Why need he trouble her further?

"Nay, but, Rachel, you shall speak, or I will stay with you here till your mother comes, and she shall answer for you. If you had disliked me I think you would have said so."

"I don't dislike you," she whispered.

"And do you love me?" She slightly bowed her head. "And you will be my wife?" Again she went through the same little piece of acting. "And I may call you Rachel now?" In answer to this question she shook herself free from his slackened grasp, and escaped away across the room.

"You cannot forbid me now. Come and sit down by me, for of course I have got much to say to you. Come and sit down, and indeed I will not trouble you again."

Then she went to him very slowly, and sat with him, leaving her hand in his, listening to his words, and feeling in her heart the full delight of having such a lover. Of the words that were then spoken, but very few came from her lips; he told her all his story of the brewery quarrel, and was very eloquent and droll in describing Tappitt as he brandished the poker.

"And was he going to hit you with it?" said Rachel, with all her eyes open.

"Well, he didn't hit me," said Luke; "but to look at him he seemed mad enough to do anything." Then he told her how at the present moment he was living at the inn, and how it became necessary, from this unfortunate quarrel, that he should go at once to London. "But under no circumstances would I have gone," said he, pressing her hand very closely, "without an answer from you."

"But you ought not to think of anything like that when you are in such trouble."

"Ought I not? Well, but I do, you see." Then he explained to her that part of his project consisted in his marrying her out of hand,—at once. He would go up to London for a week or two, and then, coming back, be married in the course of the next month.

"Oh, Mr. Rowan, that would be impossible."

"You must not call me Mr. Rowan, or I shall call you Miss Ray."

"But indeed it would be impossible."

"Why impossible?"

"Indeed it would. You can ask mamma;—or rather, you had better give over thinking of it. I haven't had time yet even to make up my mind what you are like."

"But you say that you love me."

"So I do, but I suppose I ought not; for I'm sure I don't know what you are like yet. It seems to me that you're very fond of having your own way, sir;—and so you ought," she added; "but really you can't have your own way in that. Nobody ever heard of such a thing. Everybody would think we were mad."

"I shouldn't care one straw for that."

"Ah, but I should,—a great many straws."

He sat there for two hours, telling her of all things appertaining to himself. He explained to her that, irrespective of the brewery, he had an income sufficient to support a wife,—"though not enough to make her a fine lady like Mrs. Cornbury," he said.

"If you can give me bread and cheese, it's as much as I have a right to expect," said Rachel.

"I have over four hundred a year," said he: and Rachel, hearing it, thought that he could indeed support a wife. Why should a man with four hundred a year want to brew beer?

"But I have got nothing," said Rachel; "not a farthing."

"Of course not," said Rowan; "it is my theory that unmarried girls never ought to have anything. If they have, they ought to be considered as provided for, and then they shouldn't have husbands. And I rather think it would be better if men didn't have anything either, so that they might be forced to earn their bread. Only they would want capital."

Rachel listened to it all with the greatest content, and most unalloyed happiness. She did not quite understand him, but she gathered from his words that her own poverty was not a reproach in his eyes, and that he under no circumstances would have looked for a wife with a fortune. Her happiness was unalloyed at all she heard from him, till at last he spoke of his mother.

"And does she dislike me?" asked Rachel, with dismay.

"It isn't that she dislikes you, but she's staying with that Mrs. Tappitt, who is furious against me because,—I suppose it's because of this brewery row. But indeed I can't understand it. A week ago I was at home there; now I daren't show my nose in the house, and have been turned out of the brewery this morning with a poker."

"I hope it's nothing about me," said Rachel.

"How can it be about you?"

"Because I thought Mrs. Tappitt looked at the ball as though—. But I suppose it didn't mean anything."

"It ought to be a matter of perfect indifference whether it meant anything or not."

"But how can it be so about your mother? If this is ever to lead to anything—"

"Lead to anything! What it will lead to is quite settled."

"You know what I mean. But how could I become your wife if your mother did not wish it?"

"Look here, Rachel; that's all very proper for a girl, I dare say. If your mother thought I was not fit to be your husband, I won't say but what you ought to take her word in such a matter. But it isn't so with a man. It will make me very unhappy if my mother cannot be friends with my wife; but no threats of hers to that effect would prevent me from marrying, nor should they have any effect upon you. I'm my own master, and from the nature of things I must look out for myself."

This was all very grand and masterful on Rowan's part, and might in theory be true; but there was that in it which made Rachel uneasy, and gave to her love its first shade of trouble. She could not be quite happy as Luke's promised bride, if she knew that she would not be welcomed to that place by Luke's mother. And then what right had she to think it probable that Luke's mother would give her such a welcome? At that first meeting, however, she said but little herself on the subject. She had pledged to him her troth, and she would not attempt to go back from her pledge at the first appearance of a difficulty. She would talk to her own mother, and perhaps his mother might relent. But throughout it all there ran a feeling of dismay at the idea of marrying a man whose mother would not willingly receive her as a daughter!

"But you must go," said she at last. "Indeed you must. I have things to do, if you have nothing."

"I'm the idlest man in the world at the present moment. If you turn me out I can only go and sit at the inn."

"Then you must go and sit at the inn. If you stay any longer mamma won't have any dinner."

"If that's so, of course I'll go. But I shall come back to tea."

As Rachel gave no positive refusal to this proposition, Rowan took his departure on the understanding that he might return.

"Good-bye," said he. "When I come this evening I shall expect you to walk with me."

"Oh, I don't know," said she.

"Yes, you will; and we will see the sun set again, and you will not run from me this evening as though I were an ogre." As he spoke he took her in his arms and held her, and kissed her before she had time to escape from him. "You're mine altogether now," said he, "and nothing can sever us. God bless you, Rachel!"

"Good-bye, Luke," and then they parted.

She had told him to go, alleging her household duties as her ground for dismissing him; but when he was gone she did not at once betake herself to her work. She sat on the seat which he had shared with her, thinking of the thing which she had done. She was now betrothed to this man as his wife, the only man towards whom her fancy had ever turned with the slightest preference. So far love for her had run very smoothly. From her first meetings with him, on those evenings in which she had hardly spoken to him, his form had filled her eye, and his words had filled her mind. She had learned to love to see him before she understood what her heart was doing for her. Gradually, but very quickly, all her vacant thoughts had been given to him, and he had become the hero of her life. Now, almost before she had had time to question herself on the matter, he was her affianced husband. It had all been so quick and so very gracious that she seemed to tremble at her own good fortune. There was that one little cloud in the sky,—that frown on his mother's brow; but now, in the first glow of her happiness, she could not bring herself to believe that this cloud would bring a storm. So she sat there dreaming of her happiness, and longing for her mother's return that she might tell it all;—that it might be talked of hour after hour, and that Luke's merits might receive their fitting mention. Her mother was not a woman who on such an occasion would stint the measure of her praise, or refuse her child the happiness of her sympathy.

But Rachel knew that she must not let the whole morning pass by in idle dreams, happy as those dreams were, and closely as they were allied to her waking life. After a while she jumped up with a start. "I declare there will be nothing done. Mamma will want her dinner though I'm ever so much going to be married."

But she had not been long on foot, or done much in preparation of the cold lamb which it was intended they should eat that day, before she heard her mother's footsteps on the gravel path. She ran out to the front door full of her own news, though hardly knowing as yet in what words she would tell it; but of her mother's news, of any tidings which there might be to tell as to that interview which had just taken place in Baslehurst, Rachel did not think much. Nothing that Dorothea could say would now be of moment. So at least Rachel flattered herself. And as for Dorothea and all her growlings, had they not chiefly ended in this;—that the young man did not intend to present himself as a husband? But he had now done so in a manner which Rachel felt to be so satisfactory that even Dorothea's criticism must be disarmed. So Rachel, as she met her mother, thought only of the tale which she had to tell, and nothing of that which she was to hear.

But Mrs. Ray was so full of her tale, was so conscious of the fact that her tidings were entitled to the immediate and undivided attention of her daughter, and from their first greeting on the gravel path was so ready with her words, that Rachel, with all the story of her happiness, was for a while obliterated.

"Oh, my dear," said Mrs. Ray, "I have such news for you!"

"So have I, mamma, news for you," said Rachel, putting out her hand to her mother.

"I never was so warm in my life. Do let me get in; oh dear, oh dear! It's no good looking in the basket, for when I came away from Dorothea I was too full of what I had just heard to think of buying anything."

"What have you heard, mamma?"

"I'm sure I hope she'll be happy; I'm sure I do. But it's a great venture, a terribly great venture."

"What is it, mamma?" And Rachel, though she could not yet think that her mother's budget could be equal in importance to her own, felt that there was that which it was necessary that she should hear.

"Your sister is going to be married to Mr. Prong."

"Dolly?"

"Yes, my dear. It's a great venture; but if any woman can live happy with such a man, she can do so. She's troubled about her money;—that's all."

"Marry Mr. Prong! I suppose she may if she likes. Oh dear! I can't think I shall ever like him."

"I never spoke to him yet, so perhaps I oughtn't to say; but he doesn't look a nice man to my eyes. But what are looks, my dear? They're only skin deep; we ought all of us to remember that always, Rachel; they're only skin deep; and if, as she says, she only wants to work in the vineyard, she won't mind his being so short. I dare say he's honest;—at least I'm sure I hope he is."

"I should think he's honest, at any rate, or he wouldn't be what he is."

"There's some of them are so very fond of money;—that is, if all that we hear is true. Perhaps he mayn't care about it; let us hope that he doesn't; but if so he's a great exception. However, she means to have it tied up as close as possible, and I think she's right. Where would she be if he was to go away some fine morning and leave her? You see, he's got nobody belonging to him. I own I do like people who have got people belonging to them; you feel sure, in a sort of way, that they'll go on living in their own houses."

Rachel immediately reflected that Luke Rowan had people belonging to him,—very nice people,—and that everybody knew who he was and from whence he came.

"But she has quite made up her mind about it," continued Mrs. Ray; "and when I saw that I didn't say very much against it. What was the use? It isn't as though he wasn't quite respectable. He is a clergyman, you know, my dear, though he never was at any of the regular colleges; and he might be a bishop, just as much as if he had been; so they tell me. And I really don't think that she would ever have come back to the cottage,—not unless you had promised to have been ruled by her in everything."

"I certainly shouldn't have done that;" and Rachel, as she made this assurance with some little obstinacy in her voice, told herself that for the future she meant to be ruled by a very different person indeed.

"No, I suppose not; and I'm sure I shouldn't have asked you, because I think it isn't the thing, dragging people away out of their own parishes, here and there, to anybody's church. And I told her that though I would of course go and hear Mr. Prong now and then if she married him, I wouldn't leave Mr. Comfort, not as a regular thing. But she didn't seem to mind that now, much as she used always to be saying about it."

"And when is it to be, mamma?"

"On Friday; that is, to-morrow."

"To-morrow!"

"That is, she's to go and tell him to-morrow that she means to take him,— or he's to come to her at Miss Pucker's lodgings. It's not to be wondered at when one sees Miss Pucker, really; and I'm not sure I'd not have done the same if I'd been living with her too; only I don't think I ever should have begun. I think it's living with Miss Pucker has made her do it; I do indeed, my dear. Well, now that I have told you, I suppose I may as well go and get ready for dinner."

"I'll come with you, mamma. The potatoes are strained, and Kitty can put the things on the table. Mamma"—and now they were on the stairs,— "I've got something to tell also."

We'll leave Mrs. Ray to eat her dinner, and Rachel to tell her story, merely adding a word to say that the mother did not stint the measure of her praise, or refuse her child the happiness of her sympathy. That evening was probably the happiest of Rachel's existence, although its full proportions of joy were marred by an unforeseen occurrence. At four o'clock a note came from Rowan to his "Dearest Rachel," saying that he had been called away by telegraph to London about that "horrid brewery business." He would write from there. But Rachel was almost as happy without him, talking about him, as she would have been in his presence, listening to him.

CHAPTER XV
MATERNAL ELOQUENCE

On the Friday morning there was a solemn conference at the brewery between Mrs. Tappitt and Mrs. Rowan. Mrs. Rowan found herself to be in some difficulty as to the line of action which she ought to take, and the alliances which she ought to form. She was passionately attached to her son, and for Mrs. Tappitt she had no strong liking. But then she was very averse to this proposed marriage with Rachel Ray, and was willing for a while to make a treaty with Mrs. Tappitt, offensive and defensive, as against her own son, if by doing so she could put a stop to so outrageous a proceeding on his part. He had seen her before he started for London, and had told her both the occurrences of the day. He had described to her how Tappitt had turned him out of the brewery, poker in hand, and how, in consequence of Tappitt's "pig-headed obstinacy," it was now necessary that their joint affairs should be set right by the hand of the law. He had then told her also that there was no longer any room for doubt or argument between them as regarding Rachel. He had gone out to Bragg's End that morning, had made his offer, and had been accepted. His mother therefore would see,—so he surmised,—that, as any opposition on her part must now be futile, she might as well take Rachel to her heart at once. He went so far as to propose to her that she should go over to Rachel in his absence,—"it would be very gracious if you could do it to-morrow, mother," he said,—and go through that little process of taking her future daughter-in-law to her heart. But in answer to this Mrs. Rowan said very little. She said very little, but she looked much. "My dear, I cannot move so quick as you do; I am older. I am afraid, however, that you have been rash." He said something, as on such occasions young men do, as to his privilege of choosing for himself, as to his knowing what wife would suit him, as to his contempt for money, and as to the fact,—"the undoubted fact," as he declared it,—and in that declaration I am prepared to go hand-in-hand with him,—that Rachel Ray was a lady. But he was clear-headed enough to perceive that his mother did not intend to agree with him. "When we are married she will come round," he said to himself, and then he took himself off by the night mail train to London.

Under these circumstances Mrs. Rowan felt that her only chance of carrying on the battle would be by means of a treaty with Mrs. Tappitt. Had the affair of the brewery stood alone, Mrs. Rowan would have ranged herself loyally on the side of her son. She would have resented the uplifting of that poker, and shown her resentment by an immediate withdrawal from the brewery. She would have said a word or two, — a stately word or two, — as to the justice of her son's cause, and have carried herself and her daughter off to the inn. As things were now, her visit to the brewery must no doubt be curtailed in its duration; but in the mean time might not a blow be struck against that foolish matrimonial project, — an opportune blow, and by the aid of Mrs. Tappitt? Therefore on that Friday morning, when Mr. Prong was listening with enraptured ears to Mrs. Prime's acceptance of his suit, — under certain pecuniary conditions, — Mrs. Rowan and Mrs. Tappitt were sitting in conference at the brewery.

They agreed together at that meeting that Rachel Ray was the head and front of the whole offence, the source of all the evil done and to be done, and the one great sinner in the matter. It was clear to Mrs. Rowan that Rachel could have no just pretensions to look for such a lover or such a husband as her son; and it was equally clear to Mrs. Tappitt that she could have had no right to seek a lover or a husband out of the brewery. If Rachel Ray had not been there all might have gone smoothly for both of them. Mrs. Tappitt did not, perhaps, argue very logically as to the brewery business, or attempt to show either to herself or to her ally that Luke Rowan would have made himself an agreeable partner if he had kept himself free from all love vagaries; but she was filled with an indefinite woman's idea that the mischief, which she felt, had been done by Rachel Ray, and that against Rachel and Rachel's pretensions her hand should be turned.

They resolved therefore that they would go out together and call at the cottage. Mrs. Tappitt knew, from long neighbourhood, of what stuff Mrs. Ray was made. "A very good sort of woman," she said to Mrs. Rowan, "and not at all headstrong and perverse like her daughter. If we find the young lady there we must ask her mamma to see us alone." To this proposition Mrs. Rowan assented, not eagerly, but with a slow, measured, dignified assent, feeling that she was derogating somewhat from her own position in allowing herself to be led by such a one as Mrs. Tappitt. It was needful that on this occasion she should act with Mrs. Tappitt and connect herself with the Tappitt interests; but all this she did with an air that distinctly claimed for herself a personal superiority. If Mrs. Tappitt did not perceive and understand this, it was her fault, and not Mrs. Rowan's.

At two o'clock they stepped into a fly at the brewery door and had themselves driven out to Bragg's End.

"Mamma, there's a carriage," said Rachel.

"It can't be coming here," said Mrs. Ray.

"But it is; it's the fly from the Dragon. I know it by the man's white hat. And, oh dear, there's Mrs. Rowan and Mrs. Tappitt! Mamma, I shall go away." And Rachel, without another word, escaped out into the garden. She escaped, utterly heedless of her mother's little weak prayer that she would remain. She went away quickly, so that not a skirt of her dress might be visible. She felt instantly, by instinct, that these two women had come out there especially as her enemies, as upsetters of her happiness, as opponents of her one great hope in life; and she knew that she could not fight her battle with them face to face. She could not herself maintain her love stoutly and declare her intention of keeping her lover to his word; and yet she did intend to maintain her love, not doubting that he would be true to his word without any effort on her part. Her mother would make a very poor fight, — of that she was quite well aware. It would have been well if her mother could have run away also. But, as that could not be, her mother must be left to succumb, and the fight must be carried on afterwards as best it might. The two ladies remained at the cottage for about an hour, and during that time Rachel was sequestered in the garden, hardening her heart against all enemies to her love. If Luke would only stand by her, she would certainly stand by him.

There was a good deal of ceremony between the three ladies when they first found themselves together in Mrs. Ray's parlour. Mrs. Rowan and Mrs. Tappitt were large and stiff in their draperies, and did not fit themselves easily in among Mrs. Ray's small belongings; and they were stately in their demeanour, conscious that they were visiting an inferior, and conscious also that they were there on no friendly mission. But the interview was commenced with a show of much civility. Mrs. Tappitt introduced Mrs. Rowan in due form, and Mrs. Rowan made her little bow, if with some self-asserting supremacy, still with fitting courtesy. Mrs. Ray hoped that Mrs. Tappitt and the young ladies were quite well, and then there was a short silence, very oppressive to Mrs. Ray, but refreshing rather than otherwise to Mrs. Rowan. It gave a proper business aspect to the visit, and paved the way for serious words.

"Miss Rachel is out, I suppose," said Mrs. Tappitt.

"Yes, she is out," said Mrs. Ray. "But she's about the place somewhere, if you want to see her." This she added in her weakness, not knowing how she was to sustain the weight of such an interview alone.

"Perhaps it is as well that she should be away just at present," said Mrs. Rowan, firmly but mildly.

"Quite as well," said Mrs. Tappitt, as firmly, but less mildly.

"Because we wish to say a few words to you, Mrs. Ray," said Mrs. Rowan.

"That is what has brought us out so early," said Mrs. Tappitt. It was only half-past two now, and company visiting was never done at Baslehurst till after three. "We want to say a few words to you, Mrs. Ray, about a very serious matter. I'm sure you know how glad I've always been to see Rachel with my girls, and I had her at our party the other night, you know. It isn't likely therefore that I should be disposed to say anything unkind about her."

"At any rate not to me, I hope," said Mrs. Ray.

"Not to anybody. Indeed I'm not given to say unkind things about people. No one in Baslehurst would give me that character. But the fact is, Mrs. Ray—"

"Perhaps, Mrs. Tappitt, you'll allow me," said Mrs. Rowan. "He's my son."

"Oh, yes, certainly;—that is, if you wish it," said Mrs. Tappitt, drawing herself up in her chair; "but I thought that perhaps, as I knew Miss Ray so well—"

"If you don't mind, Mrs. Tappitt—" and Mrs. Rowan, as she again took the words out of her friend's mouth, smiled upon her with a smile of great efficacy.

"Oh, dear, certainly not," said Mrs. Tappitt, acknowledging by her concession the superiority of Mrs. Rowan's nature.

"I believe you are aware, Mrs. Ray," said Mrs. Rowan, "that Mr. Luke Rowan is my son."

"Yes, I'm aware of that."

"And I'm afraid you must be aware also that there have been some,—some,—some talkings as it were, between him and your daughter."

"Oh, yes. The truth is, ma'am, that he has offered himself to my girl, and that she has accepted him. Whether it's for good or for bad, the open truth is the best, Mrs. Tappitt."

"Truth is truth," said Mrs. Tappitt; "and deception is not truth."

"I didn't think it had gone anything so far as that," said Mrs. Rowan,—who at the moment, perhaps, forgot that deception is not truth; "and in saying that he has actually offered himself, you may perhaps,—without meaning it, of course,—be attributing a more positive significance to his word than he has intended."

"God forbid!" said Mrs. Ray very solemnly. "That would be a very sad thing for my poor girl. But I think, Mrs. Rowan, you had better ask him. If he says he didn't intend it, of course there will be an end of it, as far as Rachel is concerned."

"I can't ask him just at present," said Mrs. Rowan, "because he has gone up to London. He went away yesterday afternoon, and there's no saying when he may be in Baslehurst again."

"If ever—," said Mrs. Tappitt, very solemnly. "Perhaps he has not told you, Mrs. Ray, that that partnership between him and Mr. T. is all over."

"He did tell us that there had been words between him and Mr. Tappitt."

"Words indeed!" said Mrs. Tappitt.

"And therefore it isn't so easy to ask him," said Mrs. Rowan, ignoring Mrs. Tappitt and the partnership. "But of course, Mrs. Ray, our object in this matter must be the same. We both wish to see our children happy and respectable." Mrs. Rowan, as she said this, put great emphasis on the last word.

"As to my girl, I've no fear whatever but what she'll be respectable," said Mrs. Ray, with more heat than Mrs. Tappitt had thought her to possess.

"No doubt; no doubt. But what I'm coming to is this, Mrs. Ray; here has this boy of mine been behaving foolishly to your daughter, as young men will do. It may be that he has really said something to her of the kind you suppose—"

"Said something to her! Why, ma'am, he came out here and asked my permission to pay his addresses to her, which I didn't answer because just at that moment Rachel came in from Farmer Sturt's opposite—"

"Farmer Sturt's!" said Mrs. Tappitt to Mrs. Rowan, in an under voice and nodding her head. Whereupon Mrs. Rowan nodded her head also. One of the great accusations made against Mrs. Ray had been that she lived on the Farmer Sturt level, and not on the Tappitt level;—much less on the Rowan level.

"Yes,—from Farmer Sturt's," continued Mrs. Ray, not at all understanding this by-play. "So I didn't give him any answer at all."

"You wouldn't encourage him," said Mrs. Rowan.

"I don't know about that; but at any rate he encouraged himself, for he came again the next morning when I was in Baslehurst."

"I hope Miss Rachel didn't know he was coming in your absence," said Mrs. Rowan.

"It would look so sly;—wouldn't it?" said Mrs. Tappitt.

"No, she didn't, and she isn't sly at all. If she had known anything she would have told me. I know what my girl is, Mrs. Rowan, and I can depend on her." Mrs. Ray's courage was up, and she was inclined to fight bravely, but she was sadly impeded by tears, which she now found it impossible to control.

"I'm sure it isn't my wish to distress you," said Mrs. Rowan.

"It does distress me very much, then, for anybody to say that Rachel is sly."

"I said I hoped she wasn't sly," said Mrs. Tappitt.

"I heard what you said," continued Mrs. Ray; "and I don't see why you should be speaking against Rachel in that way. The young man isn't your son."

"No," said Mrs. Tappitt, "indeed he's not;—nor yet he ain't Mr. Tappitt's partner."

"Nor wishes to be," said Mrs. Rowan, with a toss of her head. It was a thousand pities that Mrs. Ray had not her wits enough about her to have fanned into a fire of battle the embers which glowed hot between her two enemies. Had she done so they might probably have been made to consume each other,—to her great comfort. "Nor wishes to be!" Then Mrs. Rowan paused a moment, and Mrs. Tappitt assumed a smile which was intended to indicate incredulity. "But Mrs. Ray," continued Mrs. Rowan, "that is neither here nor there. Luke Rowan is my son, and I certainly have a right to speak. Such a marriage as this would be very imprudent on his part, and very disagreeable to me. From the way in which things have turned out it's not likely that he'll settle himself at Baslehurst."

"The most unlikely thing in the world," said Mrs. Tappitt. "I don't suppose he'll ever show himself in Baslehurst again."

"As for showing himself, Mrs. Tappitt, my son will never be ashamed of showing himself anywhere."

"But he won't have any call to come to Baslehurst, Mrs. Rowan. That's what I mean."

"If he's a gentleman of his word, as I take him to be," said Mrs. Ray, "he'll have a great call to show himself. He never can have intended to come out here, and speak to her in that way, and ask her to marry him, and then never to come back and see her any more! I wouldn't believe it of him, not though his own mother said it!"

"I don't say anything," said Mrs. Rowan, who felt that her position was one of some difficulty. "But we all do know that in affairs of that kind young men do allow themselves to go great lengths. And the greater lengths they go, Mrs. Ray, the more particular the young ladies ought to be."

"But what's a young lady to do? How's she to know whether a young man is in earnest, or whether he's only going lengths, as you call it?" Mrs. Ray's eyes were still moist with tears; and, I grieve to say that though, as far as immediate words are concerned, she was fighting Rachel's battle not badly, still the blows of the enemy were taking effect upon her. She was beginning to wish that Luke Rowan had never been seen, or his name heard, at Bragg's End.

"I think it's quite understood in the world," said Mrs. Rowan, "that a young lady is not to take a gentleman at his first word."

"Oh, quite," said Mrs. Tappitt.

"We've all of us daughters," said Mrs. Rowan.

"Yes, all of us," said Mrs. Tappitt. "That's what makes it so fitting that we should discuss this matter together in a friendly feeling."

"My son is a very good young man,—a very good young man indeed."

"But a little hasty, perhaps," said Mrs. Tappitt.

"If you'll allow me, Mrs. Tappitt."

"Oh, certainly, Mrs. Rowan."

"A very good young man indeed; and I don't think it at all probable that in such a matter as this he will act in opposition to his mother's wishes. He has his way to make in the world."

"Which will never be in the brewery line," said Mrs. Tappitt.

"He has his way to make in the world," continued Mrs. Rowan, with much severity; "and if he marries in four or five years' time, that will be quite as soon as he ought to think of doing. I'm sure you will agree with me, Mrs. Ray, that long engagements are very bad, particularly for the lady."

"He wanted to be married next month," said Mrs. Ray.

"Ah, yes; that shows that the whole thing couldn't come to much. If there was an engagement at all, it must be a very long one. Years must roll by." From the artistic manner in which Mrs. Rowan allowed her voice to dwell upon the words which signified duration of space, any hope of a marriage between Luke and Rachel seemed to be put off at any rate to some future century. "Years must roll by, and we all know what that means. The lady dies of a broken heart, while the gentleman lives in a bachelor's rooms, and dines always at his club. Nobody can wish such a state of things as that, Mrs. Ray."

"I knew a girl who was engaged for seven years," said Mrs. Tappitt, "and she wore herself to a thread-paper,—so she did. And then he married his housekeeper after all."

"I'd sooner see my girl make up her mind to be an old maid than let her have a long engagement," said Mrs. Rowan.

"And so would I, my girls, all three. If anybody comes, I say to them, 'Let your papa see them. He'll know what's the meaning of it.' It don't do for young girls to manage those things all themselves. Not but what I think my girls have almost as much wit about them as I have. I won't mention any names, but there's a young man about here as well-to-do as any young man in the South Hams, but Cherry won't as much as look at him." Mrs. Rowan again tossed her head. She felt her misfortune in being burthened with such a colleague as Mrs. Tappitt.

"What is it you want me to do, Mrs. Rowan?" asked Mrs. Ray.

"I want you and your daughter, who I am sure is a very nice young lady, and good-looking too,—"

"Oh, quite so," said Mrs. Tappitt.

"I want you both to understand that this little thing should be allowed to drop. If my boy has done anything foolish I'm here to apologize for him. He isn't the first that has been foolish, and I'm afraid he won't be the last. But it can't be believed, Mrs. Ray, that marriages should be run up in this thoughtless sort of way. In the first place the young people don't know anything of each other; absolutely nothing at all. And then,—but I'm sure I don't want to insist on any differences that there may be in their positions in life. Only you must be aware of this, Mrs. Ray, that such a marriage as that would be very injurious to a young man like my son Luke."

"My child wouldn't wish to injure anybody."

"And therefore, of course, she won't think any more about it. All I want from you is that you should promise me that."

"If Rachel will only just say that," said Mrs. Tappitt, "my daughters will be as happy to see her out walking with them as ever."

"Rachel has had quite enough of such walking, Mrs. Tappitt; quite enough."

"If harm has come of it, it hasn't been the fault of my girls," said Mrs. Tappitt.

Then there was a pause among the three ladies, and it appeared that Mrs. Rowan was waiting for Mrs. Ray's answer. But Mrs. Ray did not know what answer she should make. She was already disposed to regard the coming of Luke Rowan to Baselhurst as a curse rather than a blessing. She felt all but convinced that Fate would be against her and hers in that matter. She had ever been afraid of young men, believing them to be dangerous, bringers of trouble into families, roaring lions sometimes, and often wolves in sheep's clothing. Since she had first heard of Luke Rowan in connection with her daughter she had been trembling. If she could have acted in accordance with her own feelings at this moment, she would have begged that Luke Rowan's name might never again be mentioned in her presence. It would be better for them, she thought, to bear what had already come upon them, than to run further risk. But she could not give any answer to Mrs. Rowan without consulting Rachel;—she could not at least give any such answer as that contemplated without doing so. She had sanctioned Rachel's love, and could not now undertake to oppose it. Rachel had probably been deceived, and must bear her misfortune. But, as the question stood at present between her and her daughter, she could not at once accede to Mrs. Rowan's views in the matter. "I will talk to Rachel," she said.

"Give her my kindest respects," said Mrs. Rowan; "and pray make her understand that I wouldn't interfere if I didn't think it was for both their advantages. Good-bye, Mrs. Ray." And Mrs. Rowan got up.

"Good-bye, Mrs. Ray," said Mrs. Tappitt, putting out her hand. "Give my love to Rachel. I hope that we shall be good friends yet, for all that has come and gone."

But Mrs. Ray would not accept Mrs. Tappitt's hand, nor would she vouchsafe any answer to Mrs. Tappitt's amenities. "Good-bye, ma'am," she said to Mrs. Rowan. "I suppose you mean to do the best you can by your own child."

"And by yours too," said Mrs. Rowan.

"If so, I can only say that you must think very badly of your own son. Good-bye, ma'am." Then Mrs. Ray curtseyed them out,—not without a certain amount of dignity, although her eyes were red with tears, and her whole body trembling with dismay.

Very little was said in the fly between the two ladies on their way back to the brewery, nor did Mrs. Rowan remain very long as a visitor at Mrs. Tappitt's house. She had found herself compelled by circumstances to take a part inimical to Mrs. Ray, but she felt in her heart a much stronger animosity to Mrs. Tappitt. With Mrs. Ray she could have been very friendly, only for that disastrous love affair; but with Mrs. Tappitt she could not again put herself into pleasant relations. I must point out how sadly unfortunate it was that Mrs. Ray had not known how to fan that flame of anger to her own and her daughter's advantage.

"Well, mamma," said Rachel, returning to the room as soon as she heard the wheels of the fly in motion upon the road across the green. She found her mother in tears,—hardly able to speak because of her sobs. "Never mind it, mamma: of course I know the kind of things they have been saying. It was what I expected. Never mind it."

"But, my dear, you will be broken-hearted."

"Broken-hearted! Why?"

"I know you will. Now that you have learned to love him, you'll never bear to lose him."

"And must I lose him?"

"She says so. She says that he doesn't mean it, and that it's all nonsense."

"I don't believe her. Nothing shall make me believe that, mamma."

"She says it would be ruinous to all his prospects, especially just now when he has quarrelled about this brewery."

"Ruinous to him!"

"His mother says so."

"I will never wish him to do anything that shall be ruinous to himself; never;—not though I were broken-hearted, as you call it."

"Ah, that is it, Rachel, my darling; I wish he had not come here."

Rachel went away across the room and looked out of the window upon the green. There she stood in silence for a few minutes while her mother was wiping her eyes and suppressing her sobs. Tears also had run down Rachel's cheeks; but they were silent tears, few in number and very salt. "I cannot bring myself to wish that yet," said she.

"But he has gone away, and what can you do if he does not come again?"

"Do! Oh, I can do nothing. I could do nothing, even though he were here in Baslehurst every day of his life. If I once thought that he didn't wish me—to—be—his wife, I should not want to do anything. But, mamma, I can't believe it of him. It was only yesterday that he was here."

"They say that young men don't care what they say in that way now-a-days."

"I don't believe it of him, mamma; his manner is so steadfast, and his voice sounds so true."

"But then she is so terribly against it."

Then again they were silent for a while, after which Rachel ended the conversation. "It is clear, at any rate, that you and I can do nothing, mamma. If she expects me to say that I will give him up, she is mistaken. Give him up! I couldn't give him up, without being false to him. I don't think I'll ever be false to him. If he's false to me, then,—then, I must bear it. Mamma, don't say anything to Dolly about this just at present." In answer to which request Mrs. Ray promised that she would not at present say anything to Mrs. Prime about Mrs. Rowan's visit.

The following day and the Sunday were not passed in much happiness by the two ladies at Bragg's End. Tidings reached them that Mrs. Rowan and her daughter were going to London on the Monday, but no letter came to them from Luke. By the Monday morning Mrs. Ray had quite made up her mind that Luke Rowan was lost to them for ever, and Rachel had already become worn with care. During that Saturday and Sunday nothing was seen of Mrs. Prime at Bragg's End.